Praise for the Peaches Dann mysteries . . .

Is There a Dead Man in the House?

"Elizabeth Daniels Squire and her Peaches Dann have never been better than in their latest mystery-adventure set in the historic middle Tennessee landscape south of Nashville. Taking full advantage of this history, Squire integrates dashes of humor and strong characters from both past and present in creating the house and atmosphere central to her fast-paced story. And as always, Peaches' memory for names, or lack thereof, makes her a most winning and modest narrator-heroine." —Wilma Dykeman, author of *The Tall Woman* and *Tennessee: A History*

Whose Death is it Anyway?

"Peaches is back, and she's better than ever . . . absolutely the best in the series!" —*The WordShop*

Who Killed What's-Her-Name?

"Squire has a gift for characterization, setting, dialogue, plot and timing." —*Concord Tribune*

Remember the Alibi

"Wonderfully written and absolutely original . . . terrific." —Carolyn G. Hart

Memory Can Be Murder

"A page-turner that is impossible to put down." —*Rocky Mount Telegram* (NC)

"A most satisfying book, the perfect companion for an escape in a backyard hammock or a rainy day." —*The Pilot* (Southern Pines, NC)

MORE MYSTERIES FROM THE BERKLEY PUBLISHING GROUP...

CHINA BAYLES MYSTERIES: She left the big city to run an herb shop in Pecan Springs, Texas. But murder can happen anywhere... A wonderful character!''— *Mostly Murder*

by D. B. Borton

ONE FOR THE MONEY	TWO POINTS FOR MURDER
THREE IS A CROWD	FOUR ELEMENTS OF MURDER
FIVE ALARM FIRE	SIX FEET UNDER

ELENA JARVIS MYSTERIES: There are some pretty bizarre crimes deep in the heart of Texas—and a pretty gutsy police detective who rounds up the unusual suspects...

by Nancy Herndon

ACID BATH	WIDOWS' WATCH
LETHAL STATUES	HUNTING GAME

FREDDIE O'NEAL, P.I., MYSTERIES: You can bet that this appealing Reno private investigator will get her man... ''A winner.''—Linda Grant

by Catherine Dain

LAY IT ON THE LINE	SING A SONG OF DEATH
WALK A CROOKED MILE	LAMENT FOR A DEAD COWBOY
BET AGAINST THE HOUSE	THE LUCK OF THE DRAW
DEAD MAN'S HAND	

BENNI HARPER MYSTERIES: Meet Benni Harper—a quilter and folk-art expert with an eye for murderous designs...

by Earlene Fowler

FOOL'S PUZZLE	IRISH CHAIN
KANSAS TROUBLES	GOOSE IN THE POND

HANNAH BARLOW MYSTERIES: For ex-cop and law student Hannah Barlow, justice isn't just a word in a textbook. Sometimes, it's a matter of life and death...

by Carroll Lachnit

MURDER IN BRIEF	A BLESSED DEATH

PEACHES DANN MYSTERIES: Peaches has never had a very good memory. But she's learned to cope with it over the years... Fortunately, though, when it comes to murder, this absentminded amateur sleuth doesn't forgive and forget!

by Elizabeth Daniels Squire

WHO KILLED WHAT'S-HER-NAME?	REMEMBER THE ALIBI
MEMORY CAN BE MURDER	WHOSE DEATH IS IT ANYWAY?
IS THERE A DEAD MAN IN THE HOUSE?	

IS THERE A DEAD MAN IN THE HOUSE?

ELIZABETH DANIELS SQUIRE

Elizabeth Daniels Squire

BERKLEY PRIME CRIME, NEW YORK

IS THERE A DEAD MAN IN THE HOUSE?

A Berkley Prime Crime Book / published by arrangement with the author

PRINTING HISTORY
Berkley Prime Crime edition / January 1998

All rights reserved.
Copyright © 1998 by Elizabeth Daniels Squire.
This book may not be reproduced in whole or in part, by mimeograph or any other means, without permission.
For information address: The Berkley Publishing Group, a member of Penguin Putnam Inc., 200 Madison Avenue, New York, NY 10016.

The Putnam Berkley World Wide Web site address is http://www.berkley.com

ISBN: 0-425-16142-0

Berkley Prime Crime Books are published by The Berkley Publishing Group, a member of Penguin Putnam Inc., 200 Madison Avenue, New York, NY 10016.
The name BERKLEY PRIME CRIME and the BERKLEY PRIME CRIME design are trademarks belonging to Berkley Publishing Corporation.

PRINTED IN THE UNITED STATES OF AMERICA

10 9 8 7 6 5 4 3 2 1

Acknowledgments

I would like to thank all the wonderful people who enriched my knowledge about old houses and otherwise helped me write this book.

Worth and Elizabeth Squire let me set the book at the restoration-in-progress of their 1795 house in Tennessee. They were a fountain of good ideas. In addition, my son Worth, the poet, always had a way of suggesting the right word.

Vic Hood, Gary Grau, and the Leatherwood crew let me watch them at the work of restoration and were full of great ideas about what can be mysteriously lost and found in the process.

Dr. Larry McKee, director of archaeology at The Hermitage, and Dr. Brian Thomas, former research archaeologist at The Hermitage and now visiting professor at St. Mary's College in Moraga, California, initiated me into the wonders of digging up the past and made great suggestions.

Dr. Nick Fielder, head archaeologist for the Tennessee Department of Archaeology, introduced me to a skeleton buried in the mid-1800s and otherwise explained what happens when a skeleton is discovered at a house site.

Louise Lynch, archivist of Williamson County, Tennessee, not only showed me the wonders of the archives, but also told me some interesting historical tales.

The fascinating history of *Flat Creek and Its People* by Ennis C. Wallace, Sr., Jo Ann Perry, Marjorie Redmond, and Martha Ann Hazelwood interested me as much as it did my sleuth. I thank Ennis Wallace for a copy of this rare book, and I thank the four authors for allowing me to add my fictional characters to my account of this book.

Wilma Dykeman's lively *Tennessee—A History* made reading background about that state a pleasure and contained a treasure trove of anecdotes about the frontier and its heritage.

Chris Morton, Carolyn Justice, and the rest of the staff of the Vance Birthplace near my home in North Carolina were most helpful with the scene in that historic house.

Tom Tucker of Asheville, an expert on antique guns and much more as well as a consultant for historical films, told me about an Allen & Thurber Pepperbox and introduced me to the amazing history of guns.

Dr. Jack Tarleton, doctor of molecular genetics, and Kerry Crandall, genetic counselor, at the Memorial Mission Genetics Center in Asheville were helpful about DNA. Steve Weber who knows Las Vegas and Kyle Hain of Wick and Greene jewelers lent expertise.

My editor, Judith Stern Palais, and my agent, Luna Carne-Ross, were essential to the project!

My writing group—Peggy Parris, Geraldine Powell, Dershie McDevitt, and Florence Wallin—kept me on the straight and narrow path.

Lisa Franklin and Gigi Derballa were extremely helpful with the manuscript.

My long-suffering husband, Chick Squire, was helpful as always with all sorts of good suggestions and encouragement.

Wonderful people gave me memory strategies, including and especially Dr. Sharon Sweede.

IS THERE A DEAD MAN IN THE HOUSE?

CHAPTER
1

THE ARCHAEOLOGISTS

SATURDAY, JUNE 22

One man killed another in this old square-cut-log house in Tennessee in 1849. That was according to Marlowe family tradition. But I began to suspect that old murder might have fallout in the here and now. And my father, dern him, had married a Marlowe.

Just one week unchecked, and Pop ran off at the age of eighty-six and married Azalea, a wild woman from middle Tennessee whose one aim in life was to renovate the old house. Azalea believed that everything is always for the best in the long run, whether it seems that way or not.

And that was just the start. Pop rushed off to Tennessee with Azalea to help with the restoration. Help vicariously, of course—he's in a wheelchair.

Azalea took him right out to see the old house, before she even showed him her bedroom, I gather. She started up a ladder to the second floor. The ladder broke. Azalea fell, cracked three ribs, punctured a lung, and knocked over Alice. That's Azalea's granddaughter who lives with her.

So I had to leave my cool North Carolina mountains and hurry here in the heat to limit damage.

That's why I stood sweating next to the skeleton of the old house. I was watching two archaeologists dig to find clues to the past. Pop had asked me to keep an eye out for what could be wrong.

I kind of liked the house, even though I didn't want to. Even though it was half torn down, as part of restoration. The chinking was gone from between the logs, which were like an empty rib cage, two stories high. Translucent plastic, fastened to the outside of the house, flapped in the breeze. Yet the house had character. It stood as if it knew its place on the rolling land with a few young trees behind it. Like it belonged. Older than anything around it.

I stood there next to Alice, my new stepniece, so young and resilient. She had a few bruises because her grandmother fell on her. But mainly Alice was fine and busy helping the archaeologists. They hoped to date the house.

Alice's job was to spray water to separate artifacts and rocks and bones from dirt. She squirted the dirt away through the holes in a large square screen supported on two sawhorses. She uncovered a tiny amber jawbone, a piece of broken bottle, a triangular shard of white china with a brown line on it, and a button.

Alice took that washing job seriously. She was large-eyed, with wavy dark hair and a delicate body. Self-assured. She stood straight and determined. But she did seem naive in her sky-blue T-shirt and yellow shorts. I might sell her the Brooklyn Bridge. Her eyes were sad. Sad and a little scared. There was a man who worried her. I knew that. His name was Anthony.

She worked at the washing station to the left of the house. The archaeologists brought dirt over in labeled buckets. Sometimes I helped.

Azalea had told us she was sure the diggers would find that this was the oldest log house in middle Tennessee. "Us" was me and Ted, my wonderful journalism-professor husband, who was off at the library and the archives digging. He loves history and he wants to find the old records on this old house.

The young archaeologist with black hair and a President Lincoln beard strode over and joined Alice and me. His name was Hector. I pictured him in front of a museum case full of bits of the past, china shards and such. *Hector the Collector.* Maybe the museum case should have a skull or two, with marks to show they'd been bashed in. Something shocking to associate with his name. Shocking things are much easier to remember. Scholars have known that since the Middle Ages. I know that because I'm kind of a memory-trick expert. So he became *Hector the artifact-and-bone Collector.*

Hector was as square cut as the house, compact, with a precise sure voice and a good profile with Roman nose. Handsome and aware of the fact. Shoulders back with pride. He wore jeans and a T-shirt. On his belt hung a knife in a scabbard of ornately sculptured leather. I remarked on that. "That looks like some kind of antique knife," I said, wondering why on earth he'd wear it to work. It must be valuable. The handle was silver metal inlaid with brass in words that might be Arabic.

"It's for luck," he said. "I always wear it to a dig. It was my father's. He was a very lucky archaeologist." Then he told me his father's name, which I forget, but I could tell by his voice I should be impressed.

So Hector was eccentric and superstitious and proud. But if he knew his job, that's what counted, I thought.

Alice was washing dirt from his pit. He flashed her a grateful smile. She kept her brown eyes on her work.

Hector picked up the bit of china from the sieve. "That's from before 1812," he said importantly, showing off a little. "That's hand-painted. British," he said. I could feel him cataloging it in his mind, adding it to the other clues from the screen that would help date the house.

I admit my mind is like that screen, and I have to work to hold on to the bits of past that matter. I've written a book about how to use mnemonic tricks and logic and such like in order not to forget. It's called *How to Survive Without a Memory,* by Peaches Dann. And I have a section on how to recoup your losses when you do forget: how to reconstruct what you've lost. I needed to be out promoting my book, not here. Dern Pop! Still, I was interested in the dig.

The second archaeologist—brown-haired, loose-kneed sardonic Frank with the big ears—appeared next to Hector and stared at the china shard. I remembered him as *Frank the Blank* because he hadn't found anything to speak of yet. "I was sure I'd find more than you would, Hector," Frank said wryly, "because I'm digging in a place where the earth has obviously been disturbed." He turned to Alice and me: "Even if the earth was dug up a hundred years ago, it's not as hard-packed as the dirt that's never been dug. And I was sure that something had been buried where I'm digging. Even if it *is* where floorboards have covered it. So far, about all I've found is rocks."

I knew the floorboards had been taken up as part of what my father's new wife called the "demolition"—first stage of restoring the old house. Later the boards would be reinforced and put back.

Alice smiled at Frank. Her smile flashed bright like a genie let out of the bottle. She had a warm voice. "You'll find something great. Like maybe the family silver, buried to hide it from the Yankees in the Civil War."

Hector's face quivered and sharpened. He pulled at his beard. He needed to be best, I thought. To find the most splendid artifacts. "I hate to tell you," he said, "but what we're more likely to find is not silver but ancient trash dropped under the old floor."

Hector was digging in front of the hearth in the old log room or "pen" on the left. Frank dug in front of the hearth in the room on the right. They'd been at it all morning. They dug, Alice washed. Azalea sent positive thoughts from her hospital bed, no doubt.

I brought my attention back to Alice's screen. "That tiny

jawbone," I said to Hector, "must be much newer than the china to be so intact, though you found it at the same level."

Levels, I knew, were his clue to the past. I'd watched him for a while, digging out his exact square of earth, scraping out a quarter inch at a time into a bucket so that each level could be labeled and set aside. He kept the sides of his pit sharply cut and perpendicular so that each side was a map of how the soil changed from level to level. Very organized.

"This is a mouse's jawbone." He picked it up. "Yes, mice and woodchucks burrow under a house. Sometimes a fox takes over an old woodchuck den. Creatures can move things around, which makes it harder to put a date to what we find. That's why we trace animal burrows. When we took up the floor, we found a cap that Frank lost the day before. A rat or woodchuck must have dragged it under."

"Can you tell each kind of bone apart?" I asked. Something about the delicate little jaw intrigued me. Even a tiny fragment of this mouse told us it had lived in the house.

"I studied bones at Berkeley," Hector said proudly. "They have a collection of every kind of mammalian bone, even an elephant."

"You're not likely to find an elephant here," Alice said dryly, raising one of her dark arched eyebrows. Yes, scared. That was how her eyes looked.

"We've found pig bones here," Hector said, "which you'd expect on a farm in Tennessee." He made a disparaging face. Pig bones were not up to his standards.

"And there's a story that a man may have been murdered here," he added, glancing at me to see if I knew. "A neighbor came right over and told us as soon as we got here. Said it happened in the mid-1800s."

Alice stopped watching her screen and flipped her dark hair back with a damp hand. She shuddered. No callus on her soul yet, I told myself. Easy to hurt.

Hector shrugged. "But old houses collect wild stories."

And this house was so gray, so gaunt, yet with a certain dignity, of course it would.

"What would you do if you found human bones?" I asked.

Hector was examining the bit of bottle, holding it up to the light and smiling at it. "Any human bones would require me to notify the state archaeologist's office immediately," he said. "Also the sheriff. So I sincerely hope that doesn't happen."

"Me, too," I said. What would it be like, I wondered, trying to figure out a death that took place back in the mid-1800s? I didn't even want to be mixed up in whatever was out of kilter here now. I wanted to be out promoting my new book, not baby-sitting a house. Not even a house whose "memory" was being exposed. Certainly not a house where my job was to find out what was going wrong.

"We mustn't look for trouble," Azalea had told me sweetly as she lay in her hospital bed in the laciest bed jacket I'd ever seen. Her big blue eyes adored Pop, who sat by the bed in his wheelchair. "I am sure everything is going to be all right. I have a feel for these things," she said.

So do I, and I smelled trouble from the moment I learned that several two-hundred-pound men had gone up and down that ladder for weeks—no problem. But it broke when Azalea climbed up. She weighs a hundred and three.

In fact, as I stood there by the house with Hector and Frank and Alice, watching water melt dirt from a rock and an old spoon handle, I was suddenly aware of my back. I hadn't consciously heard footsteps, but I knew with a shiver that someone stood behind us.

I turned around quickly to see a man with black hair and a black mustache that didn't quite hide a sneer. He was square cut like Hector the Collector but with sensual lips and a high round forehead like a baby or Beethoven. He wore heavy leather boots, carefully pressed jeans, and one of those vests with pockets all over it. Several of those pockets bulged. Around his neck he wore a camera on a strap, a large fancy camera. This must be Anthony. Alice had told me about him, him and his mustache. He wanted to build a housing development here and destroy the old house. He thought he knew a way to make that happen.

He also wanted to impress me, I figured, and he did. I thought: Remember this man. He works on his outside because his inside is eating itself. I get sudden thoughts like that.

"I can guarantee that you'll find human bones somewhere around this house," this man said with satisfaction. "When you do, just come and ask me. I can tell you whose they are beyond a doubt. And when I prove whose bones they are, this place will belong to me!"

He spoke to us all, but his eyes were on Alice. And she looked back, dark eyes blazing with the kind of fury that would dissolve iron. He took a picture of her fury.

He smiled. I thought: He's one of those people who can enjoy being hated—who can get a sense of power from that.

He turned to me and said, "You're new here." He raised his camera and took my picture. I probably looked dumbfounded.

Then he stomped off, past the old house, enjoying a dramatic exit. He got into a silver sports car in the gravel driveway and drove away. Good riddance.

He was the kind of guy I'd like to see get a flat tire or step in a cow pie. I wanted him to be as wrong as possible in every single way.

You can bet I was electrified, amazed, annoyed, almost unbelieving when, not fifteen minutes after the man left, as if he'd caused it by his prophecy, Frank came hurrying from the house, straight to Hector. He walked with that sense of drama that you see in men about to make unnerving announcements. Perhaps the timing of what he was about to say struck him as eerie, just as it struck me. I tensed before Frank spoke. "You'd better come quick, Hector, and look at what I've found. I think it's human hand bones."

CHAPTER
2

THURSDAY, JUNE 13

But I'm ahead of myself. I need to go back and explain
how I actually got roped into letting Azalea disrupt my life.
I was the one who introduced her to my father, God help
me!

I saw Azalea first walking up Town Mountain Road in
a white jogging suit and a red sweatband with a daisy stuck
in it. Looking so innocent. This was mid June, a month that
can blow hot or cool in Asheville. The morning sun shone.
The day was springy and zestful. So was Azalea's step.

The smile lines on her face were deep enough to mean
sixty-five years or even seventy, but she was jaunty. She
turned to admire the trees on her right and then the view
on her left across the valley to far blue mountains. She
sniffed the air as if it smelled delicious. She saw me coming
down the road and raised her thumb with a sardonic grin,
as if hitchhiking must be a joke.

I never stop for hitchhikers. My husband, Ted, has made

me promise not to, because it's dangerous. But I could see that Azalea expected me to stop. I pulled over.

"Hello," she trilled, "I'm Azalea Marlowe. Boy, am I glad to see you. I'm tired. It's such a pretty day. I walked too far. I'd just love a ride back down the mountain." She said that as she opened the door of my car, moved my pocketbook from the front to the backseat, and climbed in on the passenger side. "Thanks for sharing this great day."

How could I say, Get out?

"Where to?" I asked, and she said just to the bottom of the mountain where she'd left her car. "I needed to walk and think."

"I have to make a stop before I go down the mountain," I said. "I have to leave off something for my father. He's an invalid, more or less, and he gets bored without new projects." She listened, breathless, as if I was reading her rich uncle's will.

"I'm not in any hurry at all," Azalea assured me. "It's nice to sit down. I think this is going to be my lucky day." She had a warm magnetic voice. Her face was lined at the corners of the eyes. Still, I should have taken note that she was a good-looking woman. My father can't see worth a dern anymore, but somehow he spots good-looking women. Azalea's mouth would rank as baby doll. Her nose was just snubbed enough to be pert. Her heart-shaped face was so full of hope that she glowed. She began to sing softly to herself, "Oh, what a beautiful morning," and sway slightly to the music.

And I thought: This woman will make a change for Pop. She'll cheer him up. So I said, "Why don't you come in and meet my father?" We were just turning into his driveway, shaded by big maples.

"What a lovely house," she cried. Pop's house is nice to look at, with the flowers my mother planted around it before she died. Lots of lilies at the moment. The rocks are an interesting shape in her rock garden. The white clapboard has nice lines, and it's a solid, well-built house.

We climbed up the stone steps to the front door, and I

banged the brass knocker to announce us and then let us in with my key. Pop is wheelchair-bound, and sometimes the sitter is off in the kitchen.

His face lit up as soon as he saw company. "Well," he cried, "who is the lovely lady with you, Peaches?" Pop is no spring chicken, but he has an interesting face, rugged and well defined. He has a mop of white silky hair and a way of sitting like a king. He likes himself.

Azalea's blue eyes widened with approval. I should have been warned. "I'm Azalea Marlowe from Tennessee," she said, "and mighty pleased to be here. What a marvelous place you have! What a view out those wonderful big glass windows! Even the clouds are lovely today, aren't they?" She danced right over to Pop, at the big round table where he likes to sit, and shook his hand.

"This is my father, Harwood Smith," I said.

"Please sit down!" Pop cried. "Tennessee is a marvelous state. The second best to North Carolina. I had a job over there when I was young. Helping to look after horses." His blue eyes sparkled under his bushy white eyebrows.

I could see we were going to stay awhile. But Pop beamed so that I was still glad. He'd been depressed lately. When he's depressed, he calls me every fifteen minutes.

Azalea was studying the books on the shelf in back of him. "I see you have a life of Andrew Jackson," she said. "He's one of my heroes. I just visited the Hermitage. What a wonderful place and a beautiful house. I'm interested in old houses."

Of course Pop said he was, too. He said he'd visited the Hermitage when he was young. I'm always learning new things about Pop, and some of them are true.

"That's why I was out for a walk," she said. "Because of an old house outside of Nashville. I was trying to figure out how to get my cousin, who lives here in Asheville, to help me restore it. It was built about 1795 or 1800, I think. And my cousin should care. He's an architect and he belongs to the Preservation Society, too."

"He should be honored that you came so far to see him!" Pop told her. If he could have stood, he would have bowed. "But please sit down," Pop repeated. "Sit here by me."

"I also came here to see the Governor Zebulon Vance birthplace just outside of Asheville," she said as she slipped into the chair beside him, "because it was built about the same time as the house I want to save. My granddaughter Alice talked me into coming. Alice went to school up here at Mars Hill College. She has a boyfriend who works at the Vance birthplace. Such a nice boy and goodlooking, too." Azalea winked at me. "Alice and I drove up together."

Azalea put her hands on the table. Small pink hands with only a few age spots on the back. They say that people with small hands tend to like to think big. "And I can keep that wonderful Tennessee house if I can finish restoring it," she said. "My father-in-law has given it to me on that condition. Imagine that!"

"He must be a generous man." Pop reached out and took her hand and squeezed it. Then kept on holding it.

"So I was walking along trying to figure how to get more money." She grinned and shrugged, as if to say she'd been pretty silly not to have figured that out yet. "I was praying for inspiration. That's why I didn't realize how far I'd come. But, say, I'm glad to be here. I'm just naturally lucky, you know that? I have been ever since my husband died two months ago."

She said that with a cherub smile.

Even Pop, who loves plot, blinked and stared at her hard.

"It was time," she said. "He was unhappy and in pain. He'd been in an automobile accident. He couldn't even speak. He wasn't himself. He hadn't been himself for a long time. He didn't like his new self. Or me. Or anybody. What's the fun in that? The man he used to be would be very glad he's free and I'm free!"

Pop nodded with gusto. "I'm sure he would!"

"Free to save this historic old house. Otherwise, my

brother-in-law gets possession and gets to sell the parts.''

"Sell the parts!'' This was my turn to be horrified. I hate to see things torn down. I don't even like to move, because when you leave a house you tear down the home inside. Someone else will build a new one, but not the same kind.

She nodded. "Yes, sell the parts.'' She could see that got to me. "Antique square-cut logs bring a good price. So does old ash flooring and old hand-cut chimney stones.''

"I want to hear more about your house.'' Pop glowed with interest. "Peaches, go get us some coffee and some cookies. I thought I was going to be bored today, but you, lovely lady, have changed that.''

Azalea seemed like such a breath of fresh air that I was still pleased. She sat near Pop, her back now turned to the big glass doors to the terrace, and the lively light from the garden lit up her pale gold hair. I was almost tempted to compliment her hairdresser. But that would not have been tactful.

I found Pop's favorite sitter in the kitchen, putting together his lunch—Eudora the aspiring actress, in a snake-skin leotard and red overshirt. Pop likes dramatic women. The last woman he chased in a romantic way was an ex-actress, but she was distracted by murder. Eudora was too young to interest him that way, and she seemed reliable, though we let her arrange her schedule so she could be in Blue Plate Special dinner theater and Theater in the Park. She had a boyfriend who was an antique gun expert for movies. She was not dull. You'd think that would keep my father amused. But he's heard her stories. He is easily bored.

I diverted Eudora from fixing lunch to coffee and cookies. It was still only eleven-thirty in the morning.

"My old house,'' Azalea said as I returned, "is on a beautiful piece of property my father-in-law bought a few years back for speculation. About thirty miles south of Nashville. Not far from my own house. He saw the for-sale sign when he came to my birthday party. The house on that property looked a wreck. But the chimneys were beautiful stonework. A friend who knows about old houses came to visit and looked the place over and said it was a gem in disguise.'' She threw her arms wide as if to embrace the house, or maybe us. ''I was so excited,'' she said. ''He said it might date back as far as 1800 and it had good hardwood floors. He said it was a fabulous house, and we should save it!''

Pop kept nodding, thoroughly unbored. I began to feel nervous, but I told myself that was silly.

''Alice did research and found out the most amazing part. That house was once in our family! Can you believe that? My family and my husband's family, too! We were distant cousins.'' Azalea squeezed Pop's hand. ''And I knew it was my fate to save that house! My wonderful granddaughter Alice says she'll help. She's interested in archaeology.''

''And you came here by fate,'' Pop cried. ''We'll give you our advice. We'll help in any way we can.'' He was as exuberant as the small Chinese laughing god on the bookshelf behind him. You rub that figure's shiny stomach for good luck. I should have done that.

I was aghast to realize that Pop had made up his mind to get mixed up in this house business. But not aghast enough. I was also intrigued by Azalea's description of the house. Azalea has that gift. To carry you along with her enthusiasm. To carry you along like a gone-berserk riptide. So that—even now—I want to see her save the old house.

CHAPTER
3

MONDAY, JUNE 17

For three days—just three measly days—I didn't get by to check on Pop. I phoned, but I didn't go to see him in person. I was busy, talking about the memory tricks in my book to a great group at the library in Hendersonville and to a book club at the Crowfields retirement community. Both groups especially loved the trick where if you're out and you want to remember something when you get home, you call and leave a message on your own answering machine. One person told me Batman used that trick once. I'm in good company, right?

On Monday, I drove up to Pop's house in a gray drizzle of rain to find a robin's-egg-blue convertible parked in his driveway and Azalea inside with Pop, showing him a scrapbook. He waved at me jauntily as I came in and called, "Peaches, come see the pictures of this marvelous house!"

He couldn't really see those pictures so well, but I guessed he didn't want Azalea to know that. He has macular degeneration, so even glasses don't help. Perhaps Azalea described the pictures as she went along.

Azalea, sitting with Pop at his favorite table, was all dolled up in a baby-blue pants suit and just-from-the-beauty-parlor blond hair. Even on this gray day her hair glowed. She held a big white scrapbook, which she proudly turned back to the first page to show me a photograph of the tackiest house I ever saw in my life.

The tired wooden porch had square brick pillars that turned halfway up into dirty white wooden clapboard pillars, which in turn tapered to the sagging porch roof. From the one-story porch roof up to the two-story house roof there was more clapboard, buckled here and there. Actually it was a fairly large house, but delapidated. Behind it, several cows looked sadly over a fence toward the house, as if to say, What a mess!

Perhaps Azalea saw my shock. "You have to have a good eye to see what's here, Peaches." She smiled a friendly challenge. "What you see is a later porch, from maybe 1920. The original one is gone. But look at this!" She pointed at what appeared to be a wide board at the place where the front of the house above the porch met the rusted tin roof. "This," she said dramatically, "is a log plate." She waited as if I might clap.

"And what is a log plate?"

She patted Pop's hand to say he and she both shared this wonderful secret. "A log plate is one single square-cut log that goes all across the front of the house. It's one imme-diate clue that square-cut logs are under the siding on this house. And look at this," she said, pointing to a big bump at the corner of the house just under what she'd called a plate. "That's a sleeper," she cried, and she hugged Pop, as if she couldn't contain her joy.

I could see, by the way she and Pop glowed, that a sleeper was something marvelous.

"What you see at each side of the house is the rounded end of a square-cut log beam. That's a sleeper at right an-gles to the log plate and holding it up," she said. "That absolutely proves this is early construction. My friend Ross, the old-house expert, has looked over the place.''

By me, the corner thing still looked like a wooden bump, but Pop gazed at Azalea as if she spoke of wonders.

''And here, inside the house, is a place where the plaster is gone and you can see square-cut logs underneath.'' She showed me the inside of a room so dilapidated that the section of wall with the plaster gone looked like a normal part of the decor. Where the plaster remained, peeling wallpaper gave it skin disease.

''Isn't this exciting!'' Pop demanded.

''This house looks like it's about to fall down,'' I blurted.

''Doesn't it?'' Azalea agreed. ''That's what my granddaughter Alice said. That's the marvelous part. If my friend Ross, who restores old houses, hadn't come by and looked at it with his restorer's eye, we'd never have known.''

''We certainly never would!'' Pop said. It dawned on me that he was acting as though he and Azalea were a team of some kind.

She squeezed his hand. ''You have such a wonderful eye for seeing possibilities,'' she told him. ''This was an elegant house when it was built. This is a gem,'' she said, tapping the scrapbook.

She and Pop gazed into each other's eyes as if she was talking about him, and he was savoring every word.

My stomach turned over. I don't like unexpected changes. I could feel one taking shape.

''There is even hogs'-hair plaster,'' Azalea exclaimed.

I felt like saying, How elegant can you get?

She explained. ''It's quite unusual for a house this early to have square-cut logs and also clapboard on the outside and plaster on the inside. That's first-class construction.''

''With hogs' hair,'' I said.

''Oh, yes. They needed to put some sort of fiber in the plaster as a binding agent,'' she said. ''Ross told me. On a Tennessee farm, they had lots of hogs' hair. The first thing they did after slaughter was shave the hair off the pig.'' I visualized that. I decided from Pop's beatific smile that he did not.

"That means the house was plastered some time before 1880. They used hogs' hair until about then. But this house was built much earlier than that. The roof construction is a very early style. Ross suspects this house was built as early as 1800, or even before."

So what was between this Ross and Ms. Baby Blue? That didn't seem to worry Pop. Nothing seemed to worry him.

"Have you had any luck getting your Asheville cousin to invest in reconstructing the house?" I asked Azalea.

"He is a man without imagination," Pop answered for her, frowning with disgust.

Azalea simply shrugged. "Alice says I shouldn't even bother with him. But Alice worries too much. I'm still working on it. My cousin takes persuading. I know that fate intends me to make this house whole. I am not discouraged. A way will open. That always happens when I have faith. You'll see."

I had a sinking feeling that I did see. She had designs on Pop. She might do anything. I felt like the time on the roller coaster when I started down the first long steep hill and left my stomach at the top. But then I tried to tell myself I was being silly. At least Azalea made Pop happy.

"There must be problems about renovating an old house like this," I said.

"The basic structure is sound. That's the amazing part. After nearly two hundred years, there's a sill or two to replace, and a lot of the clapboard on the outside and the plaster on the inside need to be renewed, but the logs are sound." A shadow drifted over her face. "The only problem is that people talk. That bothers Alice, who's a very sensitive girl," she said. "This project is as important to Alice as it is to me."

Pop leaned forward eagerly. "What do people say?"

Azalea frowned, and I could tell she wished she hadn't brought that up.

"When an old house sits empty and looks so . . . well,

so spooky, rumors start. I've heard two different ones. I'm sure at least one of them is not true.'' She said that last firmly.

"But what are they?'' Pop cried. "Tell us!''

"The first is that someone in this house killed a baby.'' Azalea's face became drawn. She was briefly ten years older.

"And what else?'' Pop demanded. He has real radar for knowing when he hasn't heard the best story yet.

"Around 1849, a young woman named Annie Thomason lived in this house. The night before she was to be married, her brother and the man she meant to marry both disappeared.''

Pop whistled.

Azalea sighed. "Those men really did vanish. A local history confirms it, and the amazing thing is that I am related to all the folks involved. When I was a kid, I heard the story about the bride who lost her lover and her brother just before her wedding day. And how nobody knew where they went or what happened. It was a story that got repeated in my family. Now I've discovered those men may have left from this very house.'' She paused dramatically to let that sink in, tapping the scrapbook. "However,'' she said firmly, "there is absolutely no proof that either one was killed.''

"Tell me all about them!'' Pop cried.

Azalea knew how to tell a story, I'll say that. Her voice became low and dramatic.

"Wilbur Thomason probably built the house. He was a lawyer and a farmer and well-to-do from buying and selling land. Tennessee was still the frontier, but he built a fine house. His son Wilbur Junior evidently inherited the house. The records say he owned it in 1829, and he was a wealthy lawyer, too, and a proud man. Annie Thomason was Wilbur Junior's daughter, the most beautiful girl in all that part of Tennessee.'' Azalea smiled and nodded. "That's what my grandmother told me. Annie was about to be married to David Holden, a man her father treated like a son.''

David Holden. Yes—to marry is to *have and to Hold-en*, to never be divided, which is like *Da-vided*. I'd remember that one. I really have to work at names.

"He was a solid man," Azalea said firmly, "a widower with a little boy Annie loved. But Annie's blood brother, Buddy, hated that man." Azalea paused and looked at each of us as if she expected us to say, How sad!

"Buddy," Azalea went on, "had quarreled with the rest of the family. But he came back for Annie's wedding and even brought his wife and young son for a reconciliation."

"But he was faking it," Pop said hopefully.

"A few nights before the ceremony, when the whole family was off at a party at a cousin's house, Buddy and the bridegroom disappeared."

"Aha!" Pop grinned in anticipation.

"A servant said he thought he'd seen them ride off together toward another cousin's house. The Thomasons' house servants had come to help with the party. Perhaps Annie or her father should have checked where Buddy and David had really gone, but spirits were flowing, and Wilbur Thomason simply said he was pleased to see them reconciled." She raised an eyebrow to show how seriously we should take that. "So the party continued." Then she leaned forward and spoke slowly for emphasis. "Neither man was ever seen again."

Azalea had managed to give me goose bumps. "Were there clues to what became of them?" I asked.

"Yes," said Azalea. "Back at the bride's house, the Thomason house, they found a bullet hole in the wall. That's what my grandmother said. In the morning, they found the groom's horse—David Holden's horse—back at his house, grazing by the barn. They never found Buddy's horse at all. Or either man or either body."

"That Buddy must have shot his sister's intended. Then he rode off in the dark with the body!" Pop announced triumphantly.

"Everyone assumed that Buddy shot once and missed, then shot again and killed the groom," Azalea continued, "but, like I said, no body was ever found. Could Buddy really get away with riding off with a dead man over his saddle? In the midst of a thunderstorm? My grandmother said there was a terrible storm that night."

Yes, I thought. The story needed a thunderstorm for proper drama.

"Buddy would have had a head start. The story says that Annie and her father spent the night at the house of the cousins who were giving the party. Not unusual in those days." She frowned and sighed. "Where would he take the body? Of course, I'd especially like to know because David Holden was my ancestor."

I was confused. "Not the bride?"

"Actually I'm distantly related to the bride because my husband and I were distant cousins. But the groom is my direct ancestor."

That sounded like the end of the story, but Azalea seemed poised to tell more, her lips still parted.

"Two years after that terrible night, a Methodist minister returning from California delivered a package to Annie Thomason. He said he didn't know what it contained, but it was powerful heavy for the small size. A young man dying after a wound in a barroom brawl begged him to find a way to get it to a girl in Tennessee. So that kind minister went out of his way home to North Carolina in order to bring it."

"And in the package?" Pop prompted.

"In the package were three gold nuggets wrapped in David Holden's handkerchief."

"So he hadn't been dead?" I asked. "Not until he died in California? But how could they tell it was his handkerchief?"

"His mother had embroidered his initials on it: D.H. She said it was his."

"So what did that mean?" I demanded. This was a strange story or family myth, or whatever.

"Annie Thomason believed that her brother, Buddy, sent the nuggets because he wanted to make restitution as much as he could for killing the man she loved. Maybe he wanted to confuse the issue about who was dead. But some folks believed it was the other way around. Her lover killed her brother and had to run away. He could switch horses, they said. That would be easy.''

"I don't believe that," I protested. "That would ruin the story!"

Azalea grinned. "I'm glad you don't believe it! Annie Thomason didn't either. She never married. She said she was married in her heart to the only man she'd ever loved, and she and her father raised David Holden's little orphan son, who was my ancestor. She lived in the house with the bullet hole in the wall until she died."

What a story! "But what happened to the house?"

"Annie Thomason's father left that house jointly to David Holden's boy and to his blood grandson, the son of brother Buddy. Old records show that. What could they do but sell it? That was way back, about 1880. And it's strange. Our family remembered the story and passed it down. But they forgot exactly where the house was. During the Great Depression, tenant farmers lived there, I think. It went downhill.

"But now we have the house back. And I am descended directly from David Holden, and my husband was descended directly from Buddy Thomason, Annie Thomason's brother. I think my granddaughter should live in that house, don't you? Alice would like that."

"Reconciliation by mixing blood. A very Southern idea," I said, "that the murder in that house would be exorcised if your grandchild, descended from the killer and the killed, lived in that house, right?"

Tears came into Azalea's eyes, but only briefly. She blotted them carefully with a tissue before the mascara could run much. "I have no daughter, and my son is dead. I raised Alice. She's like a daughter to me, a precious daughter. And quite beautiful. I like to think she looks like Annie Thomason must have looked. We don't have a picture of

Annie, but the family story says she was a willowy girl with dark hair.''

Pop patted Azalea's small plump hand and blurted out a question. "But suppose that groom did kill the brother," he said, "and buried the body somewhere near the house. It could be haunted!" He beamed at that.

"You're as bad as the local storytellers," Azalea told Pop. "Not quite as bad—some of them say that the men fought and Buddy was killed. And Annie Thomason helped her lover hide the body. But she wouldn't run away with him because he'd killed her brother, and he took off for California. That's why she never married and the body never was found."

Pop nodded. "What a romantic story, either way. A romantic story adds a certain glamour to a house."

I, God help me, agreed.

CHAPTER
4

WEDNESDAY, JUNE 19, 8:30 P.M.

"I was asked to notify you that your mother is in the hospital, and your father urgently needs your help," the man's voice on the telephone said.

This voice had somehow tracked me down to the Hampton Inn motel in Boone. I'd been speaking to the Friends of the Library there and signing books at bookstores. My wonderful husband, Ted, had come along for moral support, and we were just back from an early supper at a steak house next door to the motel, watching TV.

"I'd be one hundred percent surprised if you were right about my mother," I told the voice sharply. "My mother has been dead for years."

Ted turned back around from watching CNN and raised an eyebrow with a what-on-earth expression. He turned down the sound on some wild story about how DNA testing on Egyptian mummies could sort out their sex life and tell who begat who. I must not let Egyptian sex distract me.

"What hospital did you say this was?"

"The Williamson County Medical Center in Franklin, Tennessee," the voice told me. "Do you know a Harwood Smith?"

"Harwood Smith!" I was alarmed "That's my father. Is he hurt?" I asked, immediately sorry I'd been sarcastic. But how could they possibly think he was my mother? And what was Pop doing in Tennessee?

"He asked me to call and get you to come right away," the voice said. "His wife has been hurt, and I assumed . . ."

I sat down in the chair by the telephone. "His wife," I repeated. "In Franklin, Tennessee?"

Ted hit his forehead with his hand to mime, Not that! He'd figured it out.

So Pop and Azalea got married and then left for Tennessee. Was that it? I asked myself. But they had to allow time to get a license. How long did that take? And they never told me what they were up to. Of course not. Pop knew I'd try to talk him out of it.

"What is my mother's name?" I asked, just to make doubly sure.

The voice made choking sounds. The man didn't know what to make of me. Or maybe he didn't know the name. "Tell my father I'll start right over," I said. "What is the nature of his wife's injuries?"

"He said something about falling off a ladder," the voice said. "I work as a volunteer here in the hospital, and he asked me to call you."

So why didn't he call me himself? I wanted to ask. But he was probably in the emergency room with Azalea. I hung up.

"A ladder," I said to Ted. "She fell off. In that damned house, I bet. I hope she didn't fall on Pop, although it would serve him right. Eloping at his age! That must be what happened. No details at all from the man who called. Just that Azalea—it must be Azalea, what other wife would he have?—fell off a ladder and is in the hospital and Pop needs our help."

"It's six-thirty," Ted said as he began to repack his suitcase, folding a shirt. "We could get there by midnight. Call the hospital back and get a condition report, and ask what motel is nearby." Ted is quick on practical details and what to do first. He finished packing, adding his canvas toilet kit, while I called.

The report said an Azalea Smith was there. No condition report yet. A Holiday Inn was next door. I asked for Azalea's room number, but she wasn't in a room yet.

"Lucky Pop could find us," I said, not quite sure I believed it.

"You gave him your schedule," Ted said, switching off the TV. "And if he got one of the sitters to pack for him, she probably was smart enough to put it in his suitcase."

"But not smart enough to call me and warn me what he was up to." I was mad. I was worried. I was off balance.

Ted laughed. "If you'd known, you would have tried to stop him, or at least slow him up. Your father is not stupid."

"No," I said, "just foolish, dumb, and a first-prize stinker."

I opened my pocketbook and got out my day planner. I sure need it now that I'm out promoting a book. I glanced through the next few weeks. "Lucky I have nothing before the talk in the Weaverville Library in two weeks," I said. Then on the page for the next day I wrote, *Save Pop,* and *Make sure who my mother is.* The things I have to plan don't always fit in slots.

While I packed my suitcase Ted called and made us a motel reservation in Tennessee.

I had my suitcase on wheels, my pocketbook, and a briefcase all ready to go. "Three," I said.

"Three what?" Ted asked.

"New memory system. I have to remember I'm traveling with three objects," I said. "Suitcase, briefcase, pocketbook. Each time we move from this room to the car or the car to the next room or whatever, I just feel whether I have three things. It's much easier than remembering exactly what I'm supposed to have in hand.''

"Suppose you buy an ice-cream cone?''

"This is only for while you're traveling and not stopping to get things, and we don't have time to stop or even for you to ask these questions," I said. "All due to Pop.''

Then we left for Tennessee. Exit fuming.

We arrived in the middle of the night with me half-asleep, I'll admit. We parked at the motel, and I pulled my stuff out of the car and yawned. "Three," I said. "Or should I leave my briefcase in the car? Okay, two." We went inside, where an equally sleepy clerk gave us our room key. We called the hospital as soon as we entered the room. By this time we were awake. We were told by the nurse to whom our call was finally routed that Azalea was resting nicely, and Pop had left a message for us. He said meet him at the hospital at ten in the morning. So much for emergencies.

We decided to laugh instead of cry. "Besides," Ted said, pulling me close, "two is a very nice number. Tomorrow we'll worry about Azalea.''

CHAPTER
5

THURSDAY, JUNE 20

We slept late and finally made our way to the hospital, a low brick building with a tower, among other medical buildings. The crisp blonde at the nurses' station told us where to find Azalea. We hurried down a long hall to her room and found her lying back on her pillow with heart-shaped face bright as a valentine. Red lipstick, pink cheeks, blue eyeliner. I figured she'd live. Pop was in his wheel-chair alongside the bed.

"I'm glad to see you looking so bright, Azalea," I said, "and, Pop, you look okay, too." Her room was small but with a large window complete with venetian blinds to let in light but not view, and to give us privacy.

Pop was straight and even perky, white hair combed smoothly, wearing a favorite red, white, and blue shirt. The new bridegroom. How on earth was he managing without sitters? His arthritis was so bad he couldn't even dress him-self. Also he was half-blind.

"By the way, congratulations to you both." I was careful to keep sarcasm out of my voice. Maybe they'd be happy. I'd like that. I told Azalea, "I'd like you to meet my husband, Ted."

Much handshaking; then: "We were sorry to miss the wedding," I said.

"Oh, that," Pop said. "Just a quickie at the courthouse with Eudora for a witness." I thought of her as *You-Adore-Her* because Pop really did think she was great. "She's here with us," he said. "She said she'd always wanted to visit Tennessee. And her boyfriend is going to be down here to work on a movie." Ah. At least Azalea would not have to give her new husband a bath. I tried to envision how this threesome would work: Pop and Azalea and Eudora the sitter. I gave up.

"Exactly what happened to Azalea?" Ted asked, jumping to the heart of things.

Pop spoke right up. "A rung of the ladder broke just when Azalea put her full weight on it to get up to the second floor." He must mean in the old house under reconstruction. "She fell all the way down to the first floor. Alice screamed loud. She was there with her grandmother."

"I was holding on to the upstairs wall," Azalea chimed in, "or trying to. There's no banister right now. It's just a temporary ladder while we redo the stairs. I put my foot on one of the top rungs, it broke, and I fell."

"She's a rugged gal, or she'd be hurt worse," Pop said happily. "I was not trying to go up that ladder. I'm no climber." He patted the arm of his wheelchair.

"And could you tell what made the ladder break?" I demanded.

Uncomfortable silence. "It's a good thing that the floor had been taken up down below, so I fell on dirt, which is softer than wood," Azalea said.

"The workmen had been going up and down the ladder with no problem?" Ted pressed.

"Yes," Azalea said, "but this was after they left for the day, so there weren't any workmen around."

"Do you think somebody tampered with the ladder?" I asked.

"Tampered? Who would do that?" Pop glared at me as if I had a nerve to even suggest such a thing.

Okay, I'm suspicious. Better to be suspicious than sorry, I say. I would have asked more, but just at that moment a pretty dark-haired girl came in the door.

"Hi," she said with a big smile, and I was afraid she was going to rush over and hug Azalea, cracked ribs and all, but she restrained herself and kissed Azalea on the forehead.

"I'm Alice," she said, sticking one smooth, supple hand out to me. "I'm Azalea's granddaughter. I've been off talking to the doctor." She had a vivid, quick voice. She was dressed simply in denim skirt and a T-shirt with a bluebird on it, and wore hoop earrings. Yet I noticed she had style.

"This is Peaches, Harwood's daughter," Azalea told her. "And this is her husband, Ted. They're your aunt and uncle now." She beamed as if she'd pulled that off just for Alice. Like we should all be grateful.

"Welcome to the family," Alice said, but something else was obviously first on her mind. She looked me straight in the eye. "I heard you ask about the ladder," she said. "I was with Grandma when she fell." She turned toward Azalea. "Something was wrong." She became even more intense. "I went up that ladder the day before, and it was fine. The carpenters went up and down it. Why should it crack all of a sudden? You tell me why."

A frown did flit across Azalea's face, but it couldn't stick. "We will all keep our eyes wide open in case something is wrong," she said.

Wide-eyed, I thought. That's what Azalea is. Wrong kind of wide-open eyes.

"If anyone was meant to be the butt of a prank, it was me," she added. "I tend to be lucky, you'll admit that."

Prank! She called setting someone up to fall and maybe break her neck a prank?

"You *are* lucky, Azalea," Pop said, "but don't push it!

Maybe there was foul play." He said "foul play" with relish. He loved those words. He looked around the plain square hospital room as if he needed more complication. "Someone needs to look into this."

"Yes," Alice said. "We need to call the sheriff." She turned urgently toward Ted, who was standing by the phone near the bed.

"No." Azalea sat up so straight I was scared she'd jump out of bed, then she winced. "The sheriff will only slow us up. Don't touch that phone," she ordered Ted.

"It doesn't sound as though you have much for the sheriff to go on yet," Ted said cautiously, turning toward Alice. "He might not take this seriously just because a ladder broke."

"Why, then"—Pop beamed at me—"we'll just get Peaches to investigate. That's her hobby."

Hobby! Pop meant I'd been dragged kicking and screaming into investigating murders before. God willing, this was not going to become one! Some families tend to have crooked teeth or big feet or bad tempers or even some serious genetic disease like Huntington's chorea—that's the one that killed Woody Guthrie. But my family seems to get mixed up in murders. They're nice people, too—mostly, that is. I have so dern many relatives they couldn't all be perfect. We claim kin in our mountains.

Pop eggs me on. I won't say he was pleased that someone might be trying to hurt his new wife, but I could tell by the twinkle in his eye that he was glad life wasn't dull.

"All right," I said. "I'll spend today and maybe tomorrow nosing around if you'll agree to call the law at the end of tomorrow if I come across anything fishy."

"And I'll help," Ted said. He wasn't teaching summer school this year.

"Thank you." Pop gave us his most encouraging smile. Meanwhile Azalea and Alice eyed us cautiously as if we were fish that might be fresh or might not. They should have eyed Pop. He was the one who brought them into our family. But, then again, my brand-new stepmother fit.

Azalea was the type to pet alligators because they seem to smile.

"I will begin by finding out more about the house itself," I said. I had a hunch I should do that. "Your father-in-law knows all about its history—right, Azalea?"

She smoothed the sheet that covered her with one small plump hand. "Oh, I'd start by looking around the site!" she said quickly.

Ted winked at me. He knows I always look carefully at whatever, or whoever, someone wants to keep me away from. "Where does your father-in-law live?" I asked. I looked at my watch. Ten of eleven. "I'll go talk to him first, then go to the site."

"I'll drop you off," Ted said. "Since we're staying longer, I'll buy myself another shirt and come back for you in about an hour." I wasn't surprised. Ted has the theory that people are more likely to open up and tell me things when he's not along. Perhaps I look too naive to be a threat. He's good at logic, and he has a sharp eye for things out of place. I'm good at whatever needs playing by ear.

We left the hospital and followed Azalea's directions to her father-in-law's house—Adam Marlowe, she said his name was. Adam. Like Adam and Eve. I saw him wearing nothing but a fig leaf like a painting I once saw of the original Adam. I'd remember that. We drove down many narrow roads. Azalea's directions had been grudgingly given, but were quite clear.

We found the house, surrounded by horses that grazed and pranced behind freshly painted white fences on either side of the driveway. Green fields stretched away around the house. "The old guy doesn't seem to be broke," Ted said as he dropped me off.

Azalea had called to say I was coming over. The old man himself answered the front door.

He was gnarled like a tree: large-jointed. His face was as lined and wrinkled as an old monkey's. But then, he must be quite ancient. If he was Azalea's father-in-law, he must be Alice's grandfather. No! *Great*-grandfather. Ancient or not, he seemed in fine health. Better than Pop. I found myself remembering a picture of John Brown, the abolitionist, who had fanatical eyes. Azalea's father-in-law had eyes like that. It seemed to me that his eyes should go with a deep booming voice, but his voice was short on breath.

"Good morning," Adam Marlowe growled. "I was amazed that Azalea got married. But I'm pleased to meet her new daughter."

That was me, wasn't it?

"It's a miracle that Azalea is alive," he said, his voice harsh, but his words polite.

"Yes," I said. "She could have broken her neck. I'm relieved she didn't."

He waved one gnarled hand toward the room behind him. "Come in and sit down." Folks with gnarled hands don't easily change their minds. That's what my cousin Fern from California says. But then, I wasn't here to change his mind.

In his large airy living room we came to more horses, all framed. People and horses were intermixed on the wall. The lovely chestnut horse with his head high was in a gold frame exactly like the one that enclosed a woman in a deep over-the-ears hat and a man with a stiff collar, who could have been from the 1920s. A younger man in a World War II air-force uniform was in a frame almost exactly like the one dedicated to a black horse with a large blue ribbon, and so it went. More horses and folks were in stand-up frames on a long mahogany table. A large white leather Bible stood among them, and Bibles of all sizes and covers were in a bookshelf on the wall.

He indicated I should sit in a deep leather chair, and he sat down across from me in another. He rang a hand bell that sat on the table so loud I jumped.

"I am fond of Azalea," he said, without waiting for whoever he'd summoned to show up. Without even getting to know me, he plunged right into family talk. "Azalea stuck by my son after his accident when he couldn't even speak. All he could do was nod." The old man grabbed a framed photo standing on a table by his chair and thrust it at me as if it was some kind of proof. It showed a good-looking gray-haired man with a square chin and level eyebrows. Next to him in the photo stood a much younger woman with a dreamy face like the kind on Christmas-card angels. "Azalea was a loyal wife to my son, Hunt, and a friend to my daughter, Dolores," the old man said. He nodded to himself. Tears came into his eyes. "Dolores was killed in the same accident that crippled my son."

A stocky black woman with gray hair appeared in the doorway to the back of the house. He nodded and without even asking if I wanted any, he said, "Please get us some coffee, Mary." So was Mary a housekeeper or what?

He went right on with his story, bitterly now. "A drunk kid hit the car with my daughter, Dolores, and my son, Azalea's beloved husband, Hunt. Dolores was killed and so were Alice's mother and father. Ten years ago. Azalea helped us live through it."

"I'm so sorry," I said. "How dreadful." He stared moodily at the photo and then put it back on the table.

Finally, I said, "It's possible someone has tried to hurt Azalea at the site of this house she's restoring—a house that has belonged to you. So I wanted to find out as much as I could about the house in order to understand what's happening." I was afraid that might upset him even further, but not at all.

He wiped away the last of his tears and became alert as a dog on a scent. "You mean you wonder if it's haunted?" he demanded.

Haunted! That's what Pop evidently hoped. What a thought!

"I have never heard anyone claim it was haunted," Adam Marlowe said calmly—a man of quick-changing moods—"but it does have an unusual history." Whereupon he told me more or less the story I'd had from Azalea. He stressed the fact that no one knew for sure if one man killed the other or which was killed—or if anyone was killed at all.

I tried to remember exactly what Azalea had said. Oh, yes. The bride believed her lover was killed. Still, Azalea had agreed there was no proof. So what did this have to do with the here and now?

Why did a fanatical light flare up again in Adam Marlowe's eyes?

"Murder is a terrible crime!" he cried. "Murder must be punished."

What? He'd just said there was no evidence of murder! And if there had been evidence, there was no one left to punish after all those years. I was confused.

"Was there bad blood between Buddy Thomason and"—oh, dear, I'd forgotten the groom's name—"Annie Thomason's intended? For a long time?" I asked. "Did people know why one of them might have killed the other?"

"The sin of pride touched them all!" Adam Marlowe proclaimed, and a faraway look came into his fiery eyes. "We live here in a great valley of pride. In the Civil War, six thousand men were sent to slaughter by a general besotted by alcohol and pride. He sent them out to battle in an open field against Yankees safely entrenched and protected in the rear by a freezing river. Wave after wave were slaughtered." He waved toward the window as if the carnage might be just outside and still in progress. He snorted in contempt. "But the general was too proud to admit he'd made a mistake, and over the protests of his whole staff, he sent more men to die. That," he said, "was the terrible Battle of Franklin."

Ugly and dramatic. Human nature can be worth shuddering over. I wondered how the general lived with himself after that. But the Battle of Franklin would not explain who'd killed who about fifteen years before that. I pulled us back on the track. "And how did pride make two men disappear back in 1849?"

Mary brought our coffee so silently that we hardly noticed. She set milk and sugar on the table near us.

"Why, the father was proud, of course. Annie and Buddy's father," Adam said, holding out sugar in a lovely delicate china bowl, complete with silver spoon. I shook my head no, then sipped my coffee. Good and strong.

"Book proud," Adam said, sipping his coffee between words. "Buddy's father was a lawyer. He wanted his only son to be a lawyer, too. And Buddy couldn't do it. That's what I've heard. He was a good carpenter, but his father looked down on that. So the son took up the sin of drink as well as pride. And the father chose a young law clerk, a distant cousin, to be like a son to him. That was David Holden."

David Holden! Yes. That was the name! An *avid* lover. *D* plus *avid*. Who wanted Annie Thomason to have and to *hold*-en. My mental picture hadn't been strong enough before. I pictured him holding her avidly, fondling her breasts, kissing her throat. Putting his hand under her skirt. *D-avid-ly*. A shocking image to make it easier to remember.

"So Buddy was jealous of David Holden," I said.

"Furiously jealous because Buddy's father preferred David." The old man scowled in disapproval, so that the lines of his face squinched together. "And because Buddy drank, I imagine David had contempt for him. Had pride in his own superiority. That's a sin, too. That's how I imagine it was."

"That's the family story?"

"That's how my mother told me the family story. There's mention of it in a local history book, too, but only that the two men vanished." He put his coffee cup down. "Vanished and were never seen again."

So how much was family myth and how much was his need to see sin in it? Certainly something was terribly wrong, or two men wouldn't have disappeared. I pondered that as I finished my coffee.

Meanwhile my eyes fell on a picture of the large black horse with the blue ribbon. So I asked Adam Marlowe about the horses.

"I have two winners right now," he said, rubbing his gnarled hands together. "I am proud of my horses. They have good bloodlines. Of course, I don't bet on them myself. Betting is immoral. But they are beautiful horses, aren't they? They are my hobby.''

"Hobby?" I said in surprise.

"Yes," he said proudly. "My business was publishing Bibles." He reached out and patted the white Bible on the table. "I sent out the Good Word all over the world. That's a big business in Nashville, you know. Bibles and country music. But now I've sold the business and I can do what I please."

"Your family has been here a long time?" I asked, bringing the subject back toward the house.

"Since Tennessee was first settled," he said proudly. "We have deep roots."

"And the old house that Azalea wants to restore belonged to your family?" I noticed behind him a portrait of a man in a homespun-looking suit, vintage about 1800. He stood by a draped curtain and took himself seriously.

"Yes," he said, noticing my glance, "that is a painting of my ancestor who probably built the house. The early records are confusing. But it was in the family and then sold. Then, almost by chance, I bought it back three years ago. Azalea wants to restore it and keep it in our family. She loves tradition."

"But there's nothing unusual about the house itself? Nobody who believes it should belong to them?"

"Not except my son-in-law Anthony, my Dolores's husband—Dolores who died. He believes the house should belong to him. Dolores was my daughter by my second wife. Very dear to me. That's why I keep some of her things in the attic even now. Dolores was talented. . . ."

I could see we were off on a byway of thought. I said, "Anthony wants the house?"

Adam frowned. "Anthony wants to make money out of it, which he says Azalea never will. But I don't need the money. You know the passage about the camel and the eye of the needle?"

"So you've given the house to Azalea, free and clear, as long as she restores it?"

"Yes, she's a first-rate girl. She nursed my son and took care of him after his accident. Azalea is a fine person. She's good to me, too." His lines rearranged themselves around a smile.

The black woman had returned and was removing the cups as silently as a shadow. "Thank you," I said. She nodded.

"So you don't know of anyone who would try to stop Azalea from fixing up that house?" I asked Adam.

"Only Anthony, and he just wants the money. Unless you count me." He pointed at his barrel chest.

What? That was just the opposite of what he'd been saying.

"If something is found while they dismantle and reassemble the house that proves Azalea's ancestor killed my ancestor—killed him right there in that house—I couldn't give Azalea the house, could I? That would be immoral. That would be rewarding murder." He drew his brows together and gave me such a piercing glance that I flinched.

"She's descended from the bridegroom, and you're descended from the bride's brother?" I said quickly. Did I have that right way around?

"Yes," he said, "absolutely."

I needed to remember that. D*avid* the *avid* bridegroom was Azalea's ancestor. So, okay, azalea is a flower. They have flowers as well as bridegrooms at weddings. But that wasn't funny or shocking. I thought of Annie Thomason in a white gown with a bunch of white azaleas with a bee on it. The bee bit her and then bit David. He was livid. Which is almost like *avid*. Azalea descended from bridegroom David. Enough said.

"Therefore," said Adam *Figleaf* Marlowe, "there is a clause in my contract with Azalea which says that if, in redoing the house, anyone finds proof that her ancestor killed mine, I will pay Azalea what she's put into the house. I can afford to do that." He waved a hand at his possessions. "Then the house will revert to Anthony to do with as he pleases. He wants to tear it down. My Dolores loved

Anthony very much. He's good to me, too.''

My heart sank. Azalea had me hooked on saving the house. I couldn't bear to see it torn down and sold off. And for such a foolish reason.

The fanatical light in Adam *Figleaf*'s eyes burned bright, and I thought: He's a little bit crazy. Not crazy enough to be declared incompetent. That's the hardest kind to deal with.

"But don't worry," he said. "Anthony was so sure there was a skeleton buried somewhere around that house that we probed all around it before the work on the house even started. Those archaeologist fellows know how to do that. They have a special tool. So there is no skeleton. You can count on that.''

CHAPTER
6

LATER THURSDAY, JUNE 20

I told Ted about my visit with Adam *Figleaf* as we found our way to the old house, using Azalea's directions.

"So you learned what he's like and more about Azalea's family but not a lot else new," he said. That about summed it up.

"You'll recognize the old house," Azalea had said, "because it looks like we're tearing it down." She explained it was off the paved road, a little way up a gravel road that went on past it. If we kept going past the log house, we'd get to the house where she lived.

Sure enough, the old house looked stripped, a log skeleton, though it still had a tin roof. A thin skin of transparent plastic hung loosely around the bare logs—to keep the rain out, I supposed. The tacky front porch I'd seen in that original picture was gone. Behind that log skeleton, in one direction woods swept away up a hill, and in the other we direction cows in a fenced field grazed on vivid green grass or stared at Ted and me.

That old log house gave me goose bumps. It looked so defenseless and yet basically strong. Like a great man with pneumonia. The proportions were good. The logs looked solid. The gray-stone chimneys at the ends were well built, though they were now partly torn down and in the process of having the top few feet replaced. At one end of the house, tall scaffolding supported a platform with a pile of rocks on it, and a large muscular man in overalls was laying down mortar and then lifting a rock in place on the chimney. "Boy," I said to Ted, "I hope that man doesn't drop one of those stones as I pass by!"

Scaffolding rose in several other places around the house, with more men working here and there. I had the feeling the house was in intensive care. I could see how the idea of saving it grabbed Azalea.

Ted stopped in front of the house, and we both got out of the car. "I'll just scout around," he said, "while you talk to folks."

I started toward the building as a man in jeans with a hammer in his hand walked out of a hole in the middle of the house where a door had been, and down a slanted piece of plywood to the ground, right toward me. He wore a T-shirt with a guitar on it. He had a sharp angular face with a pointy chin but cheerful eyes. He grinned and said hello.

I introduced myself as Azalea's daughter, which still sounded odd to my ears but gave me entrée. He asked how Azalea was doing and then explained the boss wasn't on site. The boss supervised several jobs at once. "I'm the nearest you'll get right now. My name is Walt Singer," he said. "Basically I'm a carpenter, but I do what needs to be done."

Let's see, *Walt* was like *Waltz*. The *Tennessee Waltz*. The singer part was easy. I saw him at the top of the scaffolding belting out the *Tennessee Waltz* and playing that guitar on his shirt. To make that shocking enough to remember, I thought how he'd be squashed if he slipped from up there. Falls were on my mind.

"My father is worried because Azalea fell from that ladder inside, Walt," I said. Blame it on Pop. "I wonder if I could see where it happened."

Walt pursed his lips and nodded. "It seemed strange to us, too, the way that ladder broke under such a small gal when we've been climbing up and down it. No problem." He rubbed that sharp chin with a long hand with knots at the joints. He looked like a wood carving—a slightly comic wood carving. Which somehow gave me confidence in him. He was even honey-colored from the sun, wood-carving color. "The ladder is fixed now," he said, "but I asked the guy who mended it to save the broken rung,"

Guitar-shirt Walt-z led me through a doorway into the rib-cage room at the left front of the house. "Be careful," he said. "The floor is up, and we just have pieces of plywood to walk on, held up by the puncheons." He explained that puncheons were the huge flattened logs that crossed the dirt subfloor under the house in several places.

We made our way along a plywood walk to a homemade ladder fashioned from two-by-fours and shorter wood rungs. It was balanced in a square opening to the second floor.

"We took the steps out of the house because they weren't original," Walt said. "You can see the shadow of the original steps where they touched the wall." Sure enough, the interior wall was wood-paneled, and I could see the print of the edge of the stairway on it. A memory of the past.

He pointed a knobby finger to the third ladder rung from the top. "That's the one that broke." The new foothold was of cleaner, newer wood than the rest, which were marked by the passage of many shoes. I climbed a little way up the ladder and felt the rung. It was solid. "Where is the broken rung?" I asked.

He called, "Hey, Neal!" and let out a whistle. A stocky

young man with inquisitive black eyes arrived through the door at the far end of the "pen."

"I thought the piece from the broken ladder was right here with our stuff," Walt said, pointing to a Styrofoam cooler and some other things on a piece of plywood in a corner. We all went and looked closely. A red plaid shirt, four brown paper bags, probably containing lunch. No rung.

Walt scratched his head.

The two men gave each other an odd look. "By the way, this is Neal Madder," Walt-z said.

Good grief, *Neal Madder* rhymed with *steal ladder*. I mustn't let my prejudices run away with me. Besides, if something was stolen, it was a wooden rung. *Madder* was also what I'd be if he'd destroyed that rung. Real *madder*! I pictured me hitting him over the head with a ladder rung. That should be dramatic enough to fix him in my mind. In real life, he gave me an ingratiating smile. He was one of those reaching-out people whose every movement said, Please like me. That seemed to go with the fact that he had some of the longest eyelashes I ever saw on a man.

"When did you see the broken piece last?" I asked.

"After I fixed the ladder first thing this morning. Walt asked me to put the broken rung over here," Neal said in an I'm-your-friend tone. "I haven't noticed it since."

Tennessee Walt-z nodded. "I saw it here after Neal fixed the ladder. I think it was here when I came back about nine-thirty to get a Coke." He paused and frowned. "I'm not positive. Maybe I'm remembering from earlier."

I looked at my watch. Ten forty-five. If he was right, the rung had just recently vanished.

Tennessee Walt gave me a hard look. He touched my shoulder with one wood-carved-looking hand. "You think this is important, don't you? I'll call everybody together."

"Everybody" turned out to be Walt and Neal Madder and a middle-aged guy with coal-black hair and a beard, the one I'd seen working up high. Walt introduced him as "our stonemason," Goat something-or-other. That followed. He had to climb like a goat to get up to the top of his chimney. He was as impassive—as stony faced—as Neal Madder was responsive. There was a young woman with a mop of red hair, a T-shirt that said SUPPORT YOUR LOCAL POET, and a carpenter's apron. Her name was Melody, not as appropriate for a poet as rhyme or meter, but almost. Also there was a slim kid who looked about fourteen and had a Day-Glo lavender streak in his hair. Hey, that was punk. I thought the time of punk was over. Everybody called him Kid.

"I saw that thing," said Kid. Obviously he meant the broken piece of ladder. "When I came to leave my lunch in here. That thing was broken in two sharp pieces. Like wooden daggers," he said dramatically.

"It did look like that," Neal said. "And I was surprised to see it broke because we'd all been going up and down the ladder, and that little woman doesn't weigh ten pounds. I wondered if somebody broke it and then put it back together so you wouldn't notice. I did wonder that."

"Did anybody notice that the ladder had been broken and glued or anything like that?" I asked. Dead silence. "Does anybody know of a reason somebody might booby-trap it?" Everybody looked uncomfortable. Tennessee Walt rubbed the side of his neck with his fingertips. Goat, the stone man, began to blink. The young woman curled a strand of red hair round and round her finger and shook her head.

"Does anybody have any idea where those pieces could have gone to?" I asked. No answer.

"Nobody has been around here except us that I've seen," said Tennessee Walt. He rubbed his chin again. "Was that photographer fellow here? Or was that yesterday? Today, just us and the dog."

Walt turned and looked at a plump dog with red-brown fur that had come and sat down as though he were a member of our group. "This is Goat's dog, and he hangs around here. This dog could have carried it off, huh, Chubby?"

We all looked at Chubby, who wagged his tail.

"He wanders a little, and my house isn't far," Goat said. "But he never carries stuff off. He never has."

"He likes to chase a stick," said the girl hopefully. "He's a great dog."

"But it was broke in two pieces," said Neal Madder. "He wouldn't take two sticks at once, would he?"

"He might," said the Kid. "I bet he might!" The Kid was blondish, aside from the lavender streak, and pleasantly disheveled. His pants were too big, and his leather shoes were unpolished and shapeless as if perhaps they'd been dug up under the house. But he was full of excitement. Liked a mystery, I thought.

"Let's go out and throw a stick for Chubby and let's see how he acts," I said. So we all trooped out the door and down the slanted plank into the yard.

The Kid threw a broken piece of branch toward a small log outbuilding to the right of the house, and Chubby bounded off to catch it and brought it right back between his teeth to be thrown again. The Kid threw the stick in the direction of the road, then over toward the fence that separated us from the cows, then back toward the outbuilding. Each time Chubby raced off, tail high, ears pricked back, grabbed the stick in his mouth, and proudly brought it back.

"He looks more in the business of bringing things back than taking them away," I said.

They all nodded uncomfortably. "But you never can be sure," the Kid said, nodding his lavender-striped head.

"You guys better get on back to work," Tennessee Walt suggested, and all but Walt and the support-your-local-poet girl went back into the house. The sound of pounding began again. "Poet" went over to a car a little bit down the way, reached into a cooler, and drank from a bottle of water.

Good. I wanted to talk to the house crew one by one.

"Can we talk now?" I asked Walt. "Should we go out into the cool under that tree over there?" It was a nice big maple off to the side of the house.

He caught on that we might like privacy, and we went and stood near the tree in the shade. The grass under the tree was scraggly and uncut. A few old logs with rotten spots in them lay in a pile near the tree. "We've had to replace a few logs," he said. "We just splice the new ones in. You can hardly tell." I could see he was proud of their work.

"Is there anyone in this crew or any neighbor who might want to either stop this job or hurt Azelea?" I had to ask.

"You mean aside from the photographer guy—the one named Anthony who's related to Azalea? He keeps taking pictures of us and saying this house should be his. But Azalea says to ignore him. He's just crazy."

I hoped he was just harmlessly crazy.

"Aside from him, we fired a man last week," Walt said, frowning. "He was stealing rocks."

"Rocks? Just rocks?" I glanced up at the chimney. I noticed that Goat the stonemason, with his black hair and beard, was already back at work on his scaffolding, laying mortar and putting another stone in place.

"Now, stealing rocks may seem like an odd thing," Walt told me, "but the pieces of square-cut limestone those chimneys are made from are worth a bundle to restorers. You can't match them with fresh-cut stone. The only new rock you can get is machine-cut and looks quite different. This rock was hand-cut, probably by slaves. You couldn't find anyone with the incredible patience necessary for that job now."

"So how did you get the old stone for the chimneys?" I demanded. Fixing old houses was more complicated than I'd thought.

"The chimneys already were stone." He pointed. "But in bad condition. We needed a little more stone to fix them up."

I looked up again, and to my amazement I saw Goat take a cellular phone out of his pocket and put it to his ear as he smeared mortar with the other hand. Where would modern technology go next!

"The only way to get more stone was to find someone willing to sell a chimney from an abandoned house. And we did,'' Walt was saying. ''It's too bad that our workers know what those chimneys are worth. A good chimney can cost up to fifteen hundred dollars. And that's for the buyer to come and get it.''

I whistled.

''So if someone just needed a few stones, he'd pay well for them. And the funny thing was, the man who stole them was named Art Bolder. You know, boulder as in stone.'' That was convenient—a premade mnemonic! Walt rubbed his pointy chin. ''We found about twelve stones in the back of Art's truck under a canvas tarp. A storm blew the tarp off.''

''And what did the man who stole the rocks say?''

''He was pissed off and said somebody framed him.'' Walt-z kicked at one of the half-rotten logs. ''But why would one of us frame him? Art begged Azalea to be on his side, but she said it was up to Ross—that's our boss, the one who isn't here.''

''This Art''—I hesitated—''oh, yes—Bolder as in stone. And he was bolder than you'd think to just make off with the stones. Can you give me his address?'' Naturally, I was taking notes. Walt looked through his pocket and produced a small spiral notebook. He leafed through the pages and finally found an address. I wrote it down. ''But he may not be in this area anymore,'' he said. ''I don't know.''

''Anybody else who has a problem?'' I asked.

He shrugged. ''You can talk to them,'' he said in a that's-all tone of voice, jerking his thumb toward the house. His face became closed.

So he didn't want to be known as a snitch among the other workers, but he figured there were things to find out. ''I better get back to work,'' he said, and turned and went briskly up the plank, back into the house.

I was aware of the young woman with the red hair almost at my elbow. Named Rhythm? No, Melody. She beamed at me as if I was the person she most wanted to see in the world. ''I hope Azalea is going to be okay because what she's doing here is great.'' She waved toward the house.

She had on three rings. "I mean, this old house has character, don't you think?" Her eyes twinkled with pleasure. "Even half-done, like now, it has character. I want to see it all dressed up and back in business as a house." Miss Enthusiasm.

"Me, too," I said. I pointed at her T-shirt. "So you're a poet?" I said. I bet her poems were how-great-it-is poems and not the gloomy kind.

"I'm mixed up in music. I write lyrics," she trilled. "Everybody around Nashville is into music, it seems like," she said. "It's kind of nice."

"So you have a lot of competition," I said.

She laughed. "We all think we'll get our break."

She was pretty enough to be a country singer, with that cloud of red hair and delicate pink-and-white skin. She had flair even in old jeans and a carpenter's apron.

"Have you noticed any tensions around this job?" I asked. "Anybody who has a grudge or feels wronged?" Maybe they were all musicians, and somebody stole someone else's song. But that wouldn't make them booby-trap Azalea.

She laughed again. "No tensions except that two of those Romeos have decided I should be theirs alone. But that's not a problem for anyone but me."

"Which two?" I asked immediately.

"Goat," she said, "though he's old enough to be my father. He has a daughter just four years old. The daughter's a real charmer. He loves her one hundred percent. His wife's gone. I think he wants me to play mother. I love little Betty, but I'm not ready to settle down. Goat's basically a good guy. Lives right near here. You can see the house through the trees," she said as she pointed.

I strained, but all I could see was an impression of white through the trees across the road from the old house.

"He doesn't tempt you?"

She shrugged. "Not yet. If I wanted to settle down, I might pick the Kid. He's older than he looks and lots of fun. He lives in Nashville."

"Where are you from?" I asked.

"Franklin," she said. "I live right down the road from where six thousand men were killed in the Battle of Franklin. I used to work near the graveyard."

"From the Civil War," I said. I was learning.

"Which is why I like to have fun," she said, tossing her head. "You go by a big field of grave markers every day on the way to work, it sure makes you know that you're lucky to be alive."

"So, there's nothing strange around here except two guys competing for you. And that's not so strange!"

Her smooth brow contracted into a frown. She pursed her lips. "Something *is* strange," she said, "but I couldn't tell you what. We're all just a little too nervous, but I don't know why." She flushed. "I sound silly, don't I? Just ignore me." She laughed a silvery laugh.

"No," I said, "feelings often come before reasons. Please tell me if you figure out why."

She nodded quickly. "Yes, I will."

I tackled the Kid next. He was inside inserting wooden wedge blocks between the square-cut logs, hammering them in. "To brace the house better," he said.

He told me he was Jerry Wilton. *Jerry-built on* what? On a piece of property where a man had been killed, according to legend.

"Yes," said the Kid, when I asked if he'd noticed anything strange. "That ladder shouldn't have broke like that. But who'd take the pieces, I don't know. Or where he'd put 'em."

"Describe the pieces," I said. "Did it look like there was glue on them or anything?"

Jerry shrugged. "Just two old pieces," he said, "like one of the other stepping pieces you saw, that broke slantways, so each piece was sharp at one end and broad at the other." His hands were almost like that, broad across the bottom of the palm, fingers tapering. Callused. Can't-stay-still hands.

"Are you a musician?" I don't know why I asked that, except I wondered.

"Oh, yes," he said, breaking into a broad smile. "I play drums. Nashville's full of music. Build a house, the carpenter could play drums. Go out to dinner and you can bet the waiter plays guitar or something."

"Have you noticed anything else strange around here besides the ladder?" I asked.

He shrugged. He wiggled. He ran his fingers though his lavender streak of hair. "Maybe," he said. "We find stuff. Like a lock and key that maybe came from 1790. But I don't know. Not really strange. That dark-haired guy, that Anthony whatever, comes around and stares at us like a vulture now and then. He's a creep. But we ignore him. I think we're going to have a thunderstorm. That'll make you feel spooky—when the barometer's going down."

Yes, the closeness seemed to bear down on me, too, but at least the air was cooler. I thanked him and started to look for Goat.

Just as I craned my neck to see if he was still up laying stones on the chimney, he hurried past me. "My daughter is sick." He stopped for a second to tell me. "I have to get her from school. I can't get anyone else to do it." Was that what he was talking about on his cellular phone?

"I'm both the mother and father," he said. Conscientious. "If you need to talk to me, here's my number." Then he was gone.

Right then I noticed Ted off at the edge of the woods and Walt walking away from him. So they must have been talking. I knew by the way Ted jerked his head that he wanted me to come over. So I went to join him.

"The workers all seem nervous," he said. I had to agree. "But I've wandered around just waiting to see if anything suspicious hit my eye. Nothing has. Have you found out anything unusual that we ought to check further?"

"No, not now," I said, figuring I'd tell him the details back at Azalea's.

Because just then I became aware of two people staring

at us: a stocky gray-haired man and a small woman with brown hair. Walt had joined them over by the doorway. I couldn't hear them, but I could see that the man asked Walt a question. The woman listened to his answer as if she heard music. Some people have a talent for listening, and I could see she was one of those. Walt began telling them about us. He didn't point, but he nodded his head our way, and they looked back and forth from him to us. A muscle jumped in the side of the man's face. So why was he tense? What did this man and woman want?

CHAPTER
7

THURSDAY AFTERNOON

The man who strolled toward us from the old house had presence. He limped slightly, but his shoulders were back as if that didn't matter. I knew immediately, although his gray hair was casually half-combed and he was dressed in old chino pants and a rumpled cotton shirt, that this was someone important to this job. I also sensed by his stiff walk and slightly clenched hands that he was upset and trying to hide the fact.

"Hi," he said, "I'm Ross Turney. I'm the one restoring this house for Azalea." Aha, *Ross the Boss.* "I can't tell you how badly I feel that she fell," he said. He turned to the young woman with him. "This is my wife, Rose, who has demanded to see this place." He smiled at her, but I sensed disapproval. Why would he not like to show off his work to his wife?

She impressed me as much as he did, a tiny warm-eyed, fragile young woman—much younger than he was, I sus-

pected. Skin very white, cheeks rosy as if she'd been out
in a winter wind. (*Rose* was *Rosy*. Remember that. And,
hey, their names were close. Just one letter different in *Rose*
and *Ross*.)

I could have imagined this Rose teaching kindergarten.
Children would trust her. Babies would stop crying if she
picked them up. I bet she had a green thumb. She could
raise *roses*! Chubby, the resident dog, came over and licked
her hand. I noticed Rose's palms were rosy pink. Optimists
tend to have rosy-pink palms. I learned that from my cousin
Fern from California, who says a sleuth should read hands.

Nevertheless, the very gentleness of Rose's voice when
she said hello made me think she was lucky to be teamed
up with someone with grit like Ross.

I suggested we go over under the tree. The sun was getting hot again. So we trudged over, still talking.

Ross the Boss asked how Azalea was doing, and then he
turned to me as we moved into the shade and said, "Rose
is a psychologist, and she works with some people with
memory problems. We were very interested when Azalea
said you've written a book about memory."

"Only a practical book," I said as we stopped near the
pile of rotten logs that must have been replaced in the
house. "About how to remember better. Nothing deep and
scholarly."

"But that's what people need," Rose said, smiling her
warm smile. "I was interested that you said you thought
your own problem was a one-track mind."

I had mentioned that. My goodness, Rose was quick.
Azalea told her about my book, and bingo, she read it.

"My one-track mind can make trouble, I'll say that." I
laughed. Might as well laugh.

"I know a trick that might help you," Rose said. "When
you have a minute I could explain."

"That's mighty nice of you," I said.

"But you wanted to talk to Ross first, I know."

"My father asked me to talk to the folks working here
about what might be wrong, whether anyone might want to

sabotage that ladder,'' I said. ''I've done that now. Except for talking to you, Ross.''

He stiffened. His right hand convulsed nervously. Perhaps he felt I was accusing him of not looking after the job. He backed away slightly, bumping into the small pile of damaged logs.

He looked up at the chimney. Nobody working there right now, just the scaffolding, the wooden platform, and stone on it. ''There could have been sabotage,'' he said. ''I fired a man for stealing chimney stone.'' He looked back at us with a frown and told the same story Walt had—about the hand-hewn stone and the man who hid some under a tarp in his truck.

''But it's possible,'' Ross said, ''that so many heavy men climbing that ladder cracked a weak piece of wood, and we didn't notice until even Azalea's light weight was the last straw and the rung broke. From now on, we are all going to be double careful,'' he said, waving a hand toward the house.

Rose was hardly listening, staring admiringly at the house. ''Ross told me how they've found an old lock and key and bits of china and glass,'' she said. ''I love the way you're trying to uncover the real story of this house and how there are tragic stories told about it, which don't all agree. Even a tragic story has bits of heroism in it.'' Rose's eyes swept the house and the green grass and trees around it. ''I think this is a house that makes heroes.''

Ross laughed uncomfortably. ''You have a wild imagination, Rosy.'' He turned to me. ''This part of Tennessee is full of stories. That's how I got to love history. That's why I do old houses.''

''Yes,'' Rose said. ''We had everything here from bandits to Davy Crockett to Andy Jackson.'' She smiled at Ross proudly as if he'd arranged that.

''We were the frontier,'' he said. ''So the solid settlers came here and the drifters and the misfits. It could be pretty wild around here: gamblers and drunken fights and duels and frontier justice. A man who killed somebody or stole a horse was hanged pretty quick.'' He grinned at me as if he expected that a staid North Carolinian like me might be shocked. But, hey, in North Carolina we had Blackbeard the pirate.

''But this house belonged to solid settlers,'' he said, ''and then to their children. That's what I've heard. Except that two men vanished.'' He turned and grinned at his wife. ''Which intrigues Rose.''

She smiled and touched his arm, and it jumped. Boy, he was on edge. ''Now, if you folks will excuse us, I'll show Rose around, and we'll get on out of here.''

Rose held back. ''Let me talk to Peaches first,'' she said. So Ross went off and did whatever bosses do. I noticed he walked slowly and watched where he put his feet. What did he think he'd step on?

Rose and I stood and talked in the shade. I stuck out one hand flat against the bark of the tree and leaned on the arm that went with it. I kept my antennae out, but I didn't get alarm signals from her.

Rose asked me questions about exactly how my memory worked. We talked about how I have to use tricks and lists and such, and put things in front of the door so I'll trip over them and thereby remember to take them with me. She was one of those listeners who makes you want to say more.

She also gave me her opinion. ''Sometimes, people who can't hold a visual image in their minds find it hard to remember. If they can learn to hold a visual image, they can control their minds better.''

''But I can do that,'' I said. ''I can think of an outrageous image to help remember a name or a time or even the telephone number of my pizza delivery place: 254-1896. The 254 is easy because my number starts like that, and then I think of *one* big fat man who *ate nine* pizzas and is getting *sick*. The sick is not exactly six but it's close enough.''

''So you cope pretty well, but what's still bothering you?'' she asked.

"Well," I said, "let's say I get an important document and I have it in my hand. All of a sudden I think of some problem I want to solve. Like, why does someone want to steal stones? Old one-track mind fastens on that problem, or maybe on the solution—that's even better—and the next thing I know, I'm standing somewhere else without the important paper in my hand, and I have no idea where it went or how I got where I am. And you could say, 'Don't let your mind wander,' but the trouble is, my mind comes up with really useful things when it wanders. I'm grateful that it wanders, if I just wouldn't lose things."

"Ah!" she said. "You're good at doing things on automatic pilot?"

"You mean," I said, "like driving the car and figuring out what to say when I make a speech? Or cooking spaghetti while thinking out a possible killer's motivation?"

"That sort of thing, yes."

"Oh, I'm a whiz at that," I said. "Some of my best thoughts come to me while I'm doing something else."

"Okay," said Rose, "I think you're just too good at that. That's your problem. You can slip right into automatic pilot and not even realize it. And then you don't remember what you did because you were on automatic pilot."

"Maybe," I said. "Then I get in trouble. Like the time the electricity was turned off because I lost two bills in a row."

She laughed. "A house does work better if there are lights and heat."

House. Yes.

"Why were you so interested in seeing this house?" I blurted. "Ross is boss of the restoration of several old houses, right? Why does this one intrigue you?"

Rose flushed. She glanced over at the house, which sat so gracefully on the green field, even naked as it was. "I guess I'm contrary," she with a laugh. "I had the feeling Ross didn't want me to come see this particular house, and I had to figure out why. Now I'm here, and I still don't see a reason. It's going to be a lovely house, so I'm glad I came. But we've drifted away from your problem. Let's get back."

"Is there some special thing I could do?" I asked. "When idea number two is about to knock idea number one right out of my head and I need them both?"

"There's a trick that works for lots of folks," she said. "If you're walking across the floor with the electric bill in your hand and you suddenly begin to figure out something important, like how a man was killed, stop."

"Stop and what?"

"Just stop. Stand absolutely still. Then think out idea number two. And when you finish you'll still be standing there with the electric bill in your hand."

"But suppose," I said, "it's not a piece of paper but another thought—the one I had first—that I don't want to lose."

"Because you're still standing right there, you can trace back idea number one better even if it's not a piece of paper like a bill."

"You mean," I said, "it's related to what my mother always said—'think where you had it last.' That could work for ideas as well as objects?"

She nodded.

"I think I can do that," I said. "I'll try it."

"And another thing," said Rose. "If you find it hard to remember to stand still—if idea number two almost carries you away—then some people find it helps to hold the electric bill or whatever straight up over their heads."

I laughed. "At least I won't be able to forget there *is* an idea number one. Because anybody who sees me will ask, 'Why in heck are you standing there with your hand up over your head?' "

We both began to laugh. She had a wonderful warm laugh. It occurred to me that while she might be lucky to have the strength of someone like Ross the Boss, he was very lucky to have such a lively and amusing wife.

I sought him out and found him standing by the ladder that broke—now fixed—and looking up. He was alone. I said, "You know, I just have a feeling that something worries you so much about this place that you don't even want your wife to come here."

He blinked, startled. The muscle in his face convulsed again. Then he laughed. "It's never possible to tell my wife where she can't go. I wouldn't even try. But I don't like what happened with this ladder," he added. "It's especially strange that the broken rung disappeared. I don't like that at all."

CHAPTER
8

FRIDAY, JUNE 21

On Friday morning, we brought Azalea home from the hospital. We passed the house under reconstruction on the way to Azalea's house, which was just up the hill. "It's coming along," she said cheerfully. By now the old log house seemed like a friend. We waved to Goat at the chimney top. Nobody else in sight.

Azalea was released with strict orders to stay quiet. Home with a punctured lung? I had gasped at the idea, but the doctor said that wasn't as serious as it sounded as long as she was careful. She was so determined about going home that they let her go.

On the way, we talked about the old house—what else? Ted wanted to know what she'd done to find out about its history, how she'd checked the written records.

"Oh," she said. "I traced it at the archives. But the records on the house only go back to 1829, when they show Wilbur Thomason, Junior, paid taxes on it. Some of the older records must be lost.'' That was a challenge to Ted. I could tell by the sparkle that came into his eyes. Eventually he'd do something about that.

Azalea's own house was not huge but rather grand, with white pillars in front. We helped Pop and Azalea in, and I helped Alice get Azalea settled in a chintz-covered recliner. Ted helped Eudora, the sitter, settle Pop in his wheelchair nearby, looking out a big window at a grassy rolling hill.

Eudora had on a phony buckskin shirt—in honor of being in Tennessee, I figured. These dramatic people like to act things out. She was the second sitter Pop had had with that proclivity.

Pop had on a button that he said he wore just for me. It said OLD PEOPLE AREN'T FORGETFUL. THEY'VE JUST LEARNED THAT MOST THINGS AREN'T WORTH REMEMBERING. Where on earth did he get that?

I didn't ask because Alice was saying she wanted to usher Ted and me to the guest room.

We passed slogans that hung on all Azalea's walls, like a cross-stitch sampler that said VISUALIZE SUCCESS. Azalea's house was just exactly what I would have expected, with more dark shiny antiques, ruffled curtains, and framed inspirational sayings and quotations inside than I had ever seen before in one place.

Over the bed with the ruffled spread in our room, a sampler said DON'T WORRY—BE HAPPY. Rosebuds were embroidered around the words. On the bedside table was a motto in a stand-up frame: FORTUNE FAVORS THE BRAVE. I liked that one. Next to it was a fat book, *The Complete Works of Shakespeare*. Did Azalea want to improve our minds? Or was Shakespeare just a gold mine of quotable quotes? Come to that, I think he was the one who said, ''Fortune favors the brave.'' A framed sign in the adjoining bathroom said TO MAKE A RAINBOW TAKES SUN AND RAIN. That was at least more balanced.

All those mottoes on the wall reminded me of my cousin Mary, only her sayings were a little drier, like DINNER WILL BE SERVED AT THE SOUND OF THE SMOKE ALARM.

"And what room will Pop be in?" I asked Alice as she turned to leave us.

"Why, he'll have one of the twin beds in Azalea's room." Of course. How silly of me to ask. They *were* husband and wife. But what on earth, I asked myself, are they able to *do*? Impertinent thought.

"But Pop has come complete with his own sitter," I said. Yes, Eudora, the would-be actress.

Alice nodded. "She'll be in a room nearby." The edge of her mouth twitched. To my surprise, I was indignant that Alice might want to laugh. I did want Pop and Azalea to be happy and have some dignity, even with Eudora as a necessary part of a menage à trois. I hoped she wouldn't be memorizing lines out loud as she sometimes did back home in the mountains, where we'd occasionally hear a terrified scream or a loud laugh, and Pop would say, "That's just Eudora."

But Eudora was efficient. By one o'clock, Pop and Azalea were fed and napping. Eudora was out on the terrace waving her arms, proclaiming who-knows-what. Ted and I went into the kitchen to make some sandwiches.

Alice was sitting on a tall stool, writing a letter at the kitchen island, a bowl of peaches at her elbow. With the elder citizens safely asleep, she had a moment to herself and looked happier than I'd ever seen her, smiling to herself. She leaned over the paper—almost curled around it as if she wanted to be part of it, to escape into the round, forthright writing. She blushed as I glanced at several handwritten pages. She sat straight and brushed her long dark hair back from her face. "To Ed," she said proudly. "He wants to know everything that happens here. He's the one who works at the Vance birthplace outside of Asheville. He's the one . . ." Her face crumpled. "If only . . . But I need to stay here with Azalea for now."

"You're afraid something else will go wrong?" I asked.

A brief flash of terror lit her eyes. "I hope not," she said.

"I gather from the folks on the job that your cousin

Anthony keeps wandering around and watching them and making them very nervous.''

Did Anthony count as a cousin? I figured he did by Southern standards.

"They tell me Anthony even takes pictures of the folks on the job," I added. "Do you think he had anything to do with the ladder breaking?"

She shrugged and stopped smiling. "He wants to take this house away from Azalea. He's so determined," she said. "Like a tornado." She stared ahead as if she saw a tornado. She shivered. "I think that even if we killed him, he'd come back to haunt us."

I started to say, "Now, come on, don't be such a pessimist." Ted reached over and squeezed her shoulder in a comforting way. New uncle.

But she was ahead of us. "Buddy has been dead for over a hundred years, and he's still making trouble for us, isn't he? Anthony keeps saying that sometime, somewhere we'll find his bones." She folded her letter and put it in her small square stationery box. Her letter-writing mood was spoiled.

I got out the bread and mayonnaise and cold cuts and lettuce and went to work on the counter near her. "Shall I make you a sandwich?" I asked. It's easier to be hopeful on a full stomach. She nodded thank you.

She got up and went over to the refrigerator and poured herself a glass of milk, stopping to look at the magnets on the door. "Too many rainbows," she said unhappily. "Sometimes rain makes floods, not rainbows." She sat back on her stool at the counter with a plunk.

Ted went over to the refrigerator and poured beer for himself and cranberry juice for me. I stood working on one side of Alice. He sat down on the other side.

"So tell me more about this Anthony," I said, "who is part of a very strange provision in the contract your grandmother has on this house."

Alice choked on a swallow of milk, and we had to wait until she caught her breath. "He's a bastard," she said. Not the kind of language she had used when we talked to her before.

"Why?"

She looked down at her glass of milk—in order not to look at me, I decided. "Because he wants to tear down Azalea's old house and sell the parts, and the contract says he can if he can just prove that Azalea's ancestor killed Grampy's ancestor. He'd sell the parts from what may be the oldest house in middle Tennessee." She looked up, eyes angry. "Can you imagine that? Anthony worked on Grampy and made him put that in the contract."

"But why?" Ted asked, setting his beer mug down. "Will the parts make that much money? Isn't the house worth more as a house?"

"Anthony likes to hurt people," she said. "He wants to hurt Azalea more than he wants money." Alice's voice thickened with anger. "And a developer will pay big bucks for the land that goes with the house."

"But," I said as I spread mayonnaise on bread, "Azalea has too-nice trouble, not meanness trouble. Why hurt her?"

"I don't know why he acts that way," she said, squirming on her stool, and for the first time since we met Alice, I had the feeling that she was lying.

"Tell me about Anthony," I said, putting salami on three sandwiches. "How did he get the way he is?"

"Well, first of all, you have to know about the accident," Alice said. She could look me in the eye about that. First me and then Ted. But she began to tremble. "When I was eight years old, my mother and father"—she swallowed hard, but kept on—"and my grandfather, Azalea's husband, Hunt, and also Anthony's wife, Dolores, were all in the car together."

Adam Marlowe had told me about that bloody accident, but I needed to be sure I had it right.

Alice took a ragged breath and rushed on. "A drunk teen hit them and killed my parents and Dolores, and left Hunt paralyzed. My grandfather Hunt was driving. I think Anthony felt like it was Hunt's fault."

Somehow, I was sure by the way Alice squirmed that even in the middle of her real distress she was still hiding something. But why on earth?

"How tragic," I said. "How terrible for you and for Azalea—for the whole family." But I had to ask, "But because of *that,* Anthony wants to hurt Azalea? That doesn't make sense. Azalea suffered, too. She lost her son and your mother. Her husband was paralyzed. Why would Anthony want to hurt Azalea?"

"Well, Anthony was spoiled," she said quickly, pleased to have thought up a reason, I suspected. But what could she need to hide? "Anthony's father drank a lot. Even I can remember that. Though I was a kid when Anthony was a teen. They lived near us. His father drank and beat him and called it discipline. Then he tried to bribe Anthony to love him when he was sober. His mother was so upset she spoiled him, too. He was spoiled and also had a hard time. You could just tell. Next he got to be so good-looking that girls chased him."

"That was difficult?" Ted raised his eyebrows.

Alice blushed. "I think it made him feel like everybody should give him what he wanted all the time."

"But there was something more," I said. I put the tops on the sandwiches. "There must have been more to make him hate Azalea." Azalea might provoke, but she was lovable. I realized I kind of loved her myself, even while I wished she hadn't married Pop. She was so optimistic. So ready for miracles. That drove me wild but still was kind of nice. All this when so much in her life had gone wrong. Her son *and* his wife, Alice's parents, killed. Her husband paralyzed.

"Maybe," Alice said, "people like Anthony just naturally have a mean streak. And if they know how to be charming, too, whenever it suits them, that's kind of awful, don't you think?" She drained the last of her milk and put the glass down with a that's-that thump.

"Charming how?" I asked. I might as well be prepared.

"Oh, acting like you're so important as long as he can

get something that way. Smiling a lot—I don't know."

She stood up and said, "I have to go to the drugstore and get some things for Azalea before she wakes up." Very firm. Tears resolutely put away. She'd forgotten her sandwich.

I had to get this straight. "Your father was Hunt and Azalea's son? Your father and your mother were killed in that wreck, too?"

"It was awful," she said. "Awful for all of us. I don't like to be so mad at Anthony." She twisted her hands. Her head snapped up. "But I am!"

Ted was frowning. He had to be sure he had the basics straight. "So Anthony's wife, Dolores, and your grandfather, Hunt, who were both in that wreck, were brother and sister? The ages don't sound right. If Anthony was a teen when you were a kid, Dolores must have been much younger than Hunt."

She nodded yes.

"Dolores," she said, "was my great-grandpa's daughter by his second wife. That's why Dolores was so much younger than my grandpa Hunt even if he was her brother."

Now wait. I mustn't get lost. Alice's great-grandpa was Azalea's father-in-law. Adam Marlowe—the one with the horses. Who gave Azalea the house with conditions attached. Yes. The one Alice called Grampy.

"Grampy's second wife left him for a horse trainer from the circus," Alice said. "Grampy had to raise Dolores by himself." That must have been difficult for the old stick-in-the-mud.

"Dolores was pretty, and she was kind of a kid at heart. She was crazy about Anthony. He misses that." She sighed, then picked up her pocketbook, which was sitting on the floor near her stool. She turned first to Ted, then to me and said, "Thank you for helping us. I guess we seem kind of nutty sometimes."

I laughed. "Almost anybody you get to know well seems kind of nutty sometimes. Or else boring."

Alice ran back and gave me a quick kiss, then one to Ted, before she hurried out.

Ted was frowning. "In a big rush to leave," he said. "She didn't want you to ask too many questions. But basically a nice kid. I'll eat her sandwich. I'm hungry enough for two."

I thought about Anthony as I ate. I used to believe that there was bound to be some good in everyone. But I've learned there are people so warped that cruelty is natural to them. And sometimes they know how to be charming.

"I've been reading this book called *Inside the Brain*," I told Ted.

"Which relates to Alice?" he asked.

Actually, I'm always reading books about the brain, because they tell what's new in memory research. People give them to me, which is nice.

"This book explains how a young child's brain is wired to learn very fast—but all that learning power has to be stimulated, or some of it withers away. You have to learn things at the right time, or it may be too late. If you don't hear language and learn how to talk by the time you're about thirteen, you never can. Did you know that?"

"Alice can talk," he said dryly. "Maybe she's hiding something, but she could say it if she wanted to."

"I was thinking about Anthony," I said. "I don't like him. Alice thinks he's a bastard. But she knows he was mistreated and beaten as a kid. It doesn't seem fair that that happens. That being mistreated can make you nasty. Which means no happy ending. I always wish for happy endings, especially for people who've been hurt."

"And this has to do with the brain?" Ted asked.

"It said in this book that if a child grows up being treated violently during that quick-learning time, the brain can learn to be much more aggressive as a way to survive—can be wired that way. Can have more of the chemicals that make you aggressive. It doesn't always happen. Some people are born more resistant to that sort of thing than others. But some grow up kind of warped."

Ted bit into the second sandwich. "So?" he said.

"So I have to make myself remember that," I said. "Because I never *want* to believe that a person is simply wired to be evil. But I have to *allow* for that. Of course, Azalea would say I have to leave room for a miracle. The book says there are ways to reverse bad wiring. But how many miracles are there? And, frankly, Anthony gives me the creeps. I must find out more about him." And watch my back while I'm at it, I told myself.

CHAPTER
9

FRIDAY AFTERNOON AND SATURDAY

"So what do we do now?" I wondered. "What next?"

"I have an odd suggestion," Ted said. "And a more cheerful one. Let's go to the Hermitage and look at the Andrew Jackson house there. It will give us a feel for the time when those two men vanished." He didn't fool me. Visiting the Hermitage might possibly be useful. But also Ted would rather go to a historical restoration than eat. "We can see how Jackson lived," Ted said. "Jackson died just a few years before David Holden and Buddy Thomason vanished. So his house will be more or less contemporary, though more elaborate. Clothes didn't change that much in those days. I'm sure there'll be a portrait of Jackson wearing just about what David Holden or Buddy Thomason would have worn to a party—what they probably wore the night they vanished." I am always amazed at the odd facts that Ted knows.

The house at the Hermitage was larger and more ornate

than our square-cut-log house, but it made me aware of the
simplicity of cooking arrangements, the lack of indoor
plumbing in our house. (Yes, I admit I had begun to think
of it as *our* house.) And Ted was right. I stood and stared
at Jackson's portrait, and the two men who vanished became more real. I began to imagine what they looked like.
David would be solidly built, like our old house, but with
ruffles at his neck like Jackson, long-haired like Jackson.
He would have kind eyes. Maybe too trusting. Buddy
would be thin and mercurial, and angry. His clothes plainer
and more worn. He'd have a craftsman's hands with blunt
fingers. The lines in his palm would be twisted and broken
because his life was twisted.

All dreamed up from my imagination, of course. Were
there pictures of those men somewhere? I'd like to see
them. And a picture of the bereaved bride.

After we looked through the house, we wandered around
the grounds. There's nothing like exercise. Quite a ways
from the house we found two girls digging in a square
marked by string. The old slave quarters were here, they
explained. So far from the house? I asked. Oh, yes, they
explained, field hands usually lived a long way from the
house, in this case a quarter of a mile. It was like that at
our house, too, I supposed. There was so much to learn
about how people lived in the 1800s.

On Saturday, our own archaeologists were due to arrive
at our old house and do a one-day quick dig to try to date
the house more exactly. Azalea said they were sure to find
artifacts that would reveal hints about the history of the
house. Some of those would come from about the time
when the two men disappeared. Proving what? I somehow
felt as if those two men, both long dead, wanted me to find
out.

"I want to go watch every minute of the dig," I told
Ted. "I have the strong hunch," I said, "that whatever is
wrong now is related to what was wrong back in the days
when someone was killed in that house."

Ted raised an eyebrow. "I never ignore your hunches. But whatever they find as they dig will be sorted and labeled, and I can see it when I get back. I want to go by the library and the archives. I'll reconnoiter a little. Find out what leads to follow about the history of the house. But I won't stay too long today. I'll be back by about noon in case anything important comes up back here." So he took off in the car.

As for me, I felt the presence of David Holden and Buddy Thomason with me as I walked over from Azalea's to the square-cut log house on Saturday morning.

I arrived early and looked around. I went into the front left pen, thinking how that word restoration workers use for a log room seemed really appropriate when the chinking had been removed from the logs and the light shone between them. Each room was like a giant animal pen, or cage, except of course that there were windows in the log walls, some with their original glass.

The inside wall of this room was covered with paneling. That's where Azalea had said a bullet had been found lodged in the wall.

"Where was the bullet hole?" I'd asked Alice at breakfast.

"On the wall across from the fireplace in the left-hand pen," she'd said. That would be one of the interior wood walls. No sign of it now. But perhaps a new piece of wood had been inserted.

I envisioned Buddy in his old-fashioned clothes, standing in that room. Buddy with his clever carpenter's hands. Had those hands held a pistol?

Anthony meant to prove to his father-in-law that David Holden, prospective groom, killed Buddy Thomason, brother of the bride. I envisioned David Holden in his ruffled shirt. I saw David standing by that wall across from the fireplace, amazement in his eyes when a bullet just missed him, then saw him shudder with the impact from a second bullet, saw him fall. That's how I wanted it to have been. More tragic than sordid. Yes. The board that the bullet was in must have been replaced. Too painful for the eyes of the living.

There were parts of this house I hadn't really explored. Now was my chance.

Out the back door of that pen was a step down into an area that appeared to have been a room but now had no ceiling and not even temporary plywood on the floor. The dirt subfloor was sunken. There was a wall on the left but not on the right. From that area, I crossed to another log pen at the back of the house.

The fireplace there was blackened with soot, even on the outside. Long ago the cooking must have been done in this fireplace. Had there been cookpots on this hearth? "The kitchen?" I asked out loud.

I went back to the front pen and carefully climbed the ladder to the second floor. Today the rungs were firm. Upstairs I found myself in a room with a temporary plywood floor. The outside walls of the house had crude wood paneling up here, and somebody had plastered them over with newspapers, now yellowed with age. The print had faded to dark brown—the papers must have been for insulation, to keep the wind from whistling through the cracks. They were glued on every which way, overlapping each other. I began to read them. Hey, maybe these papers contained some clue to the history of the house!

Downstairs, Azalea hoped they'd find artifacts going back to the late 1700s. Up here, I didn't know what I might find or how old my discoveries would be. I read about bootleggers. That would be after 1920, wouldn't it? Oh, well. I reached out and touched a yellowed story: CRAZED BY LIQUOR, MAN BATTLES POLICE, and then, in smaller type, *Reputed Illinois Bootlegger Fares Badly with his Own Product.* No date showing. Plastered over with another paper advertising Moreland's Tonic.

I walked along the wall, drawn to a headline that said KLAN SUBMITS TO GOVERNOR, and in a smaller type: *Robes and Hoods Not to Be Worn in Public in Oklahoma.* No date. But before whenever that was, the Klan had apparently paraded around in public in full regalia.

Another headline said CIVIL WAR VETERANS TALK ABOUT BATTLES. One or two sentences about a veterans' convention, the rest covered by an ad for a shapely but bony-looking corset, no one inside the corset. Out of modesty?

DUELING DEATHS had a subhead: *In Seven Southern States*. Would that include Tennessee? How recently? Most of the story was covered by another ad: CONSTIPATION CURED BY THEDFORD'S BLACK DRAUGHT. There was a date on that one: 1907.

These papers were too recent to help.

Generosity and hotheads are always with us, I thought. Not to mention constipation. I wondered what we'd be able to read from the bits of pot and bone and such downstairs. Those should tell us more.

Still, I told myself, I must come back when I had more time and read some of the old stories, even though they were beyond the date of Azalea's legends—beyond the time when her ancestor might have killed her father-in-law's ancestor. Which I prayed he never had.

I pulled myself away and went to the back of this upstairs room. I stopped short. A door opened into space. There must once have been an upstairs to the dismantled room beyond, but it was gone. I looked out and down into a space where the dirt subfloor was lower than the rest of the house. Then I looked up at sky. Amazing how so much of an old house had to be torn down to be rebuilt. The missing part must have rotted.

Downstairs I heard Alice talking to someone. The archaeologists? She was telling them Azalea was still enjoying frail health, how Azalea had been persuaded to wait at her house, and Alice would call when there was something to see. I trusted that meant Pop was with Azalea. Out of our hair.

I knew that Alice was planning to help the archaeologists. I hurried down the ladder and met the young men. Hector and Frank. I shook their hands and said I was extremely interested to see how they went about digging the history of a place out of the dirt.

I watched them mark out their pits into exact squares with string and remove layer after layer of dirt.

Our first unusual find came when Hector cried out, "Look at this!" then picked up a small slightly lopsided arrowhead, an unusual dark orange-red with white flecks in it.

"This," he said, holding it out in his palm, "is maybe twelve thousand years old." He stood proudly as if he'd made it. As if trumpets ta-da-ed.

"How do you know?" I asked, impressed.

Hector explained with relish. "Arrowheads are made out of something called chert. That's a stone that flakes easily. We are now discovering that for thousands of years the Indians traded in chert over great distances." He smiled as if he should be patted on the back for knowing that. "Some of the best was mined near what is now St. Louis." He preened at our amazement. "Later arrowheads from around here are made of that traded chert. But this is local chert of an inferior grade—so inferior that they had to heat it up in a fire to soften it and make it easier to work. Around here we know that that kind of chert was only used until eight to ten thousand B.C."

I whistled. "How come ancient arrowheads are mixed in with nineteenth-century pottery bits?"

"We don't know, do we?" Hector smiled mysteriously. "Maybe the Indians lived on this site, or maybe a nineteenth-century child collected arrowheads somewhere else and then lost them here."

"So it's hard to figure it all out," I said.

He nodded, still smiling as if to say, But I have the skill to do it. What he actually said was, "What we see can confuse us, at least for a while. The past can be very hard to reconstruct."

Those words stuck with me when Anthony arrived like a mad prophet and predicted we'd find human bones, then Frank announced that he thought he'd found a human hand.

CHAPTER
10

BACK TO THE BOMBSHELL, JUNE 22

"You'd better come quick, Hector, and look at what I've found. I think it's human hand bones," Frank called out intensely.

We all came crowding through the door, as alert as if we'd heard a fire alarm. Anthony's prediction echoed in my ears: a skeleton! And Frank had found a skeleton hand? It was as if Anthony had conjured it up just with his voice. We hurried through the door of the first log pen and stood around Frank's pit, now about two and a half feet deep.

At first I saw merely a flat expanse of scraped earth. I was relieved. No horror. Then I saw a few small bones at one side of the dig. They were the same dark brown color as the earth. My stomach turned over. I saw skeletal fingers plainly, as if a hand beckoned us to find more. I went cold.

Anthony would shout for joy. He should have waited to see this, but I was so glad he hadn't.

Sometimes in a crisis strange ideas flit through my head.

I stared at those hand bones and remembered Cousin Fern from California, who taught me to read hands. Hands. Not the future—goodness knows this skeleton had no future—but character and prospects, partly from the shape of the hand. Folk knowledge, she called it, like using herbs to cure disease. Folk statistics, actually, because this had been going on for many centuries. This hand of bones still had a shape of sorts. The thumb was extremely large. I compared it with the proportions of my own hand. Yes, I have a large thumb. That tends to mean a strong will. Lots of determination.

The skeleton index finger was longer than the ring finger. No ring on that finger in the dirt. A long index finger tends to mean the person could take authority. Teachers, lawyers, and business leaders tend to have longer index fingers. Artists of all sorts, expert salesmen, and gamblers tend to have longer ring fingers. In a live hand, I'd balance off the shape, the lines, and much more. But I looked at that skeleton hand and thought, Yes! It would be David's! Solid David's, not the hand of Buddy, who had to follow his own whim! I felt a rush of relief. Then I laughed at myself—trying to read a skeleton's hand. God knows whose hand it was. I prayed it wasn't Buddy's.

Hector got down on his knees. The light from the small windows and door, the slices of pale light between the bare logs, still left the room dim. He peered closely. "Yes," he said. "Definitely human bones. We'll have to stop digging and call Nick."

"Nick?" I asked. "Who's Nick?"

"The state archaeologist," Frank said, rocking back on his heels. "He has to bring his folks to examine this body and find out how old it is and if it's a Native American body or Caucasian body or what."

Native American? Let it be twelve thousand years old—I was for that! If there was an arrowhead here, why not the Indian who made it? Then Anthony could go sit on a tack.

Frank went out to his car and turned on the ignition. While he called this Nick on the car phone, I tried to think what I ought to do next—besides keeping my eyes open, of course. Call Azalea? This was her business. And Alice had promised her. Where was Alice? I went back and looked in the door of the house. No Alice.

Thank goodness, at that point Ted arrived. I came back out the door to see him drive up. I ran over to the car as he lowered the window and leaned out with a look of concern. "They've found a skeleton," I said. "Or at least the hand of a skeleton. That nasty Anthony predicted it. The state archaeologist is coming to dig it up."

Ted got out quickly in that sure, ready-for-action way he has. "Do Azalea and Pop know yet?"

"I think Alice went to tell them."

"Above all else, we need to be calm," he said. "And we need to try to keep them calm. There's no way we're going to prevent Azalea and Pop from coming to see for themselves."

I was sure he was right. We hurried back to the old house. I paused in the doorway. I reached out and touched the log wall, rough but solid. I touched the bones of the house that had stood here for nearly two hundred years. "What happens now?" I asked.

Ted came back from staring into the dig hole and gave me a comforting hug. "We hope," he said.

But Hector answered more precisely.

"The state archaeologist—that's Nick Fielder—and the sheriff or his deputy both have to come and be here while the digging goes on," Hector said. He was not upset. Human bones were not a threat to him. "They have to be present while this skeleton, or part of a skeleton, is unearthed. All we know now is that we've found the remains of a hand."

We stood silently staring at those remains for several moments. My whole experience of human bones came from Halloween. White on black and orange. Make-believe. These bones were real.

"Azalea is almost certainly coming down here," I told

Frank, "and bringing my father, I'm sure. We're going to have a crowd."

"You better believe it," he said. "There'll be two or three television cameras, too. The TV folks scan the law-enforcement radio bands."

Azalea and Pop would make the most of that!

Soon a sheriff's-department car arrived and stopped with a slight screech of wheels. I peered out the door. A young man in a uniform jumped out, hurried inside, and leaned over the skeleton hand. "Dead a long time," he said in a brisk, official voice, then added more thoughtfully, "I wonder how long?"

Maybe twelve thousand years. I hoped they'd find a few chert arrowheads with the body to confirm that it was from long ago.

I heard another vehicle after a while and looked out to see a van with the Tennessee state seal on the side stop in front of the house. A plump, cheerful young man and a tall, thin dark-haired man got out. Hector and Frank hurried out to meet them and shook hands with them both. I heard the plump man say, "This is Dr. Emanuel Breitberg. He's my osteologist." *Osteo* meant having to do with bones, right? This must be the bone expert.

"We have hand bones and whatever else is attached," Hector told them.

The two men came inside, knelt by the hole, and looked. "You're the digger," Hector told Nick. "You're the expert on unearthing human remains."

Frank said, "We'll help get the dirt out of your way as we go."

This Nick wasn't in uniform but wore khaki pants and an old checked shirt. He carried a battered metal box from which he took a trowel, a small knife, a scoop like the one I keep in my flour bin, and a whisk broom. He knelt by the bones and began to remove dirt from around the fingers carefully. Hector and Frank and the tall, thin man stooped down and watched. The deputy stood and fidgeted and kept his eyes on Nick. Once or twice Frank scooped loose dirt away from the bones. The process was slow. The skeleton was not entirely under the spot where Frank had been digging, so the men had to remove layers of dirt to get down to other parts of it.

Occasionally Nick traded off with Tall Thin and let him dig, but mostly this Nick did the work. I could hear us all breathing slowly in anticipation.

Amazingly the hand seemed to keep its shape as the dirt holding it was scraped away. "Won't the bones fall apart?" I couldn't restrain myself from asking him, although I was certain Nick needed to concentrate; but he seemed perfectly willing to explain while he worked. "No," he said, "probably not."

"Can you tell how old they are?" the deputy asked. "Is this skeleton part of history or something more recent?"

"I can't tell much yet," said Nick as he used the tip of the trowel to scrape around the edge of the bones, then whisked the dirt away. Slowly an arm bone began to appear. He turned to the bone man. "Dr. Breitberg will have some thoughts as we get this uncovered."

Next a man ran up with a video camera on his shoulder. Letters on the camera said WKRN—CHANNEL 2. A bright light shone down on Nick and his trowel. A TV reporter.

"Who's dead?" the reporter demanded.

Nick looked up and grinned. "Hi, John," he said. "You know I don't know that yet. I won't know much for a while. But we can tell from the size of the bones that it's an adult and not a child."

"So who do you think it is? You must have some idea." The reporter held out a mike to Nick. I was afraid he was leaning so close, camera pack on back, that he might fall on top of the bones, but he didn't.

Nick just grinned and shook his head.

"Hey, that rib is broken." The reporter got excited. And sure enough it was. In fact, as Nick dug, it became clear that two ribs were broken. But he said he couldn't comment on what it meant yet. I thought it must mean a violent murder, but I didn't say that out loud.

The reporter went over and began to ask the deputy questions—still getting very few answers, I gathered by his look of frustration. He had hair that kept falling in his eyes. He kept having to toss it back.

At that moment Alice and Azalea appeared. Azalea walked in a gingerly way. Talk about ribs. I knew hers were strapped under her loose blouse and that nothing would stop her from coming to see for herself what was going on. Alice told me Pop was just outside in his wheelchair. I knew he'd never forgive me if I didn't get him inside where he could see, too.

I pulled Alice aside. "Can you get a small straight chair for Pop to sit in?" I asked. "We can make a seat with our hands and bring him in."

I will say this for Alice; she was accommodating. She found a chair in a nearby barn. Weathered but sittable. She put it inside the pen, a little back from the dig, on the part of the floor where the log beams that had held up the floor were still in place, and were covered with plywood for walking on. That part was too jerry-built for the wheelchair. We made a handseat and brought Pop in to sit in the chair. The deputy and archaeologists were too focused on the bones to even notice.

"I suppose that's the skeleton of David Holden," Pop said loudly. The deputy was by his side in a minute. The TV cameraman was not far behind. Pop referred them to Azalea with her old family story. The TV cameraman spotlighted her, and Azalea told her story—and told it well, as usual, not suggesting there was any doubt that Buddy killed David Holden. Two more TV reporters had rushed in with camera and lights. They ate the story up.

Meanwhile I watched Nick. The digging seemed to take forever, but he was the one who might discover whose body was really being unearthed. Finally he had two arm bones, the top side of the skull, as well as the top of the ribs in sight. The skeleton had not been dumped helter-skelter but carefully laid out long ago when it was a body. In my mind I saw it fleshed out, clothed. David Holden, gray with death. Some bad wound to his chest. Oozing blood.

The deputy was leaning over, staring at the bones. "So can you tell how old it is yet?" he asked Nick.

"No." He turned to his bone man. "What do you think? Look at these teeth."

"The eighteen-year molars have come in," the bone man said thoughtfully, "and between that and the shape of the bones, I'd say it's a male in his early twenties. Also, I can be pretty sure it's not a Native American."

I hadn't really expected it was. Still, my heart sank. If this had been a Paleolithic skeleton, my life would sure be simpler.

"How do you know it's not an Indian?" the deputy asked.

One of the reporters heard that, and he and the others flocked over, catching the tall thin bone man in all their lights.

The bone expert got down on his knees and pointed to the skull. He and Nick had liberated the front teeth from earth. "See these teeth?" he said. "The front teeth of a Native American are likely to have a distinctive shape. There'd be shovel-shaped incisors. These teeth do not have that shape."

"So you can be sure it's not an Indian," crowed the original TV reporter.

"No," he said. "I can't be positive yet, but it's probably not."

"And you don't know what killed him?"

"We'd like to finish here before we say anything for sure," Nick said firmly. Sweat poured off his forehead under the lights. Or was something about this discovery upsetting to him?

The broken rib cage of our skeleton now stood high above the dirt. The arms and legs were entirely exposed.

"You'd better call the medical examiner now," Nick told the deputy. "We've got this almost to the point where he can look at it." The deputy went off, and I heard his car radio squawk in the distance.

"Why does a skeleton last so long?" Pop called to Nick. Pop was assuming it was old.

"Because the soil here isn't acid," Nick said, gently raking dirt from the rib cage. He seemed completely unflappable.

Suddenly he said, "Oh, look at this!" We all leaned over together. If we'd been in a boat, we'd have capsized.

I saw a white glimmer down in the rib cage. He dragged out dirt with his scoop and placed three small white objects in the palm of his hand.

"Now we have a hint of the date," he said dramatically. The TV cameras zoomed in. "This skeleton was probably buried here between 1840 and the turn of the century."

"How can you be sure of that?" a TV reporter challenged.

"I can't," Nick said, "but I can have a pretty good idea. These are Prosser buttons, a kind of white glass button made between about 1840 and 1900."

"I told you so!" a voice called out. Anthony. He was pulled to the bones like a vulture to carrion. He stood in the doorway, blocking the light from outside, his face in shadow. Then he was glowing with TV light. How could the head of such a nasty person be shaped so much like a baby's? But his mouth was hard. He had predicted the worst and now he was here to proclaim it to the world, his eyes shining with triumph. My stomach cramped as if I'd tasted poison.

"You'll find that this is the body of Buddy Thomason," he told the TV boys. "Buddy was murdered by David Holden in 1849," he proclaimed. "Then David ran off to the Gold Rush in California."

The TV boys went wild like sharks in a feeding frenzy, asking questions all at once, finally getting Anthony's answers onto tape. I all but groaned.

"He has no reason to believe that!" Azalea cried. The lights zoomed to her. She gave those TV boys a dazzling smile. "It was the other way round, just like I told you. Buddy Thomason killed David Holden." Now the TV boys had a controversy going. Azalea versus Anthony. They'd play this big. But they didn't know what the stakes were: the very life of this old house. I heard rain begin to splatter. Oh, great. And we had to get Pop and Azalea home.

"I hope to goodness," I said to the deputy, who was standing next to me, "that you'll be able to prove this is the body of David Holden."

The TV boys turned to him. The deputy shook his head. "No. If the forensic-anthropology folks at the University of Tennessee study this body and agree that it goes back to about 1849," he said, "I doubt if we'll investigate it. There's not going to be anybody to punish even if there was foul play, is there?" How could he be that complacent?

Meanwhile we'd all but forgotten Tall Thin, who was taking a turn at unearthing the bones. "This man was shot," he announced dramatically. "Whoever he was." He pointed at the grinning skull. Then with his trowel he gently edged a small round ball about the size of a large pea out of the rib cage, where it lurked in the dirt near the backbone. As we stared he held that in one hand and dug out another bullet with the other. He looked around the circle of faces as if he wanted someone to blame. Dead silence all around. He kept digging until he had the backbone entirely clear and four bullets in hand. Four bullets. TV lights devoured him. He held out the balls in the palm of his hand like an accusation. More thunder. Raining hard now. "These could have broken the ribs," he said.

So this was an especially violent death. Four shots, enough to break two ribs. The killer was in a rage. That's how it added up. So we could never say this was an accident. I figured that was for sure.

I looked around at the circle of faces. I'd been concentrating on Nick and Tall Thin and on the skeleton. Now I needed to know how all people involved felt about the skeleton, about the violence of four shots.

Azalea looked prayerful, asking her guardian angel, no doubt, to prove her ancestor was innocent. She stood by Pop, one hand on his shoulder. Pop looked fascinated, his eyes wandering from Anthony the doomsayer to the skeleton and back, as if he hoped for more fireworks. Hector the Collector was talking to Frank, who could certainly no longer be called Frank the Blank. I might think of him in a Halloween skeleton suit. Frank the Prank. But this was obviously not a prank.

I heard still another car arrive, wheels whishing in the rain. A man in a dark suit came in and conferred with Nick. I heard the words "medical examiner."

"I'll see that these bones get to Dr. Bass and Dr. Marks at the University of Tennessee," Nick said, "for a more detailed examination." Dark Suit nodded assent and then proceeded to photograph the skeleton from every angle.

The deputy said, "I'm glad this is your problem, Nick, not mine!" But he did go over and talk to Azalea and Pop and Alice and took a few notes. "Let me know if there's any more excitement," he said to Azalea. Rain continued to patter outside.

"I'll invite you all to our party to celebrate when the house is finished," Azalea said, clasping the deputy's hand between hers. "We don't look for any more trouble."

Standing beside her grandmother, Alice winced. She looked as pale and distraught as if she'd seen a ghost.

How awful, I thought, if Anthony does get the right to tear down this house. He's the kind of bully who will do it and laugh.

CHAPTER

11

LATE AFTERNOON

The TV people left. The thunder and lightning had subsided—just steady rain now. One young woman with a notepad stood near the pit—or should I now say the grave?—talking to Nick as he began to put pieces of the skeleton in paper bags.

"So, next those bones go to the University of Tennessee?" she asked. She was taking notes in a spiral notebook.

"Yes," he answered as he wrote *right arm* on a brown paper bag with a marker. "The forensic-anthropology people will be able to tell more exact things about the body, such as what traumas it's had, and they can confirm the age more exactly."

Azalea hurried over to the young woman. "I'm Azalea Marlowe Smith. You're a reporter from the *Review Appeal*?" she asked.

"Yes," the young woman said. "I'd like to know the

local angles to this story. Are you the one who's restoring this house?''

Azalea beamed. "Yes. We may prove this is the oldest house in middle Tennessee!"

The reporter was so impressed that she hardly noticed that behind her Dr. Breitberg had brought over a small cardboard box lined with plastic foam padding, and Nick was packing the earth-stained skull into it like a fragile present to be mailed. He put the small box into a large cardboard box.

Meanwhile Azalea was beginning to lead the reporter on a tour of the house. The deputy had departed, evidently figuring the murder didn't concern the here and now.

Alice, Pop, Ted, Frank, Hector, and I continued to watch Nick, the state archaeologist. Anthony watched with satisfaction, seeming to breathe more than his share of the air. Alice was still pale, hardly breathing at all. Pop was plainly hoping for more drama.

Nick gently loosened the bones from one arm and hand from the dirt beneath them and put them in the marked bag, then put that into the big box with the skull already in it. Dr. Breitberg was marking bags for left arm, right leg, left leg, and such. These guys were matter-of-fact, like Christmas-gift wrappers in a department store.

Anthony said, "Won't you search the dirt around and under this skeleton?"

"Yes, of course we will," Nick said. "I will, and Hector and Frank will." He looked at his watch. "Good grief, it's six o'clock."

I realized how hungry I was. Ted must have had the same thought. "I'll get us some food," he said.

Nick was slipping the bones from the left leg into the appropriately marked bag. "I'll get pizza," Ted said. "Do you all like mushroom, peppers, and pepperoni?"

"The more toppings the better," Nick said. "I'm starving."

"We'll need a blanket from the house to sit on in the

back room," I said to Alice. The idea of eating next to the grave seemed too macabre.

Alice turned to go and get the blanket. I noticed the rain had let up. "Don't you want to go back to the house?" she asked Azalea and Pop. They both looked exhausted, but they both shook their heads

Alice was just walking toward the door to the pen when Nick, who was still digging, said, "Will you look at this!" in a startled tone. He held something out to Frank. It was a ring, a ring with a flat gold nub where a stone might have been. He rubbed it to get the last little bits of dirt off, but some still stuck in a depressed design.

"There's an initial in the gold," Frank said. "Hand engraved. Look here. It's a *B*."

"*B* for Buddy?" Pop blurted.

Anthony peered close. "And don't say that was just a nickname," he said with a malicious grin. "His birth name was Benjamin: Benjamin Thomason, brother of the bride. B for Benjamin." We were all struck silent.

CHAPTER
12

EARLY THAT EVENING

Nothing else of note had turned up at the pit where the skeleton had rested. Without the bones, the dark brown dirt looked so ordinary I could have believed our grisly find never existed. Even the faint skeleton-shaped imprint was gone, because Nick had explored the dirt a little deeper. Yet the hole in the ground still seemed like a grave.

At one end of the oblong-shaped hole, stones that formed the base of the fireplace were visible. One long wood beam or puncheon, which had held up the floor, ran straight across the room over those stones and in front of the hearth. Just beyond the end of the pit, more puncheons held up the plywood where Pop had sat. A long time ago a bullet had been found lodged in the wall on the other side of the room from the fireplace and the grave—so Azalea's story went. Perhaps the first attempt at murder had happened on the other side of the room from the grave, then the four shots as the man tried to defend himself or tried to escape.

By now the light through the door and window holes had become a luminous blue gray. We wandered around and mostly just digested the day.

Quiet at last. No TV lights and clamor. When Nick had finished examining the last resting place and thanked us for the pizza, he'd driven off in the state van with Dr. Breitberg and the cardboard box of bones. He'd given the gold ring to Frank, who hoped he could date its manufacture. I'd immediately asked Alice to get her camera and photograph it against a piece of black paper.

Of course, it was Anthony who intended to use that ring as evidence that the skeleton belonged to Buddy Thomason.

Who else, he'd demanded loudly, would have a ring with a *B* in the gold!

But on the other hand, in case the ring could be proved not to be Buddy/Benjamin's—maybe inherited from an ancestor of the bridegroom, called Bruno or Bob or whatever—I wanted to have a picture. Just in case the real ring vanished. I've known that kind of thing to happen. I also quietly asked Frank if he could put the ring in some very secure place. He said of course.

Anthony was loud in claiming victory. "It's my house now!" he crowed. His eyes were full of spite. "Just wait until I tell Adam about this!" He leered at Alice. "I hope you'll be pleased!" Such animosity toward Alice. More than the rest of us. He left singing a song about "Why is tomorrow better than today?" A song that Azalea often sang.

Azalea looked sick. Pop was tired as death. Alice was shaking. Frank and Hector seemed confused by all this, but Azalea did not explain. Hector said he and Frank would send a written report of what they'd found. They put tarps over the digs and left.

Ted and Alice and I managed to get Azalea and Pop into Alice's car. Alice said she and the sitter could handle things at Azalea's, and I said I'd like to stay in the old house just a few minutes and mull over the day. So Ted and I stayed briefly and conferred in the shadowy room, where the ghosts of the past seemed part of every log and every board.

Ted stood leaning against the ladder to upstairs. The ladder that broke with Azalea. "This is not necessarily what it seems," he said firmly. "That's what we have to impress on folks."

"That's the kind of thing you're good at," I said, glad that at least Ted looked firm and solid in that shadowy room. "Sensible logic. Thank goodness." I gave him a strong hug and a glad-to-be-alive kiss.

Ted hugged me back, but his mind was still on the ring. "Signet rings tend to have the last initial or both initials, not just the first, as in *B* for Buddy," he said. "That certainly looked like a signet ring. Still, I suppose a man could have his first initial on his ring if he wanted. And David Holden had no *B* in his initials at all."

"Perhaps that skeleton belonged to somebody else entirely," I said. But I knew that was unlikely.

Ted pulled the tarp off the empty hole as if he expected some revelation. In the distance I heard a hoot owl. A car passed on the road. Ted kept frowning as if some crucial thought was forming in his brain. Finally he said: "It wouldn't be easy." He looked down at the dirt that had once been under a wood floor and gently nudged the puncheon by the fireplace with his toe. "Not easy to take up the floor, bury a man under it, and then put the floor down again so neatly that no one suspected." He leaned down and touched one of the wood puncheons to which the floor had been attached. "But a carpenter like Buddy Thomason could do that job more easily than a lawyer like David Holden."

"Yes," I said. "The house itself is trying to help us. Azalea's family story said the rest of the family did not come back until the next day, so if that's true, Buddy had time. I wonder how much of an old story like that you can count on. Was Azalea's grandmother really right about a thunderstorm that night, or did she add it in for atmosphere?"

"That had to be true," Ted said. "To explain why no one heard the shots."

Now, why didn't I think of that? Meanwhile, in the here and now, the sky became darker every moment. No more inspirations came. But the rain started again. Hard and steady. I was tired.

I remembered the bullet that hit the wall. I turned toward the place on the wall where the bullet was said to have nicked the plaster—or was it the paneled wall, the place on the other side of the room from the dig? I backed away so as to see the whole wall and see where the supposed nick place was in relation to the hole under the floor. So don't ask me how old One-Track Mind here forgot exactly where the hole was. Suddenly Ted yelled, "Stop!" Too late. I fell backward into the hole. I lay there startled, with the breath knocked out of me. Me in a grave. In the dirt where the skeleton lay. It was like taking a bath in somebody else's dirty water. Only much worse. My skin crawled. Let this not be an omen.

I had a choice. I could cry or laugh.

"Are you all right?" Ted gasped. He reached to pull me up.

"I'm doing research," I said. "If you want to know how a person feels, walk in his shoes. If you want to know how a skeleton felt . . ."

Ted didn't laugh. "I really worry about you sometimes, Peaches," he said.

I had knocked some dirt off the side of the hole in my fall. As Ted pulled my right hand to help me up, I pressed down on my left hand. It touched something hard in the newly loosened dirt—something small and hard and smooth. Something that belonged to the dead man! It must be. First I dropped it. Next I thought, Maybe a clue, and felt myself grinning. I grasped it again and stood up. I held it out in my hand, loose dirt bits and all. It was a locket. I picked it up with the other hand. It was on a chain. God bless gold. It lasts.

We were both so excited, I forgot my bruises, and Ted

forgot to worry. We couldn't manage to pick it open, and we certainly didn't want to break it. So we re-covered the dig with its tarp, jumped in the car, and drove up to the house where there'd be better light and some sort of tools.

The house was quiet. Eudora must have helped Pop into bed, and presumably Azalea had helped herself into whichever bed she preferred. Azalea must sure need comfort. I did myself.

Ted found a bottle of wine in the refrigerator and was pouring a glass for me and one for himself. "Medicinal," he said to me, "and if anything really hurts, we'll put ice on it." Nothing hurt that bad. "I suppose Alice may know where some tools are. Maybe an eyeglass mending kit. There'd be a tiny screwdriver in that. Just right for prising this open." I laid the little oval locket on the kitchen table and looked up and saw Alice.

She was fighting back tears. "You've got to help me," she said. Her voice cracked with desperation. Ted and I both came to attention.

"This is all my fault," she said. She clenched her fists.

Alice's fault? That didn't make sense. She wasn't even around to shoot whoever in 1849. But Alice was the one who had seemed most stressed out all day.

"I don't know what to do next. Because I've been dumb, the thing my grandmother cares about most in the world could be destroyed. And she's been good to me. She trusts me, and look what I've done!"

"What *have* you done?" I asked, waving her to sit down at the kitchen table. Ted and I sat down, too. The locket lay waiting for us. It wouldn't go away.

She sat and stared at her hands as if they could give her the right words. "Anthony," she said, and pressed her lips together. She tossed her head up and said, "Oh, he's predicted this before—kept predicting we'd find bones. But now we have, and he'll make trouble because of me."

I figured he'd make trouble no matter what, but I kept listening.

"You've only seen the ugly side of Anthony," she said. "When he wants to be, he's charming."

"Yes," I said. "That's what you said." I thought: Charming like a rattlesnake.

"He's angry inside. But that can be sexy. Until you understand how it works." She flushed and bit her lip.

"Understand what?"

She got up and walked over to a small linen hanging that said AND ALL SHALL BE WELL, AND ALL MANNER OF THINGS SHALL BE WELL—ST. JULIAN OF NORWICH in a medieval-looking scroll.

"I hate these things now," she said, and jerked it down from the wall and rolled it up.

"What happened?" I asked gently. "You can trust us."

She sat back down, put her head in her hands, and began to shake with angry sobs. Ted and I sat silently and sipped our wine until Alice cried herself out. I will be patient, I told myself as the locket pulled me.

She jerked her head up and said again, "This is all my fault because I should have known that leech likes to draw blood!"

"How?" I asked.

"I thought he was so sexy," she said. "And how could it hurt, just a few times—to enjoy that." Warm, impulsive Alice. She'd needed to be cold and logical and look out for herself.

Long silence. "And . . . ?" I said.

"We went to Las Vegas for the weekend. That was the most exciting thing I ever did in my life." She perked up just remembering. "You wouldn't believe the lights! Everything was open all night. Casinos, restaurants, hotels. One had a pyramid in front. Ours was like a castle. One place had a million dollars under Plexiglas where you could see it, all in ten-thousand-dollar bills. I've got to tell you, I was dazzled." She stopped and frowned and then laughed ruefully. "I was out of my mind!

"And Anthony *was* sexy. But he was mean, too. He could mimic people behind their backs. He was good at that. He was funny. I'd seen him mimic before but not so much. Not so cruel. He'd get annoyed with me and mimic me, and after a while I hated that. I didn't want him around anymore. He made my skin crawl. I certainly didn't want to go to Las Vegas again. Besides, after that I met Ed.''

Her eyes softened, then got an angry glint. "But you don't leave Anthony. He can't take it. He goes crazy. But I didn't know that. And now I just can't—I can't make myself—not even once. He says that unless I come back to him, he'll destroy that house that means so much to Grandma. Just to hurt me. So I'll know what it's like. The house is historic and ought to be saved—she'll feel terrible. Because of that damned Anthony. And what can I do?''

"Does your grandmother know this?" I asked.

"Oh, Lord, no! She mustn't know. Promise you won't tell her! She's had enough trouble, and I don't want to make it worse. I have to figure some way to save the house. Except I just can't think how.''

Ted spoke for the first time, summarizing the situation. He's good at that.

"So you expect Anthony to go to Adam Marlowe, your great-grandfather, and persuade him that the skeleton with the initial ring must be his ancestor Buddy Thomason, killed by Azalea's ancestor David Holden, and therefore, according to the contract, Azalea loses the house, and it goes to Anthony.''

"Yes!" cried Alice. "I'll bet he's there right now. What can I do?''

"First of all," Ted said, "I think we need to go see Adam ourselves and tell him this has not been proved. And we are going to find out who killed whom and why. There are old records. The gal at archives tells me there are some old papers that just turned up and haven't been sorted yet. We don't know what's there until we look.''

"But suppose . . .'' Alice began.

"Whatever we discover," Ted said, "if Adam will just agree to wait until we find the truth, we will have a reprieve. We'll have time to regroup and decide what to do next.''

"Ted," I said, "you're wonderful. But then I knew that!''

"We're all going to have to be wonderful," Ted said, "in order to prove that skeleton isn't Buddy Thomason's.''

"I'll help," Alice said, "in every way that I possibly can." She smiled at Ted. "A reprieve. That'll give us time to take action. Like, shoot Anthony." She smiled even more broadly at the thought. "Or hang him." The panic ebbed away, and she focused on reality. "Hey, what's that?" She pointed at the locket.

I reached out and held the locket in my hand, light and smooth, oval and quite plain—about an inch long and not that wide. With the dirt wiped off, it had that soft gold patina of something that has been worn next to the skin. The chain was slithery and slipped out between my fingers. "We found this," I said, "where they found the skeleton." I told her how.

Alice quickly found a fruit knife with a thin blade in the table drawer, and that turned out to be just the tool to prise open the locket. We all leaned forward, hoping. Were we going to see a picture of the bride, a picture of David Holden, or what?

What we finally saw with the locket open was a curl: one lock of hair. Dark, like Alice's hair.

"Oh!" Alice groaned. "That's all!"

Ted laughed. "We'll find lots of temporary disappointments on the way to the truth. And even wrong turns." He paused and frowned. "The ring with the *B* was a wrong turn." He stood up. "And that's what we'll have to convince Adam Marlowe as soon as possible."

CHAPTER
13

9:30 THAT EVENING

Alice used the phone on the kitchen counter to call Adam *Figleaf* Marlowe to see if he was awake and if it would be all right for us to come over at nine-thirty at night. Ted and I hovered.

"Do you think I can sleep?" Adam asked in such a loud voice that I could hear him right through the phone. "I'm so upset about what Anthony told me, I've called my lawyer. He's coming here first thing in the morning."

"Anthony doesn't know the whole story." Alice's voice quavered with fear. Her elbows on the counter held the rest of her steady. "Please don't do anything until we get there. Please!" she begged.

"He hung up," she groaned, and slammed down the phone. "He's going off half-cocked. He does that. We need to go right over." Anguish lined her face. She drew in her breath. "Oh, I've goofed again! Eudora wanted to go out tonight to a movie. It's the night she's supposed to have off. Pop and Azalea were asleep. I was distracted, and I said okay. I can't just leave them here alone in the state they're in."

Ted put his arm around Alice. "That may be a blessing," he said. "You're too upset. That's the very kind of state that could mean you'd put your foot in your mouth. Right? You stay here and let Peaches and me handle the old man. If that doesn't work, you can go see him tomorrow."

She nodded unhappily. "But don't expect to persuade Adam of anything," she told us. "He hasn't changed his mind in thirty years." She looked down near the phone, and there was one of Azalea's inspirational plaques. Positive thoughts even on the kitchen counter! It was a small bar of wood with words lettered in green. She read it out loud: " 'All things come to him who has faith.' Azalea believes that," Alice said. "I'll try to believe that."

Personally, my slogan is "The Lord helps those who help themselves."

Suddenly at the back of my mind something I almost remembered tried to come to light. Something I knew I needed to remember, only it wouldn't come. I was about to say that when Ted said, "We need to hurry." Even the shadow of whatever it was slipped out of my mind.

So we set forth. It was late. By the time we got to the old man's house through the pouring rain, it was quarter of ten. The horses were in the barn or at least out of sight. Adam Marlowe had floodlights trained on the front of his house with the white columns. Quite dramatic in the rain-drenched dark. The wet white fences on each side of the driveway reflected the headlight glare.

Adam came to the door more stooped than before. The floodlight brightness made his face look haggard. "I don't like this," he said. "I don't like any of this. I like peace."

We led him to a chair in that living room full of Bibles, framed relatives, and horses. We sat down on either side. I introduced Ted.

"I suppose Azalea is upset," he said, "so she sent you over."

"She wasn't in a condition to come herself," Ted said, "and Alice had to stay with her."

"It won't do any good," the old man said. "You should have stayed with her, too. That house is Anthony's now," he said. "I don't like that, but it had to be."

"Don't jump to conclusions without getting the facts about that skeleton," I said. "You'll feel bad later." Once more that flash of a half memory came to my mind. What was it?

"Pictures don't lie," Adam said, and caught my attention. He thrust out the Polaroid picture Anthony had taken of the ring. Anthony had managed to catch the light and shadow so the *B* showed clearly. "That *B* shows the body belonged to Benjamin Thomason. And the four bullets they found with the skeleton show he was murdered, brutally murdered by a man who couldn't stop firing. He was in a rage! So it couldn't have been self-defense. How do you justify that? Azalea's ancestor brutally murdered mine." His eyes flashed anger.

"Pictures can give a false impression," Ted said calmly. "I know, I used to be a newspaper reporter."

"They're all crooks," the old man bellowed. "Reporters and politicians. I wouldn't trust a one." A horse picture just behind his shoulder seemed to sneer.

"Are you sure you can trust Anthony to have the facts?" Ted asked.

The old man stopped bellowing and frowned. "He couldn't fake a picture," he said, "and I have to trust Anthony. He's my son-in-law. He's all that's left of my daughter except her things in the attic. All her things are still there. I had a beautiful daughter."

"Anthony could make a photograph seem like proof for something that isn't proved," I said. But my heart sank. If Adam Marlowe felt he had to trust Anthony because of his daughter, logic might not help.

"We don't have all the evidence yet," Ted said. "There was a skeleton—pretty gruesome—and a ring. The ring wasn't on the skeleton. Someone could have dropped it.

The ring had a *B* on it, but the first name of your ancestor began with a *B*. Signet rings usually have the first letter of the last name on them. Your ancestor's last name began with a *T*."

Adam eyed Ted through narrowed eyes. "Why do you care so much?"

"I'm Azalea's"—Ted groped for the relationship— "new son-in-law. And I don't think history should be destroyed, certainly not without trying to find out what really happened here."

The old man did seem to be listening at last. So Ted told him his theory about how difficult it would be to kill a man, take up the floor, bury him, and put the floor back down without a trace to cause suspicion.

"A carpenter like Buddy Thomason could get away with that if he had all night to work, and the story says he did. A lawyer like David Holden could never do it."

"That's not proof," the old man said defiantly. He clenched his fists.

"We want to find you proof of what happened, whatever it was," I said, aiming to sound as calm and reasonable as Ted. "We need to be positive whose bones were under the floor."

Once more that glimmer. What on earth was trying to find its way up into my mind?

Adam laughed scornfully and chased that glimmer away. "Proof of what happened way back then? What will you do—interview the neighbors?"

"Newspapers were pasted on the upstairs walls," I said, "maybe to keep the wind out, and some of them are nearly a hundred years old." Then I bit my lip in frustration. I realized that wasn't long enough. "I'll bet the *Review Appeal* has older ones. They could help."

"If anybody knew back then." The old man shrugged. "But how would they know?"

"You can find proof of the past," I said. "The archaeologists who dug up artifacts at that house today found an arrowhead made twelve thousand years ago. Which proves that Indians lived here then. There are more clues to one hundred and fifty years ago. We'll find the clues we need.''

The old man did not seem to have any answer to top that. He sagged, as if he was suddenly tired. He shrugged again. "All right. See what you can dig up." He laughed at his own pun. "I'll give you six days."

"Only six days!" I said, shocked. "Why six?"

But Ted said, "We'll accept that if you'll agree that if we begin to find evidence that David Holden did not kill Buddy Thomason, you'll give us a little longer. That would be fair, and I understand you are a fair man."

Mr. Figleaf could hardly disagree with that.

As soon as we were out the door in the quiet night, my glimmer came back. Ted said, "Where do we start looking into all this?"

I tried to ignore him. I stood perfectly still. Lucky the rain had stopped. Ideas for what we should do first rushed at me. I held my hand up straight over my head.

I wondered if Rose's memory-saver trick would work for a memory that was trying to be born.

"Listen," I said. "Some idea keeps knocking at my brain. I need to figure out what it is."

"When did it start?" Ted asked as he opened the car door.

"We were talking about proof," I said.

"And what else?"

"About bones," I said, keeping my hand safely high.

"Proof and bones?"

"I think it has to do with an Egyptian mummy," I said, surprising myself. "They had bones. But that makes no sense at all."

"Yes, it does." He burst into a big grin. How come he understands what I think better than I do? It's not fair, but it sure is useful.

"We were listening on the TV to a report about how DNA testing was able to sort out the sex life of the Egyptian pharaohs, remember that?" he said. "To prove who was really descended from whom. In the motel in Boone, just before we came here. It was such a wild idea that it stuck in my mind, and I bet it stuck in yours, too! So you're wondering why don't we ask for DNA testing, to prove who the skeleton was, isn't that right?"

"Yes!" Hey, that was smart of me! Or at least it was halfway smart of me and the other half smart of Ted. "And why hasn't *Anthony* asked for testing if he's so sure he's right?" I asked in a rush.

"I thought about that myself when they sent the skeleton off to UT to the forensic-anthropology department," Ted said. "No mention of DNA."

"So thanks for sharing your thoughts! Why didn't you say something?"

"Because I believed Anthony never would ask for DNA testing. He's not sure who the skeleton belongs to and he knows all he has to do is convince Adam that it's Buddy Thomason's. If a DNA test, comparing cells from the skeleton with cells from Adam, shows conclusively that it's not his direct ancestor, Anthony has lost his case. That's final. Otherwise he can keep working at Adam."

"And we don't want a test for the same reason?" I asked. "Because we don't want final proof until we know exactly what that proof would show. Otherwise, we may gain time by not knowing?"

"Exactly," he said. "And those tests are expensive. The sheriff doesn't care about a murder back then. He's not about to pay for tests. And by the grace of God, Adam hasn't thought of it. For God's sake don't tell him about King Tut or whoever proved that DNA can unscramble the distant past.

"You can take your hand down now," Ted added.

I realized it was still up in the air. I had forgotten about my hand. I pulled it down and got in the car.

"What we need to do first is call Alice," I said.

So we called Alice on the car phone as we drove along— I guess Ted is right, the phone is handy—and told her we had a reprieve for six days, and it could maybe be extended.

We'd need to work fast.

CHAPTER
14

10:45 P.M.

By the time we left, the rain had stopped. There was full night and a full moon. Mad men are madder on the full moon, I thought to myself. Why that? We were investigating a murder that happened over a hundred years ago, and a kind of blackmail now: *Come be my carnal love, oh Alice, or the house goes.* There was no reason for madness or the moon to explain either of those facts.

I'm a little spacier myself on the full moon. Is that why I fell into the grave? More crimes are committed when the moon is full, I reminded myself. More babies are born. Very influential, the moon. The face in the moon was especially clear. Good evening, sir.

I dozed off thinking of the round shining face. Ted was driving. I woke up to music. Guitar music, rather weird. The car had stopped, and we were in front of the old house. I woke to attention instantly. The light of the moon made everything clear. The plastic shroud around the house moved slightly in a night breeze.

Ted got out of the car, and I heard him open and close the trunk as quietly as you can close metal on metal. He came back with a wrench in his hand, a menacing silhouette and yet still familiar. Ted, with his glasses reflecting the moon and his hair sticking at odd angles the way it does when he's run his fingers through it. "I'm going to find out what's going on," he said. "It's probably just some kids who think this is a prank, but I'm armed."

I got goose bumps. "Well, I'm not going to stay here unarmed all by myself," I said firmly. I reached in the glove compartment and got out the small flashlight that lives there. We wouldn't need it in the moonlight, but the house would be darker inside.

Ted went first, wrench in hand. The moon was so full that we had no trouble finding the plywood ramp to the opening where a front door had originally been—now just a black hole. We came so quietly we could have been ghosts ourselves. No one was in the right-hand room. We went through the door to the left. Someone was sitting next to the open grave with his back to us, lit by an eerie flickering light. I caught my breath. Who on earth? He was lower than we were. We were up on the puncheons that had held the floor. He was down on the dirt that had been under the floor. His arms moved in a strange way like the legs of some insect.

I realized he was playing a guitar, playing a guitar and singing, "And all that's left are the bones, oh," in a mournful tone. He turned his head. It was Tennessee Walt-z. We walked closer. I saw his source of light: a candle in a 7UP bottle. Just beyond it, I saw the open dig hole again, half-blackened by shadow. Not far from that, the flexible blue plastic tarp lay in a heap. I flashed my small flashlight beam around the hole. It didn't appear to have been disturbed, not beyond my falling into it earlier.

Walt grinned at us. He didn't even get flustered.

"Hello," he said. "I'm writing a ballad about what happened here." He spoke in this happy dreamy tone as if the skeleton had shown up just for his inspiration. "This is going to be the best thing I've done. I'll get my break from this. Maybe even get on TV." He strummed several chords on his guitar. He stood up in one motion, unfolding himself to full length, turning his whole body toward us, guitar and all.

The candlelight made his wood-carved features sharp.

"How long have you been here?" Ted demanded.

"As it happens, I know," Walt said. "When I left Goat's house, he was just telling his daughter she had to go to sleep because it was already ten o'clock. He really takes good care of that kid."

"Have you touched anything here?" Ted asked. "Dug anything?"

"Of course not," Walt said. "Except for moving this plastic away so I can get in the bones-were-here mood. I've been too busy trying to get this song right. The place I dig is down in my creative mind. Down where the music lives." He strummed a couple of more chords. He smiled broadly, and his eyes twinkled, very pleased with himself. "But if you think something might be hid around here, I'll show you something."

He leaned down and put the guitar into its case, which sat on the dirt underfloor. He handed the candle in the bottle up to Ted and then climbed up onto the nearest puncheon. He led us through the inside door, into the other front pen, and over to the other gray-stone fireplace. He pointed to the big slab of hearthstone. "See how one end is cracked?" Yes. Someone must have dropped a heavy pot there, I thought. But this wasn't the kitchen. Still, a narrow crack went across the hearthstone from front to back.

Ted held the candle high, and I shone my puny flashlight so we could see as well as possible. Our shadows wavered against the dirt floor and log walls. Walt began to work at the hearthstone, trying to loosen the cracked end. His shadow wobbled against the wall. Finally the crack widened. He managed to pull up that section of stone. My heart thumped. Ted gasped.

"What's there?" I demanded. There was a dark cavity below the stone. Not a deep hole, but certainly a fine hiding place for something secret or something valuable. In answer to my question, Ted moved the candle around so that we could see that the cavity was lined with rock and absolutely empty. I felt a pang of disappointment. I added my flashlight beam to the illumination. Nothing but flat rock lining the hole.

"What was in it when you found it?" I asked. There must have been something! I hoped. And why hadn't Walt or someone mentioned this before?

Walt shrugged. "We found it empty. But we decided to leave it as it was as a memento of the past. And Azalea asked us not to talk about it. Said someday she might hide her jewelry there." He smiled, as people do at Azalea, then became more serious. "But certainly you should be allowed to know about this." He cocked his head. "What do you suppose the people who built this house had to hide?"

"And why would this place be empty now?" Ted wondered. Very disappointing, very odd. "You'd better close it if Azalea wants to keep the secret."

Outside I heard the rain begin to fall again, tapping gently on the tin roof. Walt was working to get the stone slab back in place just right, getting it to fit so exactly that it would stay in place. "Is there anything else we ought to know?" I asked.

Walt shook his head emphatically. "Not that I know of."

When the stone was snug, he led the way back into the pen where he'd left his guitar. He climbed down by the hole where the skeleton had been, picked up his guitar case, and said, "I reckon I'd better get on home." The rain was plunking louder.

"I don't see any car," Ted said. "Do you need a ride?"

"I'm staying next door," he said. "Goat said I could sleep on his couch. He plays the fiddle. He knows how it is when the inspiration gets you. My car is over in his drive.''

Goat was the one with the sick daughter, right? Nothing catching, I hoped.

''You'll get soaked,'' Ted said, looking out the front-door hole at pounding rain.

Walt-z glanced at his guitar case. Was he afraid it would leak and the rain would hurt his guitar? ''A ride would be mighty nice,'' he said.

''I'll stay here,'' I said. ''You'll be back in a minute. By then, the rain may have let up, and I won't get soaked on the way to the car.'' Also, I simply had a hunch we should look around the old house more and not leave it unguarded before we checked it out. If this were a modern crime scene, it would be sealed off with yellow tape, guarded until every nook and cranny had been examined. But since this murder had taken place in 1849, as far as we knew, the law enforcers hadn't taped the site. Logic said no one had guarded it since the middle of the nineteenth century, so why now? My intuition told me we shouldn't have left it unguarded, even to go talk to Adam Marlowe.

Ted said he'd be back shortly. ''I'll run out to the car first and unlock the doors,'' he told Walt.

Walt-z handed me his candle. ''I won't need this in the rain.'' He slung his guitar case on its strap over his shoulder, ran down the slanted plywood in front of us and out to the car. His door slammed. Ted's door clicked shut, the engine revved, and off they drove, headlights making the rain into long thin slits of light.

Inside the house, the candle was brighter than my little flashlight. I turned off the flashlight and put it in my skirt pocket and looked around the room where I stood. Not much new to see: two wood-log skeleton walls, with dark shadows between the logs, moving in the candle flicker. Two wood-panel interior walls, also the door holes, one out front, one in back, one to the side. Windows on each side of the fireplace still had glass panes that reflected the candle. The dig hole where the skeleton had been was shadowed on one side.

I put my hand on the ladder up to the opening in the floor above. And in the corner by the ladder, I saw the shadow of the stairway that had once been there: the imprint of the edge of the stair treads on the wall. I felt the past strongly with us. Did Annie Thomason go up that stairway to bed every night with a candle in her hand, never knowing that, under the floor below, her lover's body slowly turned to dirt and bones? I looked through the door hole to my right. At Hector's dig hole in front of the fireplace over there. Buckets for carrying dirt. Nothing new or surprising. Hector's cap—the one that always sat on his head, indoors or out—lay on some plywood near the buckets. Odd that he left it. I guessed he took it off after there was no more chance of going out in the sun.

I came back to the ladder. Holding the candle carefully, I climbed part way up, holding the ladder with my other hand. Then, when I could reach, I set the candle bottle on the upstairs floor above my head and climbed the rest of the way with two hands. At the top I pulled myself up onto the floor. No more rain noise on the roof. I was right. That was just a passing shower. Shadows danced as I picked up the candle. I heard a creaking noise. Just an old-house noise, I told myself. But another part of me thought: Someone else could be hiding in this house. I felt a chill. I looked around the upstairs rooms. Just me and the light and shadow. But I felt a presence. I went to the back door hole of the upstairs room on the left. The door that looked out on space and then on the room at the back. Nothing unexpected there. Someone could push me, I thought, and my stomach turned. I walked back to the door hole to the room on the right. That room was empty. I made myself go look out the window onto the pipe scaffolding around the chimney. Someone could crouch on the platform out there. Nothing there but a platform made of heavy planks with stones on it. Ready for work in the morning. The rain had stopped. I crawled back

down the ladder, walked through, and looked at the back
room, walking close enough to the fireplace to see that no
one lurked in the shadows. I looked out the rear door hole.
A drip of water from the roof above landed smack on my
candle and put it out. Dern—no matches. The room went
black. The moon came out from under a cloud, and I
jumped into the light outside. My feet squished in mud, but
I welcomed the moon! I could see nobody was lurking outside. What was taking Ted so long?

The moonlight was more friendly than the candlelight. It
didn't flicker. So instead of walking back through the
house, I walked around it—even though the ground was
wet and my shoes were getting soaked. Still, someone could
be hidden behind the hulk of the Dumpster. I picked up a
piece of wood lying on the ground. It was about three feet
long. Sturdy and splintery in my hand, but a weapon if need
be. Scaffolding around the chimney loomed ahead of me,
the scaffolding where Goat was working in the daytime.
With all those stones on his high platform. Those expensive
stones.

Then I became aware of something lying at the foot of
the scaffolding. My stomach lurched. It was a man—half-
moonlit, half in shadow. Automatically I reached in my
pocket. I'd forgotten the flashlight was there when my candle went out, but under stress, my hand knew it was there.
I pulled the flashlight out quick and shone it where the
moon shadows lay. The body was belly down, its face
turned away from me. The top of the head was caved in,
and near the head lay one of the antique hand-hewn rocks,
with blood on it. Near the outstretched hand was a knife,
glimmering in the light. As if this man were trying to protect himself when someone stove his head in. The knife
had an inlaid handle like the one that Hector— I shone the
flashlight on his features. Good Lord, it was Hector the
Collector!

I heard a car drive up and prayed it was Ted. I called
out, and he came running. He took a good look at the body,
then looked up at the scaffolding: pipes crisscrossing, plat-

form on top. "The rock must have fallen, or been pushed, from up there," he said.

Thirty-pound rocks don't throw themselves, that's for sure. "I was just upstairs," I said. "There was no one up there. No one anywhere in the house." Walt had been inside, but certainly he wouldn't . . . "Besides," I said, "Hector has a knife near his hand. The one he always wore for luck. He must have been protecting himself from someone down here."

We looked at the ground for footprints. If there'd been footprints before ours, the rain had washed them away.

The moon went behind a cloud, and I felt the dark press in around us like a cloud of evil. Who would want to kill Hector the Collector? Hector who knew so much about old bones and other clues to the past. Hector believed in luck. That was ironic. All his knowledge and skill were destroyed by one rock. He'd been so proud of himself. Which was a little annoying, but impressive, too. He'd wanted to be someone important. Now he'd never have a chance. His dreams had been flattened by the killer's rock.

Ted put his arm around me. "I'm sorry I left you to find this alone. Goat grabbed me. He's so upset that Anthony may get the house. But obviously I should've come sooner." He looked down at Hector's crushed head. "This must be murder."

And that murder must have happened before ten o'clock if Walt-z was telling the truth. I hoped and prayed he was not involved. I liked his song.

CHAPTER
15

EARLY THE NEXT WEEK

Late into the night on Saturday, the sheriff's deputies questioned Ted, questioned me, and, I gathered, most especially questioned Walt-z, though I wasn't in on that. The deputies were closemouthed about what was going on. Asked a lot and told very little. On Sunday and Monday, the deputies questioned Azalea and Pop and Alice and all the workers on the house. Since I'd found the body, they grilled me more than Ted. Somewhere they'd heard I'd solved a couple of crimes. They took a dim view of "amateurs" and suggested that I confine my efforts to telling them anything useful that I might happen to hear.

But I thought I had a right to help Pop and Azalea sort out what was going on. It was my own kin who might be in danger.

Ted agreed and said he figured that the more minds that focused on a crime, the more likely it was to be solved. So he got busy quietly asking each person where he'd been at the probable time of the crime and making one of his time charts. He's very good at that.

Meanwhile I talked to Frank on Monday. That wasn't hard. He came by Azalea's house in the morning to tell me what he thought. I guess he felt the way Ted did. The more minds, etc. "I know you've been able to unravel some crimes, so I wanted you to know about Hector," he said.

I was out in front of Azalea's house about to pick some zinnias to cheer myself up—Azalea's recommendation. "Let's go for a walk," I told Frank. "The morning is still cool, and there's a crowd inside." The crowd was only Pop and Eudora and Alice and Azalea, but I felt I could learn more with just Frank and me.

Frank seemed disorganized. The buttons of his khaki shirt were done up wrong. He'd been loose-kneed before, but now the parts of his body didn't quite seem to work together. The hand that pulled one earlobe seemed out of sync with his hurrying feet. One foot seemed out of rhythm with the other. "This has thrown me for a loop," he said, groping for words. "I feel like it's my fault—well, partly my fault—that Hector's dead." He ran his fingers through his hair like Ted does when he's upset.

"Why?" I asked as we walked down the gravel road beyond Azalea's house. Young woods were on both sides of the road.

"Because I should have guessed. I should have known that Hector was in some kind of trouble or danger. You see, we've worked together once or twice, and I've heard him talk about his father. He hero-worshiped the man. He felt he had to try to live up to him. Well, that's all right, but he felt that because his father handled all sorts of dangers like Mexican bandits and snakes in the jungle and things like that, he had to handle anything that went wrong all by himself. That's what he told me on the last dig when he broke his leg and splinted it and got to the doctor all by himself. He couldn't ask for help."

"And you think that killed him somehow?" A bird flew up from the side of the road. I jumped.

Frank pulled the other ear. He stopped in his tracks. "But that's not all. He had this temper. I hear he got fired at one dig for telling off the boss."

"Why does all that make you feel guilty?" I stopped, too. The sun was getting warmer.

"Because he'd been acting so angry. He said, just out of the blue, 'Nobody can get away with bullying me,' and I asked him what he meant and he said that's just how he felt about life. But I had a feeling there was more to it. And he wore that knife you saw."

"He told me he always wore that to a dig, for luck," I said.

"Not on the ones he's worked with me," Frank protested. Perspiration broke out on his forehead, but he ignored it and still stood in the sun. "Hector had a short fuse," he said. "He met this Anthony Wolf at Ross's house a while back—Hector worked with Ross a lot—and recently I heard Hector yell at Anthony like you wouldn't believe when the man took his picture. I gather Anthony's a nut, but it didn't help to shout so. All those things should have warned me that something was wrong, that Hector was in a bad state. And I didn't do anything."

"What could you have done?" I asked. I was sweating myself.

"Made him tell me what was wrong. But he never would have. And I had this totally illogical feeling that finding that skeleton made things worse, because it made me look smarter than Hector. Which I'm not. But it seemed like when he felt somebody had outdone him, he got antsy. I just feel bad about the whole thing."

He let out a long sigh. "I didn't really know Hector well," he said, "but I should have known he was in trouble."

So had Hector done something to get himself killed? And if so, what?

CHAPTER
16

TUESDAY

We sat around the table at the breakfast end of Azalea's kitchen on Tuesday morning. Ted and me and Azalea and Pop and Alice. Eudora had eaten early. Pop had rolled his wheelchair right up to the antique wooden table in front of the stone fireplace at the far end of the kitchen. He was wearing a T-shirt that said IF I COULD JUST REMEMBER YOUR NAME, I'D ASK YOU WHERE I LEFT MY CAR KEYS! Where on earth had he gotten that? He said he was wearing it to cheer me up and show me that someday I would get back to promoting my book about memory. Pop was positive and upbeat. Wow. Marriage was good for him, although there were certainly side effects, if you count murder.

We needed cheering. I hated to think about that yellow crime-scene tape around the old house, looking bizarrely modern and artificial near the hand-hewn logs. And I kept seeing Hector in my mind, seeing his body lying in the moonlight and trying to figure, Why Hector? Frank had helped me understand a little, but not much. Now all that knowledge in Hector's skull was erased with one stone. Had he known something that could threaten someone to the point of murder?

Azalea was upset about Hector, too. "He was such a talented boy," she said. "Such a loss. So young." But after she said she felt badly about Hector, she went on to be determinedly cheerful. That was because she was upset. I was beginning to psych Azalea out. She was upset not only about Hector's death, but also that this would divert us from proving that the skeleton had belonged to her ancestor. In other words, that David Holden wasn't a killer. The ruckus did divert us some, but by Tuesday morning the dust was settling.

"While we're all together," Ted said, "I'd like to go over this chart of who was where when and see if there is anything any of you know that should be added to it." Tense moment of silence. Not upbeat. The chart on his yellow legal pad was basically a suspect chart.

"You have us all on that chart?" Pop asked, putting his coffee cup down.

"Yes," Ted said. "I even have myself here, although I don't think I did it."

Alice laughed nervously.

"We have two main dates to check—late afternoon of Wednesday, June nineteenth, when someone seems to have sabotaged the ladder—probably between five and six-fifteen P.M., because Azalea fell about six-fifteen, according to Alice. Also we need to check this Saturday evening, just three days later, when someone either dropped a stone on Hector or was strong enough to raise it up and bash his head in with it. Not necessarily a strong person, if the stone was rolled off the scaffolding platform. But the person needed to have good aim or be very lucky."

"Or unlucky, if they get caught," Pop said. "I have an alibi for that one. I can't climb up to the second floor or lift a stone."

Ted turned to Pop. "You were on the scene on Wednesday when the ladder broke, Pop—you and Alice. Was either of you alone so you could have sabotaged the ladder?''

Another small shocked silence. Alice said, yes, she got there before Pop and Azalea had arrived, complete with Eudora pushing Pop's wheelchair. ''I was there about six. But I sure didn't fiddle with the ladder.''

Pop said he always needed someone to push his wheelchair, so he was never alone.

''Speaking of what you need,'' Ted said, ''Eudora tells me that Azalea and Pop stopped to talk about the outside of the old house, and Eudora was so curious about the inside that she went in and looked around, and then came back outside to help wheel Pop up the ramp. So she had the opportunity to sabotage the ladder, though she swears she didn't touch it.''

''And,'' I asked, ''what possible motive would she have?''

''Jealousy,'' Azalea said, and winked at Pop.

''Then, on Saturday evening,'' Ted went on, ''Pop and Azalea and Alice were all together at Azalea's house, right?'' They agreed.

Alice said, ''Eudora was there early on. Then she went to a movie. At least, that's where she said she went.''

Ted nodded. ''That's what she told me, too. Also I found out from the workers at the house exactly where they were on the two critical dates.''

Whoops. I had forgotten to ask them where they were on Wednesday afternoon! That's why Ted and I make a good team. He claims I find out the offbeat things that he would never think of.

''On Wednesday afternoon, right after work, all the house crew went to Fat Boy's for a drink to celebrate the Kid's birthday. Ross was on hand, and he joined in. If one of them tampered with the ladder, he'd have had to do it with the others coming and going. That would be possible but hard.

''On Saturday,'' Ted went on, ''the regular crew was off while the archaeologists were digging. So, as far as we know, nobody but Walt came on the site. He says he'd heard about the skeleton from the TV, and it caught his imagination. He came over and wrote a song about it. He said he arrived about ten P.M. Peaches and I found him playing his guitar and singing by the open hole where the skeleton had been. That was about ten forty-five. He'd uncovered the hole but didn't appear to have disturbed it otherwise."

"Very strange," Alice said.

"Hector could have been killed anytime after the last of us left around eight P.M. until we found him dead about eleven. I hear secondhand that the medical examiner thinks he was killed early in the evening," Ted said. "So Walt is a suspect."

"But he has no motive, and maybe Walt's song will bring him fame and fortune," Azalea said, and she began to sing—at breakfast, yet—"I'm Looking Over a Four-leaf Clover."

"I found out what the members of the crew were doing Saturday evening," Ted said. "Ross went out to dinner with his wife, Rose, and her sister and brother-in-law to the Macaroni Grill. They were together until about eleven, just about the time we found Hector already dead. Melody and the Kid had dinner in Nashville and spent the night together. Goat was home alone with his daughter, and Neal Madder was home entirely alone."

"Neal Madder's the one you notice the least," I said. "He's always pleasant but quiet, even though his name does rhyme with 'steal ladder.' But, of course, we're not looking for anyone who would simply steal a ladder. We want someone who booby-trapped a ladder and committed murder."

"And how about Anthony?" Alice asked. She pushed her cornflakes around the bowl. She'd hardly eaten a bite.

Ted made a grimace. "He says it's none of my damn business where he was and when." Anthony must have enjoyed thumbing his nose at Ted. I felt hot thinking about that. I suddenly saw Anthony's hands in my mind's eye.

"Anthony held his hands curled shut," I said. That position means he plays his cards close to his chest, which doesn't surprise me since he's a sneaky type. "Of course," I added, "sometimes people who are not sneaky have a reason to keep things to themselves, and they hold their hands that way, too. Ross the Boss holds his hands closed. So does Adam Marlowe. I notice things like that since hand reading helped solve my cousin's murder. I jot down a few things that might be useful."

"What else?" Ted asked. He has a theory that I often know more than I know I know.

"Ross's wife, Rose, has the open pink hands of a natural optimist," I said. "Walt-z has knots at his finger joints— the sign of someone who makes up his mind slowly and changes it slowly. The Kid has the broad base on his palm of someone who is active and inventive. But none of that relates to murder."

"That we know of," Ted said with a sigh.

I took another bite of my own cornflakes and then another sip of coffee. A picture of St. Francis of Assisi feeding the birds was behind Pop's head on the wall. Behind Azalea was a handmade sampler of an angel with a small child. It said, GOD IS LOVE. What a contrast to our life.

Alice was pale with fear and guilt, warming her hands on her coffee cup, but not drinking her coffee. It's a wonder, I thought, that a girl raised among so much sweetness and light didn't rebel by becoming a hellion. Was it all that upbeat talk that caused her to be fascinated by Anthony, then frightened of him? Was she warped by too much good-cheer-no-matter-what? How much good cheer was too much?

And had Anthony committed murder? I wanted to think so. I freely admit I was prejudiced against him. But why kill now, just when he seemed to be getting his way?

I think every single one of us felt Anthony had set up Azalea to fall and had killed Hector, even though I could only speculate why. "Maybe Anthony thought if Azalea was hurt, it would stop work on the house, or at least slow it up,'' I said. ''Maybe Anthony thought that Hector had discovered something that meant Anthony had to kill him to hush it up. But what on earth?''

No one answered.

''Something about the past?'' I asked. ''Would he actually kill to get possession of the house and spite Alice and Azalea? He may be unbalanced, but that seems extreme.''

Still no comment. Pop was relishing his scrambled eggs, while Ted gazed at his list.

''I am so sorry that talented young archaeologist died,'' Azalea said as she poured herself a cup of tea from a pretty pink pot, ''but it will mean the sheriff will guard our house more carefully. I'm thankful for that.''

Life must go on. ''I am going to find this Art Bolder today and talk to him,'' I said, sipping more coffee. ''The one who got fired for stealing stones before the trouble started. Stealing possible murder weapons, as it turns out. He's the only worker we haven't talked to.''

Alice put her spoon down. The corners of her mouth lifted. All of her seemed to become lighter. Her eyes sparkled. ''You won't find him around here,'' was all she said, but her words sang.

Everyone at the table turned to look at her. Now, wait a minute. Alice was in love with someone called Ed, who was up in the mountains, near my bailiwick. So why did the very mention of the stone thief light her up like a carnival?

''He'll be back with his family now,'' she said. We all waited for more. ''I know him well,'' she said. ''We were at Mars Hill College together.''

Oho! Mars Hill was up in the North Carolina mountains. So she hoped we'd go there. The sheriff had said to stay in touch. He hadn't said we had to stay put. I have a car phone. So why shouldn't I go where I pleased?

''Only, Art got expelled.'' Alice stirred her tea until it formed a whirlpool. She shook her head at Art's expulsion. ''I liked him,'' she said firmly. ''I figured he hadn't done what they said." She looked from one of us to another. "I mean, why would he steal a shirt two sizes smaller than he was and a wristwatch when he already had one? And some CDs when he didn't have a CD player?"

Nobody answered. Pop waited expectantly to hear more.

There was more to this—I could feel it. Azalea smiled her dazzling congratulatory smile. "Is that why you suggested he get a job down here? To help that poor boy out? But Ross says he didn't rise to the occasion."

Alice looked down at her cereal. "He'd worked in the summer as a carpenter," she said in a please-understand tone. "But coming here didn't turn out well, did it?" Dead silence around the table. Some of the lightness went out of Alice.

"So, I guess he does steal. I'm sorry," she said. "I'm making a mess of things. But he wouldn't hurt anybody. Except for stealing, he's a nice kid. Maybe he was framed or something." Alice wanted to believe that.

Azalea smiled and nodded and passed me the pitcher of orange juice. "I'm sure this will turn out for the best." She began to sing—something about a bluebird of happiness. A song I'd never even heard before. Her snatches of song never lasted. They were musical exclamation points.

How could Azalea go right on looking at the bright side, I wondered, after all that had gone wrong in her life? She'd lost her son and his wife in a car crash, and her husband had been paralyzed in the same crash. He'd been unable even to speak for nearly ten years. Why didn't she weep and pull her hair out and wait for the worst? Maybe her constant good cheer was a kind of nervous breakdown inside out. No, I thought, more a comfort. Something to hold on to.

"So, Alice," I asked, "do you know where Art Bolder will be?" That's what I needed to find out.

"Oh, yes," she enthused. "I went to visit his family. They live not far from the college. He was the first one in his family who ever went to college, and his mother was so proud. He's everything to her." Alice stopped and frowned. "I don't think his father liked his getting an education. It made him different. His father is a farmer and a carpenter. That's how Art got good at woodwork." Her frown deepened, then exploded back into a smile. "I'll come with you, Peaches. I can show you exactly where to go! And Art's a smart kid. He notices things. He'll help."

And maybe you can see your Ed, I thought. Hence euphoria. "It would be nice," I said, "to slip by home in the mountains and check on the neighbor who's feeding the cat and get some clothes in case we're here awhile longer. But can Alice and I both leave Pop and Azalea?" I turned to them. "Would you feel deserted, Azalea?"

Ted jumped in. "Not when I'm here. I'll stay and do some more research at the archives and the library," he said. "I've found some good leads."

"I went to the newspaper," Azalea told him, "and looked for old stories about how Buddy Thomason and David Holden disappeared. But the records didn't go back that far." She sighed. "Even the archives didn't tell the story. And there was nothing much in the library. The first library in Franklin wasn't started until the 1920s in a room in the Masonic Hall—and even then it was only open part-time. But I hear they've just found some new historical papers. That sounds promising. I haven't had a chance to go look."

"Yes." Ted beamed at Azalea. "Now they've found boxes of old papers that were evidently given to the library back when it was in the Masonic Hall, and stored somewhere else because the library was so small." He turned to me. "Stored in someone's attic. Old diaries, letters, that kind of thing. They're still completely unsorted. They're in the archives now, and a volunteer from the Historical Society is sorting through them and says she'll let me help. It's a long shot, but maybe I'll find some clue to what happened in 1849."

Azalea sang a phrase of "Blessed Be the Tie That Binds" and reached over and squeezed Ted's hand. "I'm so glad to have you in the family, Ted. I know you'll find something that helps."

"So I'll go search," Ted said, getting up from the table. "Besides, it always helps to talk to an archivist. They know all sorts of resources. Just bring me extra underwear from the mountains, Peaches."

Pop said, "And bring me the rest of my summer shirts. Eudora missed some when she packed."

So Alice and I left for the mountains, and Ted stayed to keep Pop and Azalea on an even keel and do more research. I didn't even need to pack an overnight bag. I was going home. All I had to keep track of was my pocketbook and the map and an umbrella in case it rained and the list of who wanted me to bring back what. One, two, three, four things to keep track of on the five-hour drive home. I put the list in my pocketbook. Not four anymore. One, two, three. Travelcount. Much easier than remembering the names of the objects that must be kept in hand on a trip.

Travelcount was a good trick but not foolproof, of course. There was the time I forgot to bring underpants because they were inside the suitcase and so not part of the count. I crossed them off my inside-suitcase list by mistake. Then the overnight laundry didn't get dry, so I had no underpants to wear the next day. But I knew I wouldn't get in trouble unless I had a wreck or stood on my head. I managed not to do either.

And one thing was sure, I intended to be cautious on this trip. Too many things were going wrong.

CHAPTER
17

OFF TO THE MOUNTAINS

I noticed Alice looked carefully in every direction as she prepared to get in the car. "You never can tell what a jealous man might do," she said. "If there's one thing that drives Anthony wild, it's for me to be with Ed. The last time I went up to the mountains with Azalea, he mailed me a dead rat."

I turned and stared at her, my hand on the door to the car. "What on earth did you do about that?"

"I threw it in the garbage," she said. "I thought if I just ignored Anthony, maybe he'd stop. I didn't know what else to do."

"If he does anything like that again, call the sheriff," I said, though I could see that would be sticky. Anthony was more than a troublemaker, I decided. He was off balance. Alice might not recognize how dangerous he was. An idea slammed me hard. Alice was with Azalea when the ladder broke under her weight. Perhaps the ladder was an Anthony trap meant for Alice! I hoped to God he wasn't that vindictive.

But Alice was thinking happier thoughts. "I called Ed, and we're going to get together this evening." She glowed at the very idea. "I hope that's okay. I'm going to call him when we get there." But her voice still had a nervous edge. "I asked Pop and Azalea and Ted not to tell Anthony where we've gone. He'll know I'll see Ed if he hears I'm in the mountains."

As I started the car I looked around carefully myself. I wouldn't like to be followed by a man who might have dropped a rock on Hector, who might have booby-trapped a ladder. A man who mailed Alice a dead rat.

On the other hand, I wanted to meet this Ed to see who set Alice aflame.

We went forth through the heat, already steaming at nine o'clock. Air shimmered. This was going to be a scorcher. I looked forward to the mountain cool. Our ride was quiet. Nobody following that I could see. Blue sky. We didn't talk much at first. Alice navigated. She knew the route. Otherwise she was quiet, dreaming of Ed, no doubt. I was going over every angle of what had happened, wishing I knew more about Hector. I'd have to find out more.

After Murfreesboro, we drove east on Interstate 40, pleasant with trees on both sides. Lots of cedars with their dark green. We crossed the eastern continental divide and came to huge twin smokestack towers on the left. That was the Clinch River power plant, Alice told me, the plant the conservationists managed to stop from becoming a breeder reactor. She said she thought it was because once the process of an endless chain of atomic reactions got started so no more fuel would be needed for the plant, how could you be sure you could stop the chain reaction? "Anthony is like that," she said bitterly. "Something started a chain of anger inside of him, and it feeds on itself."

"Tell me more about Anthony," I said as we drove through the edge of Knoxville, past big high motel and restaurant signs. "I'd like to understand him."

Alice squirmed in her seat and readjusted her seat belt. "I'd like to feel sorry for him," she said, "because he had a hard time. Then his wife died so soon after they were married. That was about ten years ago. He never has been happy since. But why did he have to turn so downright evil?"

"He couldn't live past that?" I asked. "He couldn't reach out to other people?"

"He never could reach out to other people."

After grief, you have to learn to live and laugh again. I learned that after my first husband died.

A sign for a chicken restaurant caught my eye. One bull stood on another bull's back, painting the sign with his hoof (not real bulls, of course). The sign said EAT MORE CHICKEN.

"Anthony has no sense of humor, does he?" I asked. "I think a sense of humor helps a person not to be evil."

"When he was a teen, he was a scrawny slight kind of kid. And his family always hid what was going on." Alice considered that. Did she think it had to do with having no sense of humor? "His mother tried to hide the fact that his father got mean when he drank. Sometimes we kids could hear him yelling, with the windows shut tight. His house was right down the street. We couldn't hear the loud yelling, just an echo. But that made it eerier."

She stopped talking and watched an old jalopy struggle in the next lane. The windows were open, and a frazzled-looking woman with uncombed hair was yelling at a small kid with his arm stuck out the window.

"Anthony's mom was smart, and she had a good job. That's what was so strange," Alice said. "She was a college professor. She should have done something to help Anthony, right?"

I nodded. The strange ways people run their lives amazes me. VISIT THE KNOXVILLE ZOO. OPEN EVERY DAY, a sign on the right said. Life is a zoo.

"Anthony's father was an artist. He was a big powerful man. But very moody. He drank in binges. He was a lot of fun when he was sober. That's what was so confusing. Us kids all loved for him to come out in his yard and sing funny songs for us. 'Lydia, the Tattooed Lady' and 'Who Put the Whiskey in the Well?' and 'Oh, You Can't Get to Heaven,' and lots more. He was fun for maybe a week at a time.'' She became quiet, mulling that over.

"Then he'd hole up in the house. And soon you'd see Anthony and his mother with bruises. Once Anthony had a broken arm.'' She sighed as we passed a sign that said FIREWORKS.

"Once in the summer, when the window was open, I heard his father tell Anthony what a damn fool he was. How he'd never amount to a hill of beans. It wasn't just what Anthony's father said, but he had this sneering tone of voice.''

Alice got a faraway look in her eyes. "The next week, Anthony would have new clothes and a new bike or a portable radio and be allowed to go to the movies on a weeknight. We were impressed with him. Sometimes he'd let us listen to the radio or he'd ride us on the back of the bike. Next time he'd tell us to get lost—we were dumb babies.''

We rode through rolling hills and woods again. Finally I said, "So sometimes you liked him?''

"He kind of fascinated me. Even as a kid. It was confusing. It was so different from home. His mother was so different from Azalea.''

I could imagine. "So what happened next?''

"He learned to take pictures. He was good at it. He had a darkroom in the basement. Sometimes the newspaper used one of his pictures, like a car that hit a telephone pole. That made him seem important, too.''

"So you were impressed?'' I might have been, too, as a kid.

She shrugged. "Anthony was angry all the time, even when he made us laugh by mimicking people. Angry seemed sexy when I got older. I don't know why now. He filled out and wasn't wispy anymore. I was his friend, too, because I felt I knew why he was mean sometimes. I just stayed out of his way when he was in a crummy mood.''

''But now he's angry at you, and he also wants to hurt you,'' I said.

She nodded. ''I hate that.'' She shut her eyes as if to shut that out.

By the time she opened her eyes again, she had to steer me through Greeneville, then onto a country road. We began to follow a stream and go slower around sharp curves. The road was narrower now, and the branches of trees almost touched above us. There was pine and rhododendron, too, and the mountains rose steeply on each side of the road. If Anthony had followed us, he could catch up with us now, and find us out of sight of human help. As Alice said, he wasn't wispy anymore. He had muscles.

I told myself not to be paranoid. But my mind was still on the man who could mail a dead rat. ''What does Anthony do for a living?'' I asked.

''He became a professional photographer,'' Alice said, sitting up straighter in her seat. ''He even takes great baby pictures. Can you imagine Anthony with a baby? I guess he does okay at it, or he couldn't have taken me to Las Vegas, could he? Fool that I was to go.''

We came up a steep rise, still on a narrow road. ''You see,'' Alice said, ''there was this Amy Lee Self, who had a big part in *Oklahoma!* when the summer theater at Mars Hill did it last year. She and Anthony hit it off. Then Amy Lee ditched him and fell for the guy who played Curley. A lot of girls fell for Anthony and then changed their minds.''

''Which freaked him out?'' I guessed.

''Yes. But I was nice to Anthony when Amy Lee left him. I played up to him, I guess. So he noticed me. I wasn't a little skinny kid anymore, and he took me to Las Vegas. When even I, his little kid friend who'd been impressed— when even I left him, he went off the deep end.''

''And you didn't know what to do,'' I said as we passed a weathered barn.

''No, I didn't. I guess he'd been ready to blow up for a

long time. He was jealous of anyone who had a good life. He could get what he wanted, but he couldn't keep it. I think that's why he mimics people and tries to make them look like fools. I didn't see that for a long time. I didn't want to see it.''

She turned to me. "I've told you all this, but you won't repeat it, will you? The only thing that Azalea lets herself worry about is me. That's why I didn't tell her about me and Anthony. And, please—you mustn't either.''

"It might help her understand what's going on," I said.

"If we can't get around him," she said, "and if she needs to know, I'll tell her. But, please—I told you because I trust you. Please don't tell.''

"If he'd just get lost," I said. "Permanently lost. Now, tell me where to turn next, or that may happen to us.''

We were driving up a steep hill. We were in North Carolina now. Home. At last we had a view of the mountains around us, the near slopes and the far blue shapes. My heart thrilled. *I will lift up my eyes unto the hills from whence cometh my help.* I remembered my grandmother reading that aloud from the Bible. If you've lived among mountain peaks, nothing else is the same. Art Bolder is a fellow mountaineer, I told myself. I can appeal for his help. And still no sign of Anthony following us. I was thankful for that.

But Alice had him on her mind. She sighed. "Anthony's a great photographer," she said. "So why does he need to be hurtful? Oh, I don't mean the baby pictures or the brides. He takes wonderful pictures of gnarled old trees or houses that have burned down or street people. Moody and actually beautiful. There was a girl who ran an art gallery in Nashville who gave him a show. People bought a few of his pictures. But you don't really want a photo of a sick bum hanging in your living room, do you? I don't. In a museum, but not at home. When people didn't buy his pictures, I think that made him even more cynical. I wish I never had to see him ever again in my life.''

We were approaching the small college town of Mars

Hill. Alice pointed out a small attractive white house not far from the road and nicely shaded by a large oak. I pulled into the driveway. This was Art Bolder's house. We hadn't told him we were coming, so we'd run the risk of missing him and having to wait around. On the other hand, if he'd expected us, he might have disappeared on purpose. Mountain folks can be particularly good at that.

"I'll stay in the car," Alice said. "Art knows me, and Azalea fired him."

I walked up a stepping-stone walk flanked by freshly mowed grass and knocked on the screen door. No answer. I walked around the house and heard a radio or television going. I came to a glassed-in side porch and saw a young man sitting in a wood rocker, among a jungle of potted plants. His whole attention was on a TV set. I knocked and he jumped, reflexes on double time. Why?

He got up and came over toward the door and stood to block it. His eyes were large with startle, but he smiled and said, "Can I help you?"

He hardly moved his lips, a pale, sensitive-looking young man with an air of being lost among the begonias and ferns. Somebody here had a green thumb. The begonias were covered with blooms. As for Art, the front top of his head was bald, but with plenty of wispy hair all around, which made him look like a vague intellectual instead of a carpenter.

He'd been watching TV at four in the afternoon. The set still blared. So he probably hadn't found another job.

"I do need your help," I said. "And I might be able to help you. A friend of mine believes you were fired from a job unfairly. Something is going wrong at that job. Someone has been killed there. I wanted to talk to you about it."

I thought I was being tactful—I hadn't even mentioned murder—but the alarm in his eyes increased. A vein at his temple began to beat. He folded the hands at his sides tight shut, large hands with knots at the joints. What was he hiding?

"My mother is upstairs sick, and I can't let you in," he said. He reached to pull the door shut.

"I've come all the way from Nashville just to talk to you." I actually put my foot in the door. "I'll be quiet and not disturb your mother and I'm willing to take my chance with germs."

I pushed forward like an overzealous salesman. I was almost ashamed of myself.

He backed up and let me in. "Please sit down," he said, so quickly that I figured he didn't want me to walk around.

I sat in a wooden captain's chair that also faced the TV. He didn't move to turn it off.

"You were working on Azalea Marlowe's house in Tennessee," I said.

He blinked, not denying that.

"Three things have happened since you left," I said. "A ladder broke under suspicious circumstances, and Azalea Marlowe cracked several ribs. Also, they unearthed a human skeleton under the floor. Worst of all, one of the archaeologists who came to date the place was found dead near the house."

"I know," he said dolefully, waving toward the television. "A deputy came all the way up here to see me. Thank goodness I was at the dinner at the firehouse the night that man got killed. I have lots of folks to say I was there." Relief was in his voice when he said that.

He leaned forward as the TV host extolled the softest toilet paper, and said, "I'm not surprised there was trouble. I didn't trust that Anthony guy who kept hanging around Azalea's house."

He finally turned the TV off. "After I was fired," he said, with just a hint of bitterness, "Anthony came to my place in Tennessee. He caught me as I left. He said he knew I wouldn't steal." Art looked out through the glass walls, avoiding my eyes. "He wanted to know any dirt I'd heard on the job. He said a murder had been committed there years ago and he'd pay me for anything I'd heard about that or anything I'd found on the job to help prove that. I figured he was looking for anything at all to make trouble."

He looked me in the eye for just a second, then down at

his hands. He kept inspecting his hands as if to see if they were dirty. "We kept finding things," he said. "But they weren't bad things. We found a broken flute, just a wooden one. Around the door frames, we found old keys, and on top of one door was a lock and key that matched. Ross said those went back to 1800."

"So you told Anthony everything you found?"

He flushed right up into his bald pate. "I did not!" he cried. "Alice is my friend. This Anthony hoped something they found could make her and her family look bad." Pride lifted his face. "I would never help him do that." I could see why Alice believed Art. And yet . . . His face sagged. "Now there's another murder. That's what the man who asked me questions said."

"Yes, a young archaeologist had his head bashed in with one of the chimney stones."

The very mention of the stones made him squirm. "I never met the archaeologist. I never even heard of him." His jaw stuck out, belligerent.

I believed him because Azalea said Hector and Frank came that day we found the skeleton for the first time. What a first time!

But why was Art so nervous on the edge of his chair? Why hadn't he wanted me to come in this house? "My mother used to collect begonias," I said. "There are some lovely ones here." I stood up quickly and strode toward the other end of the porch as I said, "If you don't mind, I'll look around."

"Yes, I do mind!" He tried to get in front of me and knocked over a potted fern. "My mother doesn't like people snooping around her house."

But I was near enough to the other end of the porch to have seen the arrowhead on the windowsill. It was next to what appeared to be a gold watch chain, a small wooden flute, and a small box—about the size of a candy box, but made of inlaid wood. The arrowhead was exactly like the one that Hector said was ten to twelve thousand years old. I recognized the red color and the flecks of white.

I pointed to it. "I know that's from Azalea's house," I said. "It's made of the kind of chert that was used in middle Tennessee twelve thousand years ago." Oh, if I could just remember not to lose an umbrella as easily as I remembered strange little facts about what happened twelve thousand years ago! Strange little facts just pop into my head, usually when I don't need them. But this time I did.

Art Bolder's face was full of panic. I could see him struggling to decide what to say or do.

"You can't be bribed," I said. "You're proud of that. But you steal things you don't even need. Maybe you need help." That was the best light I could think of to put on this. It could be true.

"That's what Mr. Easley said, back when . . ." His voice seemed to have failed. It came back gravelly. "But my father said I just needed to pull myself together. He was mad. I tried. I did try. It's like something makes me do it! The way some people drink." He gave me a look of desperation. "And then having those things where I can see them is part of it somehow."

"And what does your family say now?"

Terror flashed in his eyes. "They don't know I was fired. They think the job ended, and I was lonesome for the mountains. This is my mother's plant room. My father won't come in it. He says it's a damn jungle. And my mother—she thinks they gave me those things because I found them."

So his mother was another wishful thinker like Azalea.

"You can have those things." Sweat broke out all over the bald front of his head. "That's all I took, I swear. Please don't tell. I'll get you a bag to put them in. You can take them back."

He went out of the room, and while he was gone I looked around further. Nothing else seemed suspicious. Perhaps contemplating his latest theft stayed his hand for a while.

He brought back a paper bag, and we carefully put the inlaid box in the bottom of the bag. "Where did you find this?" I asked. "That's important to know." How, I wondered, did it stay so well preserved? Then, even before he told me, I knew.

"I was removing the wood floor by the hearth in the room on the right in the old house. I tripped over a wooden measure that someone had dropped," he said. "I fell against the hearth, hard," he said. "I knocked the hearth-stone and one end of it tipped. I could see something was underneath. I pushed it back in place so no one would know—in order to find it when I was alone and prove I was the one who could discover historic things. That may sound dumb to you. Maybe it was. But that's how I felt. And then, before I had a chance to be there by myself, they fired me. So I went back that night. That night was my last chance. I pried up the stone, and this was hidden under it. I was so angry—at myself and at them—that I was glad they'd never find it." A very screwed-up young man.

"Thank you for giving these to me," I said.

He put the arrowhead and the flute and the chain on top of the box. "I just found these around," he said. "The flute was between two logs, and the arrowhead was in a place where the dog dug—you know, that dog of Goat's that hangs around the house? I saw him digging near the front door, and he dug this up, and I hid it in my pocket quick, before anyone could see."

I suppose he hoped that would satisfy me and I'd leave, but I said, "Sit down," and I sat back down myself. He sat, too, uncomfortably. He wiped the drops of sweat on his bald pate with his bare hand, but more formed.

I tried to sound reassuring. "You can be a big help to me, even beyond this," I said. "Now think. What was strange or out of kilter about that job in Tennessee?"

He moved uneasily in his chair. He made a wry grin. He wanted to please. Wanted to get even with the world and wanted to please all at once. "You mean, strange aside from me," he said dryly. "Well, Anthony kept coming around, which made people nervous. He kept taking our pictures. Azalea just said to ignore him. He had this obsession about a skeleton. Everyone thought he was nuts. But then, I hear, they found a skeleton.'' He eyed me as if he expected I might explain more. But I outwaited him. "And Ross was so polite to Anthony,'' he said. "Because Anthony was related to Azalea, I guess. But Ross didn't trust him. I could see that Ross kept an eye on him whenever he was there.'' Ross the boss. My young thief or kleptomaniac or whatever rocked in his chair thoughtfully. "Walt was okay. A little bossy. But Anthony nosing around, that's what made us all uncomfortable,'' he said. "I wouldn't be surprised if Anthony found out about me somehow and told Walt and Ross to watch me. That's how Anthony made you feel. Like he was watching for a flaw to make trouble for you.''

"He came every day?'' I asked.

"No. It just seemed that way.''

Beyond that, I didn't learn anything important from Art. I thanked him. I mentioned that we were probably going on to the Vance birthplace, which was built about the same time as Azalea's house. I asked him how long it would take to get there, and he said about half an hour.

As I left I gave him a little hug. That embarrassed him, but never mind. If he was telling the truth, it might encourage him. If this was all an act, he *should* be embarrassed.

"Try to get some help,'' I said, "before you get in serious trouble.''

I hurried back to the car and decided to get out of that place before Mama got up from her sickbed or Papa came home and asked me what I was doing there. I couldn't wait to look in the inlaid box.

CHAPTER
18

TO THE VANCE BIRTHPLACE

Alice drove and kept having to slow down. Her foot wanted to press the gas pedal—to get to Ed quick. I opened the box. Inside were sheets of paper, yellow with age, and covered with old-fashioned handwriting. My heart beat fast. I read the top one out loud, slowly, to be sure I got it right. The *S*'s and *L*'s were much alike, but I could make out the sense.

Dear Mother,

I have taken up my pen, though I can never send this letter. Writing it will ease my pain. And, even in heaven where we must someday meet, perhaps you know what happens here. Perhaps you can send me comfort.

Still, I must not write all I know. Because the world is not sure, and must not learn, what

happened to my beloved David or our poor Bud.
Only let me say that each one was betrayed by fate.
And I loved them both.

"Damn," I said. "This must be written by Annie Thomason. This is an incredible find. But do you suppose she
really won't tell what happened?"

"Keep reading," Alice said. "Don't stop now." So I
read on, hoping Alice wasn't so fascinated she would forget
the traffic as a truck lumbered by us.

I cry for them both till my eyes ache. I miss David
like my right hand. He was my life. I see him now,
taking my arm as we went to church together. Once
I slipped, and he held me steady, would not let me
fall. David with his broad shoulders and his warm
eyes. I shall ever remember his passionate loving
words when he asked me to marry him. But Bud had
been my child, because I raised him after you died. I
tried hard to shield him from father's anger. His
birth took you away. Father could never forgive Bud
that.
Father might have been kinder if Bud had been
like him, and reflected Father in a good light. But
Bud was awkward, not clever in the way that Father
wanted, a vexation to him.
I remember the day when Father found Bud out in
the barn fixing the hayrack. He could fix anything.
But he should have been at his books. Father raged.
"My only son is a fool," he said, "who won't stay
at his lessons." Books were not alive to Bud. He
learned to build behind Father's back, slipping away
to help a neighbor raise a house. "I have a
changeling son," Father said. "Not mine at all." I
knew how that hurt Bud, but still Bud couldn't be
anything but what God made him. I could see that
so clearly. I wish you could have been there,
Mother, to soften Father.

*I prayed for Bud. And for Father. They both had
that Irish temper. As Father's father had before him.
Both good men in other ways. Quick to be generous.
Quick to love. As you know. But anger took them
like an earthquake.*

*Bud could not stand our father's anger and ran
away. And I was so relieved when he apprenticed
himself to a carpenter in Carthage. We had a secret.
He wrote me through HIM. Such a good and helpful
servant of God, who showed me the way to have
compassion for our father and for Bud.*

Wrote through HIM? A very cautious girl, our Annie.
Hiding facts that could hurt. Who did she fear might find
these pages?

I tried to pull the first page up and read the second, but
the edge crumbled. "Don't stop there," Alice begged. Her
foot actually lagged on the gas. For the moment she'd forgotten we were on our way to see Ed.

"I have to wait till I have a flat surface," I said unhappily. "Then I can gently turn out all the pages and read
them without harming them. I certainly don't want them to
crumble away." I stared at the fragile papers in the antique
box. "But what if Annie Thomason never tells who killed
who?"

"We'll find some clue," Alice said. "We're bound to."

I stared at those yellowed pages in frustration. In the left-
hand margin, something was scrawled as an afterthought,
perhaps put there when she went back and read these pages
later. It was hard to make out. *The S-something-or-other
will keep our secret.* Was that a name with a capital *S* or
just an *S* written big? Was it spiders? I pictured black-
widow spiders protecting some other document or artifact
so we could never reach it. Yes. I was almost positive the
word was *spiders*.

Alice gasped. "Oh, I've forgotten to call Ed and tell him
we're through with Art and on the way." She picked up
the car phone, dialed, and pushed *send*. A smile of complete

beatitude softened her face. I knew who had answered.

"Yes. Yes, we will," she said breathlessly. "See you very soon." To me, she said, "I guess I told you he's working late today. He wants us to meet him at the Vance birthplace."

Actually that suited me fine. The Zebulon Vance birthplace, now a North Carolina historic site, was about the same vintage as the old house in Tennessee and made of square-cut logs but without clapboards outside on top of the logs or hog's-hair plaster inside. Azalea's ancestor had gone elegant. Governor Vance's ancestors had kept their square-cut logs uncovered on the outside and used wood paneling inside. With spiders hiding in the corners?

What mattered now was finding a flat table at the Vance birthplace for gently tilting the papers from the box. I was sure there'd be one. I thought I'd die of impatience before we got there and I could read what happened to Annie.

Finally the Vance house came into view, with a sharper-peaked roof than the Tennessee house. A weathered split-rail fence surrounded the yard, and flags fluttered from three tall flagpoles: the Stars and Stripes, the North Carolina flag, and a version of the Confederate flag with a wide red stripe across the bottom.

"Ed says that one with the red is the Confederate flag that's not for battle," Alice said. I could almost feel her pulse fluttering like the flags in the wind as we approached. We drove down a drive to a modern stone welcome center in back, and Ed let us in through two large glass doors. He beamed when he saw us. Alice ran and hugged him hard.

I liked Ed right away. Nice looking in a quiet way, with level eyebrows, friendly gray-green eyes, and sandy hair with a cowlick in back, a few hairs bounding skyward. Not like Anthony at all. Thank God. Shy but responsible, I thought. One of those people who check last thing at night to see that the doors are locked, or who make sure that any old people or kids in a group are keeping up with the other folks and are okay. Ed had that solidity.

He grabbed my hand firmly and shook it as Alice introduced us.

"I'm just making some last-minute phone calls about the reenactment tomorrow," he said. "We're going to have a Revolutionary War skirmish here. I hoped I'd be through by the time you got here, but I'm not quite. Maybe you two could look around." He had hold of Alice's hand again, as if he'd never let go.

I explained that what we needed was a table to turn out nineteenth-century letters that might contain a clue to a murder. That got his attention. He hugged Alice's shoulders and said, "I want to hear more soon." He led us through a small office into another office, a small brightly lit room without windows, where he indicated a desk with a chair. He pulled up another chair and said, "Will this do? You two work here. I have to be on the phone at the other desk."

I noticed a copying machine on a small cabinet on the left and thought, Now, *there* is a wonderful memory device. Yes. Copy what you might lose, and then you can lose one and still have one. I do that with very important papers. I would certainly copy these fragile pages. But I was in such a hurry to read them that I decided to do the reading first.

I did notice a gray cardboard box on a bookshelf near the door into the office, the kind of box that comes with a dozen eggs in it. I noticed because it seemed so out of place. Why eggs in an office? I thought it didn't matter.

While Ed was busy at his phone, arranging logistics, I gently turned out the papers onto the dark wood desk. A pile of empty manila file folders was on one end of the desk. Alice held one up to Ed, and he nodded yes. His eyes threw her a kiss. Ah, young love!

I carefully edged the antique papers into the folder, turned the folder over, then moved the top sheet that I'd already read into another folder. I marked those folders big with a red felt-tipped marker from the jar on the desk. I sure didn't want to get Annie's stuff mixed up with Ed's papers. I wrote *Annie Thomason's letters 1849*. Then I began to read the faded writing on the second page:

When Bud married and had a son, I hoped this would cure his hurt. But word came back to Father that Bud was drinking. That upset me. And yet Bud still wrote. He still found work. I hoped his life was better than our father thought.

And I who had helped nurse Bud through the pox at three and a half, and scarlet fever when he was thirteen, just on the verge of manhood. I who'd feared for Bud's life, then saw him grow strong. (Except for those two illnesses, he was healthy as an ox, as they say.) Now I was afraid that he'd destroy himself with whiskey. I prayed for him.

Bud was so unlike David. David was a sickly child. He told me he'd had pneumonia at two and typhoid at four and measles at six, and some mysterious fever at eight, yet he became a strong and cheerful man.

"Two, four, six, eight," Alice said. "He sure paced himself." I continued reading:

David came to work in Father's office. David was like fair weather. He had the gift of never stirring Father's anger. He even thought of ways to make my father's work go smoother. When he laughed, you had to laugh with him. And yet, he had a serious side. My David had thought of becoming a minister, but changed his mind and went into law. In some ways he may have been too kind, not demanding enough for himself. But I loved him even more for that. I knew my life would be a better life with David by my side.

"Like Ed," whispered Alice, who was reading over my shoulder. I turned and saw that she was crying silently. Oh, brother! I went on carefully to the next page, aware of Ed's warm voice on the phone at the other desk talking about where the cook tent would be.

> *Thank God I have David's little son, David, whose mother died. I am his mother now. But I grieve when I see Catherine Holden Riggs with her brood of little ones. Catherine who looks so much like me, or so they say, except that I have only one child to comfort me for my loss.*

Catherine *Holden* Riggs. Was she related to David? Not a word about that.

> *I was so happy when David and I agreed to marry. And—*

We were interrupted by loud pounding on the outside door. It sounded as if the door could literally be battered down. Ed hung up quickly and hurried out into the entry-way to find out what was wrong. Old Curious, here, put the paper carefully down, closed the folder, and laid it on the desk. Then I went out, too. Ed opened the door. He really was a trusting type. There in the doorway was Anthony.

Get out of here, I thought. You've done enough. It was like magic the way he'd found us so quickly. I was scared he'd beat up Ed just for existing. He looked angry enough.

"I knew it!" he said to me. "I knew that you'd come up to the mountains and talk to Art Bolder. You think you're so smart," he said. "And I knew Alice would have hot pants for this nicey nicey young man!" He smiled a nervous smile, mimicking Ed's, and held one hand with the other like Ed was doing. But somehow he made the smile look really stupid.

I thanked goodness Alice had had the good sense to stay in the inner office out of sight. "Art can't keep a secret," Anthony said with a sneer. "He told me exactly where you'd be. And here you are.'' He strode into the first office, swept it with his eyes, and looked into a storeroom on the left as Ed said, ''Now wait a minute—you can't come in here!'' Ed couldn't sound mean enough to make an impression.

His words just spurred Anthony on toward the inner office. Ed and I were right behind him.

''The Vance birthplace is closed,'' Ed said louder. He was not used to dealing with headstrong Anthony. He needed to trip him, not just say, ''I'm afraid you'll have to leave.''

Fat chance. By that time Anthony was in the little office, where Alice pressed against the back wall as far from him as she could get. He glared at her. ''You little bitch. First you led me on, then you dumped me like some pile of crap.'' He aped her outraged grimace and wrung his hands to add to the silly effect, though Alice was holding on to the desk with her hands. He sent fiery glances at me and Ed, lest we think we were not included in his rage. I stood near the copier, not sure what I ought to do. Ed hesitated, wondering, I figured, whether he would make things worse if he tried to get between Anthony and Alice. He picked up the phone and called the sheriff's department.

Anthony even ignored that.

''I thought it might please you to know I really am a skunk,'' Anthony hissed at Alice. In fact, he smelled of anger, an acrid smell almost like car exhaust and body odor mixed. He turned to me. ''I'm suing you and Alice and Azalea for a hundred thousand dollars each. I thought that might help keep you out of trouble.''

That seemed unreal, but then I remembered seeing some television show about the ruinous cost of protecting yourself from an unfair suit. ''What on earth have you found to sue us about?'' I demanded.

''I'm suing you for harassment,'' he said. ''For mailing me a dead rat.'' He laughed loudly. He knew how ridiculous that was. But he could still do it. He raised his camera and took a picture of my outrage. He kept looking around the office and clicking that damn camera.

"You're suing me for trying to find the truth about that skeleton," I said. "Of course *you* know how a person mails a dead rat, since you sent Alice one."

"Says you," he said with another sneer. "The rat that came to me has Alice's fingerprints on the inner box," he said triumphantly. "Also Azelea's. And I'll say you helped them. What do you think of that?" By what trick had he managed prints?

He glared at Ed. Rage was like hot fumes shimmering around his skull. I was afraid he was going to lose it and have a dogfight with Ed after all.

"Get out of here. You're trespassing. There's a law against that," Ed said to Anthony, who was beyond hearing.

Ed had knotted his hands into fists. My eyes begged him to do what he could to avoid a fight. Begged him not to do the natural thing and sock Anthony. Anthony was ready to go berserk. To get violent.

I looked around for a weapon. What could we do? Hit him over the head with a calculator? Ram him with a chair?

When I looked back, he was opening the box of eggs. What on earth? "I'm glad you have fresh eggs," he said, suddenly cheerful. He took two out, and balanced them on his palm, as if admiring them.

Ed blinked in surprise at the change. "Country friends dropped them by," he said, obviously trying to keep things calmer, or maybe stall for time while he figured out what to do next.

Alice watched Anthony fearfully. Fast as lightning he pulled the hand with the eggs back and threw them at Alice so hard they crushed and splattered egg and shell over her face. The gelatinous egg dripped over her nose, and when she opened her mouth to breathe, it sucked into her mouth. I thought she was going to choke. Ed grabbed a handful of tissues and wiped her nose clear. I admit I was so startled that for a moment I froze, eyes on Alice. I thought, Anthony is a master of pointless meanness. I was wrong. This meanness had a purpose—cover for escape.

Ed turned back toward Anthony in a rage, green eyes glinting, but all we saw was Anthony's back vanishing out the door. Before we could catch him, he revved up his motor and was gone with a squeal of tires.

At least I could breathe easier. The room had been jammed with fury.

Alice finished wiping her face and wiping egg out of her hair. She looked almost normal again. Ed put his arms around her. They did look right together. About the same height. Alice slight, Ed solid. Alice dark, Ed light, enclosed in love like a cocoon.

I sat down in the chair by the desk. My knees were weak from shock and surprise. I took a few deep breaths. Ed was kissing Alice as if he'd almost lost her. She was kissing him as though the world had melted away. I sighed. Love is a great cure for despair, except when love is not really love but obsession. Anthony was going to cause some terrible kind of trouble. That's where he was headed. Without brakes. Or maybe he had already, if he'd crushed Hector's head. But thank God he was gone from this small room. That was my first thought.

My second thought was panic. I looked down at the desk. The two file folders, marked *Annie Thomason's letters* in large red letters, were gone. Anthony had grabbed the folder with the pages we'd read—*and* the folder with the pages we hadn't read. I stared half unbelieving at the empty desk, the expanse of dark wood with a few books and a stack of file folders at the end and the jar with felt-tipped markers. I could have screamed. Why did I mark those folders in red, so Anthony couldn't miss them? Why hadn't I noticed sooner? Oh damn! If only I had copied those pages before I read them.

I wanted to kick myself, but I forced myself to remember rule one from *How to Survive Without a Memory.*

Don't linger over what you should have done. You need your energy to think about what you can do next.

I tried to speak calmly. "Anthony has made off with the letters. He threw those eggs to divert us, and it sure worked."

"He'll burn them!" Alice screamed the way I wanted to. "We'll never know what they say! We've got to stop him!"

"We don't know which way he went." I groaned. "He could have gone toward Asheville, or turned off to the Parkway via Ox Creek Road, or gone over Maney Branch Road to Paint Fork and beyond." This was my neck of the woods, so I knew which way he could have gone. A lot of good it did me.

"I've called the sheriff," Ed said.

Alice sagged. "Anthony will say those letters belong to him, because the house is his!"

How could we prove those old pages were ours, no matter who the house belonged to? Nevertheless, Ed put in a call to the state highway patrol. At least we might prevent Anthony from destroying the letters till the question of whose they were could be settled.

Ed called the Tennessee Highway Patrol, too. I didn't expect them to pull out the stops for a few old letters, but we could hope. Tennessee folks care about history.

Gradually the adrenaline stopped roaring in my veins. "There's no way we can guess how to find Anthony," I said. "Considering the back roads he could take to Tennessee, the highway patrol may not see him either. We'll just have to pray he won't destroy the letters. Certainly he'll read them first. There could be something in them that will prove his point. God forbid."

Discouraged silence, then: "What should we do?" Alice cried, looking all around her as if she, too, was ready to jump in any direction.

"I don't believe that chasing Anthony will work," I said unhappily. "There are too many chances for him to slip away. This may sound crazy, but I'd like to ask Ed a question about the Vance birthplace before we go anywhere."

"But Anthony will get away!" Alice groaned.

"Yes. He's slippery as a snake's elbow. He could even go up a side road and wait for us to pass. If he wanted to destroy the papers, he could do that in some mountain cove near here as well as anywhere else. I have a hunch we should do what we can here. This may sound really odd, Ed, but in what part of any old house like the Vance house would there be the most spiders?"

He laughed. "Spiders? This house is treated against bugs. I don't know!"

"Is there something here that could be scrawled to look like *spider*?" I told him about the scrawl on the side of the page on Annie's letter.

He thought about that a long time, then shook his head. "There's something we call a spider in the kitchen, but that's not what you mean. It's a kind of a cook pot."

"I'd like to see it," I said.

So we walked up a gravel path, through a gap in a gray split-rail fence, and onto the porch of the old house. Ed unlocked the door, and we stood in a dim wood-paneled room with the largest fireplace I ever saw in a small house, at least six feet wide. It was warm red brick with a gently arched front, deep as well as broad. In front of the fireplace stood a small baby's cradle.

Annie didn't need a cradle. She never married, never had a child. She was shocked to barrenness, except she raised her lover's child, David's child. That thought hit me in the stomach.

This fireplace was bigger than Azalea's, twice bigger. These mountains were colder than middle Tennessee, so the luxury in Governor Vance's North Carolina mountain childhood house was this huge generous fireplace. Each old house had its own unique personality. This house, at least, had been saved. Azalea's might not be. Another wrench in the stomach.

Ed led us through a doorway into a cheerful room with a table in the middle and another fireplace backed up to the one I'd seen in the room where we entered.

The Vance house kitchen fireplace was equally huge and

filled with cast-iron implements. I recognized some: a spit for turning a roast above the fire, a huge hanging stew pot, A Dutch oven on legs with a lipped lid. My grandmother made corn-bread in one of those whenever she had a fire going in her fireplace. She put the corn-bread batter in it, raked coals underneath, then put more coals in the lipped lid so the corn bread cooked from top and bottom. The best bread I ever ate. That's why Grandma did it that way, as her mother had.

I realized Ed was pointing at the Dutch oven. "There," he said, "is the spider." And then it came back to me. I'd heard someone call a pot like that a spider. Because of the black legs, I guessed.

Of course, I thought. The spider sat on the hearth when it wasn't in use, on top of the cavity in the hearth that hid Annie Thomason's letters. So the spider helped hide her secret. I felt hollow with disappointment. The spider was only a clue to what we'd lost.

CHAPTER
19

TUESDAY EVENING

We called Ted as we drove back down the mountain to Tennessee and filled him in on our catastrophe. He said he'd go watch Anthony's house, beginning about nine o'clock. Even with the one-hour time difference in his favor, Anthony couldn't get back from the mountains before that.

We called Azalea on the car phone, too, and told her what was up. She was indignant and said she'd call her father-in-law and tell him how Anthony stole the letters. She rang us back to tell how Adam said he was sure there must be some misunderstanding and that Anthony had just borrowed the letters.

Borrowed, my foot! "Anthony sure must do a snow job on the old man," I told Alice.

"He's good at that," she said bitterly.

As we drove through the lights of Knoxville, Ted called us to report that Anthony's house was locked and dark. He said he'd continue to watch, and we should meet him there. All of us were determined to waylay Anthony.

By ten o'clock, Alice and I drove through Nashville, then out of town on Lewisburg Pike. We'd just passed a new house under construction when Alice said, "There it is," and nodded toward a peak-roofed house with a sign out front dimly lighted with one bulb. It said ANTHONY WOLF STUDIO—PHOTOGRAPHY and gave a number to call. No lights on in the house. We turned into the gravel drive and around in back, where we found a parking space.

My headlights picked out Ted's car, then another car, then Ted talking to someone next to the clapboard wall of the house. I was pleased and scared. My first thought was that Anthony had arrived. But the man was too short for Anthony, and he stood defensively, shoulders stooped. Anthony would never do that. Then I noticed his punk hair. It was the Kid—the carpenter who liked the lady carpenter with the Support Your Local Poet T-shirt, the girl named Song. No, Melody. She'd said the Kid was fighting over her with Goat. What was the Kid doing here?

I parked and turned off the car lights. I didn't want to scare Anthony off if he did show up. The moon was covered by clouds. My eyes weren't accustomed to the blackness yet.

"Stay in the car and call for help if you see anything go wrong," I said to Alice.

I got out of the car and walked over to the place where voices came out of the dark.

Kid's voice: "Anthony said he had something important to tell me, that I should meet him here." He said this loudly, as if he wanted us all to hear clearly.

"Something to tell you at this hour?" That was Ted.

"Yes. He said it was important. He was damn close-mouthed about what."

"When did you talk to him?" Ted asked.

Silence. I had the impression that question threw the Kid for a loop. But he answered after a pause. "About five o'clock."

"At five o'clock I happen to know that Anthony was in the mountains," Ted said.

The Kid did a double take, but he had an answer. "He telephoned me. You can do that from anywhere, right?"

"And he told you not to meet him until ten o'clock?"

"Yes," he said defiantly.

Would the Kid lie about Anthony? He sure gave that impression. I wished I could see his face.

"I don't believe that's why you're here," Ted said. "I think you're trying to find out something just like we are. You drove by and saw the house was dark, and maybe you hoped it was unlocked."

Maybe it *was* unlocked. No, Ted had told me on the car phone he'd tried the doors.

"Anthony never leaves it unlocked," the Kid said. So the Kid was well acquainted with Anthony's house. Why?

I was near enough now to see the Kid's shape darkly. I reached over and touched him. He jumped. "He's blackmailing you," I said. It was a wild guess, but it kind of fit.

"No," he said in a trembling tone. "No, he's not!"

A long silence. A car approached on the pike, but it didn't stop. The sound of the wheels faded into the distance. A dog barked somewhere nearby, and another one answered.

"But I think Anthony *is* blackmailing Goat," the Kid blurted, "so when Anthony asked me to come here, I was scared not to come. Because maybe he's figured out some way to make me look bad with Melody. I was scared of that."

"Why is he blackmailing Goat?" Ted demanded. I could see his shape vaguely. Suddenly the clouds moved, and we were all clear in moonlight.

The Kid blinked. "Goat got mixed up in some kind of brawl last year. Broke a guy's jaw. He's on probation. He didn't want Ross to know about it, and he didn't want Melody to know either." He leaned toward us confidentially.

So Goat was afraid he'd lose his job and his chance with

the girl he liked. Still, he'd be crazy to get mixed up in paying blackmail.

"You kept his secret for him when you both were after the same girl?" I asked.

"We both like Melody—but, yes, I did," he said. Belligerent again.

"How did you find out Goat was on probation?" Ted asked.

"When we took up the floor in the back room, there was a letter down underneath. I figured it must be an antique letter and I opened it before I noticed his name. It was from his probation officer."

What? How could that be possible? But then I remembered what Hector had said. Poor smart Hector. Animals dragged modern things under a house to mix with the older artifacts. He'd found one of the workmen's hats when they took up the floor. That had amazed me. So Goat had inadvertently dropped that letter—and the Kid was so curious he just opened it, old or not.

"Wouldn't you know Goat came along right at that moment and caught me reading that letter and freaked out," the Kid said. "He went, 'Oh my God, I forgot it was in my pocket. I was so upset because my ex-wife called.' He hates that she's a druggie. Then he told me what happened so I wouldn't think it was worse than it was. And he went, 'If I lose this job, I can't take care of my kid. What will I do?' But to tell you the truth, as long as Goat does a good job, I don't think Ross would give a damn if he was on probation. But Goat thinks he would. That's all I know."

The Kid stood on one foot and then the other, not just nervous but impatient. Quivery in the moonlight. I thought, He wants us to go away.

So I said, "We want to ask Anthony something, so we're going to stick around until he shows up."

That seemed to really get to the Kid. He began to crack his fingers, an odd, uncomfortable sound. "He's not coming," he said. "He's already nearly an hour late. There's a girl he shacks up with in Franklin. He probably went there.''

"And just left you standing here?''

"He might do that,'' he said, cracking a finger so loudly that I winced.

"What's her name?''

"Damned if I know,'' he said. "It's not always the same girl.'' He shrugged. "I guess he's not coming. I'll go on home.''

After he left, Alice slipped out of the car and hurried down to join us, figuring the danger was gone, I guess. I said, "We need to leave, too.''

"But suppose Anthony does come?'' Alice asked.

"Let's go park in the next driveway,'' I said. "I'll bet you five dollars the Kid will be back when he thinks we're gone. Let's see if he wants us out of the way.''

"That half-built house over there has a lot of space to park in the yard,'' Ted said, "and I noticed a van's been left there. We can park behind it.'' Alice and I got in my car. Ted got in the one he'd borrowed from Pop and Azalea. We followed him over to the partly built house. So different from the old log house. Here the ribs of pale wood framing, picked out by moonlight, were largely vertical with large spaces between. We parked, and Ted sat with Alice and me so we could talk while we waited. The clock on the dashboard said 10:20 P.M. Would the Kid come back? Not right away.

"Anything you haven't told me about your trip?'' Ted asked.

I said I figured I'd kept him pretty well briefed on the car phone. "So what did you learn at the courthouse?'' I asked. In the distance an owl hooted. Eerie.

"I learned a lot, but not as much as I'd like,'' Ted said. "Azalea is right that the records on that land go back to about 1810, when Annie Thomason's grandfather paid taxes on it. I can't find any mention of the place before that. Some records must be lost.''

"So that's all you learned?'' Alice asked.

"There are old records in leather-bound books," he said. "Back to the 1790s. The archives gal was a big help telling me about what went on, too. Apparently Revolutionary War veterans from North Carolina got land grants in Tennessee in lieu of pensions. Tennessee was part of North Carolina then, the wild part. Soldiers got thousands of acres. The Thomason property was probably part of a Revolutionary War grant of three thousand acres, given to Wilbur Thomason's father, Joshua, in 1794. A copy of the original grant is in the archives."

"What a pension!" Alice said.

"The state was short on money, long on land," Ted continued. "Of course, those grants got broken up; parts sold off, parts divided among children, parts given for schools and churches."

"But all that was long before 1849," I said, trying not to sound impatient. "How can it help?"

"I wanted to trace the land as far back as possible and then down to the present," Ted said. "I did discover something interesting that happened later. The Thomason property line was moved in 1916 after a survey of the land next door."

So Azalea's family got the land because of a war and lost some of it right before World War I. That was easier to remember than 1916.

Alice said, "You mean, our neighbors claimed some of our land?"

"Yes. The shed that's in the pasture, beyond your fence on your neighbor's place, probably used to be on the land that was claimed by your ancestors. I don't know how the surveyor ever figured out where the line should be. The old surveying marks were trees and rocks, and the woman in charge of the archives says that old-timers measured the boundaries with chains, but most of the time the chains were wet ropes.

"In fact, the archives gal told me that one of those old-timers with a four-thousand-acre Revolutionary War grant divided it into seven supposedly equal tracts to give his children and then discovered there were about six hundred acres left unaccounted for.''

A car drove by slowly. Could have been the Kid's car. We went quiet, straining to see. Clouds were over the moon again, making it dead dark. After the car faded into silence, I said, "So what else did you discover, Ted?"

"Wilbur Junior left the land to Annie for use in her lifetime and then to his own grandson, Bud Junior, and to David Holden's little son, David—whom Annie raised after big David's death. They sold it to a John Williams in about 1900. After that, it changed hands several times and was evidently rented out to tenant farmers. It fell into the sad state you saw in Azalea's pictures.''

"That's it?'' I asked. I'd hoped for some major breakthrough.

"All but the gossip,'' he said. "Historical gossip is always interesting. Did you know there had been a murder down the road from Azalea's old house? It was back around 1900. It seems a man threw his wife into the well, and then he threw rocks in on top of her, but he didn't stop to make certain she was dead before he ran off to his girlfriend in the next county. Two drunks came wandering along and heard her screaming for help, and after about half an hour it dawned on them where she was yelling from, and they pulled her out of the well and saved her.''

"That's not a murder,'' I said.

"Not yet. Two friends of the woman went after her husband with a shotgun, knowing where to find him with his girlfriend. They made him climb up on the iron railing of a bridge then shot him down dead. The man who pulled the trigger had to run away to Texas.''

I was so absorbed in Ted's story I almost didn't notice the same car coming back. It passed, then turned around quite near us and went back toward Anthony's house and turned into the driveway.

"The Kid,'' we said in unison, though his car was just a passing dark shadow with a blast of headlights in front. What was he looking for?

We got out of our car as quietly as possible, Ted with flashlight in hand—but he didn't turn it on. I had my own small flashlight I'd stuck in my pocket. We felt our way with a tiny bit of light, for the moon was mostly under clouds.

Alice refused to wait in the car alone this time, but we made her stay back from Anthony's house in a clump of cedars, where she could see if we got in trouble and then run back to the car and call the sheriff.

The Kid was nowhere in sight.

We walked up to the front door and tried it, but it was still firmly locked. We crossed the lawn to the driveway and walked along the grass at the edge of the gravel drive to the back of the house. The grass muffled our footsteps. Just as we got to the back the moon came fully out from under a cloud. We saw the Kid's parked car at the top of the driveway, rather than down in back of the house. Which seemed odd. But still no Kid in sight. He must be inside. We had to walk on gravel to get to the back door, and even when we picked our way as quietly as possible, our steps made some noise. A windowpane in the back door was broken, and I was not surprised to find the door unlocked. So it wasn't us who broke into the house. We merely looked to see what was wrong. Ted turned on his flashlight. Glass flashed. Framed pictures all over the walls. No Kid. The Kid made himself known by a slam of the front door. In a moment we heard the engine of his car cough, and finally the whir of wheels speeding away. His car was at the top of the drive for a quick getaway.

We stepped inside the house, and Ted shone his flashlight around on a brown couch and a couple of chairs. He raised it to one picture after another. I was amazed. Alice was right. Anthony took stunning pictures. I got my own flashlight out so I could study them one at a time. They represented a different side of Anthony, one I had never seen. Each caught the essence of a mood. There was a homeless man in layered clothes and a stubble of beard, flicking away the last glowing butt end of a cigarette. His expression was both wry and full of anguish, as if he thought his life was like the butt, fit to be flicked away. He was still able to be sad about that. But not, his faded eyes said, able to change it.

Next to him hung a picture of a baby crowing with joy and with all the hope in the world shining in his eyes, waving his arms at nothing in particular. So Anthony could catch more than one mood. But the way Anthony hung the baby by the picture of the bum seemed to say he knew where hope led.

A bride stood resplendent in a white dress that glowed with satin and embroidered pearls. Her bouquet, complete with white rosebuds and lily of the valley, was a valentine, and her white lace veil had the look of an heirloom. The bride herself was a pretty little thing who seemed insignificant compared with her clothes and a pair of dramatic Victorian pearl earrings. Probably an heirloom, too. She seemed almost alive in Ted's moving flashlight beam.

I figured that a bride looking at that picture would think, Wow! Look at how much this photographer can make of me and my wedding dress! And I, from the vantage of more years than I care to mention, felt a pang of sadness for the young bride so overshadowed by the trappings of a ceremony. A ceremony for a marriage that had maybe one chance in four of lasting through the years. I knew that that was exactly what Anthony wanted this picture to say. To the bride and to eyes like mine.

How could Anthony catch so much of these people in their photographs, make them so human, and still be a man who liked to sneer, to mimic with malice? It didn't make sense.

The bride's picture got to me. I stood closer to Ted and felt deeply grateful that our marriage was more than a contract. We could depend on each other. I reached out and touched him and felt the electricity of that. Dependability without electricity would not have been much fun. I prayed Alice would find for herself what Ted and I had. But we mustn't stand and stare at pictures.

"Where would Anthony put the letters if he'd brought them back here?" I asked. Even as I asked I realized that what with Ted watching the house earlier, Anthony probably hadn't brought them here. Still, I wanted to look at his office to see if there were any clues to blackmail.

"One of us should stand watch," Ted said. "We may need to get out of here fast like the Kid did if Anthony shows up. At least we need to be warned."

"We both need to look at the office," I said. "We have an eye for different things. You go first, then we'll switch." Ted and his flashlight took off, and I stood by the door. The moon disappeared under a cloud again. I wondered if Anthony could reach that back door without my hearing. The dark felt dangerous.

I stood and listened to another car go by on the road, to insects making small noises, to the dog still barking in the distance.

It seemed forever before Ted finally came back, the bouncing beam of his flashlight arriving before him. "I've been over the whole house," he said. "Anthony doesn't keep much paper. He must have an accountant somewhere else who does his books. I even went through the trash, and I found a couple of things that could be useful, but probably are not. This note says *Buy rose.* That could have to do with a wedding bouquet. On the other hand Ross has a wife named Rose." Yes, the small delicate wife of Ross the Boss.

"Or," Ted said, "here's a note to Anthony, I guess." He handed me a note that had been crumpled, then spread back out. It said *I'm going to be late. Please give me time for the rest,* and was signed *G.*

"Goat?" I asked. "But that's a nickname."

"I'll look on the back of the pictures on the wall," Ted said. "That's always a handy hiding place. No sign of anybody coming to join us?" he asked.

I said no, not so far as I could tell.

I took the flashlight and went back into Anthony's office. Here I noticed the character of the pictures changed and became much grimmer: a gaunt burned-out house against a setting sun that gave the illusion that the fire still hovered round the house.

In another picture, a car was horribly smashed, its front end pushed back into itself against a thick tree. Through a distorted window I could half see the form of a man, slumped forward, head down over the steering wheel, limp as death. A second car seemed to be hitting the rear end of the first with maybe a glancing blow. But the first car must have been done in before the second even arrived. I thought this should be titled *Anticlimax.* All like a modern painting of bizarre and twisted lines. So close up that not all of either car was in the frame. How depressing it must be for Anthony to have that picture over the desk where he worked.

The third picture was most cynical of all. A huge old tree with a deep gash where a car must have hit it, and wreaths of plastic flowers fastened to it. The tree somehow kept its dignity, but the flowers were faded by sun and rain and wind and looked like trash. So much, the picture seemed to say, for keeping alive the memories of the dead. A little boy was standing nonchalantly in front of the tree, eating a Popsicle.

But one picture sitting in a stand-up frame on Anthony's desk was not grim at all. My eyes were grateful to find it: a young woman, maybe twenty-two or twenty-three, with blond curly hair and an elfin smile. She looked into the camera adoringly.

Her identity hit me in the solar plexus. Dear God, it must be Anthony's wife. The one who'd been killed in an automobile accident. And, because it was so sad, I remembered what Adam *Figleaf* said about her: All he had left of his daughter were her things in the attic—and Anthony. This accident photo that hung above her on the wall—it couldn't be the one she was in. That would be too much. Even for Anthony. How could he even bear to look at his wife's picture near any wreck at all? I couldn't understand. I felt sick.

I looked back at the lovely young woman. She had a

sensitive mouth and gentle eyes. I had the oddest feeling of gladness that she'd been killed before that adoring look went sour for them both. I was shocked at myself.

But I was being honest. It seemed to me that Anthony could not hold on to love for long. He'd have turned both their lives bitter if she'd lived. Now I was being as cynical as he was. At least he had something unspoiled to remember. I was glad. Maybe that made some small part of him decent enough to appeal to in a pinch. God willing.

I didn't find anything else that seemed useful except a calendar with appointments written on it. Most were for wedding and baby pictures since next to the name he'd written *B* or *Wed.* There was something that set me to thinking, however. There were a number of baby-picture appointments for people named Payer. I noticed there was an *R. Payer* and a *H. Payer* and an *E. Payer*.

Old Active Imagination here wondered if those were appointments for blackmail payments. None on the day Hector died. But something had been erased on that calendar slot. My flashlight was getting dim. I needed new batteries. But I could just make out the dates: June 15, June 18, June 22, June 25. That was today! Had he told Kid to meet him here to pay blackmail and then been diverted by us? When he didn't come and didn't come, had Kid searched the house? Where was Anthony?

Was blackmail Anthony's real business, the photography a cover-up? Maybe Azalea wouldn't pay because she figured everything was bound to be for the best in the long run.

But then, why was Hector dead? Because of something in the present or something in the past?

Ted came in and joined me. I showed him the calendar entries. I turned my flickering flashlight off and put it down on the desk so I could turn the calendar pages for him while he shone his bright light on them. I wrote them down in my notebook. Then I froze.

Wheels on gravel meant a car in the driveway. "He'll come in the back way," Ted whispered. We slipped through the house to the front door. I prayed Ted had figured that right. We stopped to peek out the front window. No sign of anyone approaching the house that way. Behind us we heard the back door creak open. We slipped out the front door, shut it behind us as quietly as possible, and hurried toward the cover of the cedar trees. The moon, God bless its heart, blacked out. We had to feel our way toward the building site next door and our car, praying the moon would stay under.

CHAPTER
20

WEDNESDAY NIGHT AND THURSDAY

We arrived home exhausted. Eudora, Pop's sitter, had on a green face as she read at the kitchen table: a book called *Theatrical Makeup Made Easy*. I felt as if I was already dreaming. "I'm taking a mail-order course in makeup," she explained. An ambitious girl. Never dull. She had a box of all sorts of paints out and had turned herself into a monster with not only a green face, but also puffy cheeks. She mumbled as though she had padding in her cheeks when she said Pop and Azalea were sound asleep.

"In the morning," Ted said as we walked toward the guest room, "remind me to show you a book I managed to steal."

I was so exhausted after a day in two states and finding the letters and having them stolen and all that, I didn't even ask, What book?

As my eyes closed I noticed Ted reading Shakespeare.

He reads when his mind is racing too fast to go to sleep. But *Shakespeare*? Never mind. Nothing could keep me awake!

In the morning, I woke up early, and for a minute I forgot where I was. Then my eyes focused on the REST EASY. BE HAPPY sign. I lay under Azalea's ruffled canopy with my mind teasing at our problems. First of all, why would anyone kill Hector? Suppose he was mixed up in blackmail—wouldn't he be worth more alive than dead? Or suppose Hector had discovered some secret that proved that the 1849 murder had not been committed by Azalea's ancestor? Anthony wouldn't have the chance to tear down the old house. Would he be so bent on spite that he'd kill to prevent that fact from spoiling his revenge? He *was* unbalanced, I was sure of that. But *that* unbalanced? It would seem more natural for someone to kill Anthony. Could Hector have been mistaken for Anthony? Now, there was a thought! They were both tall and dark. Hector had that Lincoln beard, but I realized that from the rear or in the dark they were ringers.

The clock by the bed glowed six-thirty. I couldn't sleep, so I got up and went in the kitchen to make coffee. I took a cup to Ted. "Just tell me where to find that book," I said. "If you really went to all the trouble to steal it, I ought to read it. Tell me, then go back to sleep if you want to."

But that woke him all the way up. He slipped on his clothes and brought a large flat book and another smaller book into the kitchen. He carefully washed and dried the tabletop, even though it appeared already clean. He laid the flat book on the table in front of me. "This is irreplaceable," he said. "Actually someone lent it to me without telling the rest of her family. If anything happens to it, she and I will both be shot. I won't even tell you her name. Don't put your coffee near it."

It pays to have a charming husband who can get unnamed women to go out on a limb for him. I hoped he didn't have to lose his virtue in the process. No. He wouldn't. "What is the book?" I asked. There was a picture on the cover of a long ago farm scene with hay wagons loading and men in overalls, but no title.

"This is the history of all the early families who came to settle in this area," he said. "There are only a few copies. The one in the library is kept behind a locked gate, and special permission is required to use it. Families who have these books guard them with their lives. But you, you lucky girl, get to look at this one in the comfort of your own home, or at least your stepmother's home."

I opened the book at random in the middle. I often do that so that if the author is trying to fool me in any way by determining the way I read the book, I will have him thwarted. It always annoys Ted. "That's not the way a book is designed to be read," he says, and I say, "Exactly."

I opened to a page about Gillespies. Boy, Ted sure was right about how North Carolina gave big tracts of land for Revolutionary War pensions. One Thomas Gillespie got four thousand acres. This was carefully reported, including the page of the deed book where it was officially recorded. Later Gillespies, whose lives must have been easier because of land in the family, stared out of old tintypes with earnest eyes.

I ought to look for the Thomasons. But somehow I wanted to get the lay of the land, the feel of the book, and let the Thomasons open under my fingers as a surprise. Azalea had said there wasn't much about them that she'd found in books and records. I didn't want to start by being dissapointed.

I flipped a few pages and looked down at John Hardiman Bruce. An impressive man with a huge mustache. I turned back to the family description, which said that *the best way to describe this line is simply "pure Scotch."* A pun? Seemed the family was probably descended from Robert Bruce, crowned king in 1328. Well! That was impressive. The Bruces came to Tennessee via Virginia, and the man in the picture had been a community leader, the book said—a farmer, a mule trader, and owner of a cotton gin around 1800. One of seven children. "Boy, they all had big families," I said to Ted, who was looking over my shoulder. "The book says Bruce's descendants are still around. Folks like to stay here."

I read about a Joshua Holt, who came from North Carolina and erected a mill on Flat Creek in 1814. That mill might still have been grinding when Buddy and David disappeared. David. Azalea said he came from out of the area. His family wouldn't be in the book.

I read on at random. Another David, a David Riggs, came from North Carolina by 1814, bought land at Cross Roads and contributed to building roads, including Fishing Ford Road, the earliest traveled thoroughfare in middle Tennessee. So the early settlers even had to help build the roads. No picture of David Riggs. Just a picture of a monument to his ancestor, Edward Riggs II, who helped found Newark, New Jersey.

Farming, community involvement, and pride in who they were, whatever—that's what the book told about families. A man called Ples Biggers was commended for his hog-trading talents. These folks sure had to go to great lengths to trade in animals. Hiram Joshua Edde disappeared while driving livestock to market in Mobile, Alabama. That wasn't until 1867—after Buddy and David vanished. I guess with bad roads and poor communication, it was easy for someone to simply vanish back in the nineteenth century.

But I was impressed by these people who came to the frontier and made a good life for themselves and helped each other. It must have been a wrench for a young man—Buddy, I hoped, but maybe David—to have to pull up stakes and disappear. On top of that, he'd had to leave the ones he loved forever—because of the dead man under the floor.

Riggs. That name seemed to be trying to say something to me. *Riggs.* Why? I looked at the pictures. Gideon, born 1790. The book said he built his house from bricks made right on his property in 1830 or 1840. Buddy and David and Annie knew him, I'll bet. I came to a picture of Catherine Holden Riggs, a pretty woman with her portrait painted in a shawl. She had wide-set dark clever eyes, high cheekbones, a full sensual mouth that was nevertheless set with determination. Beautiful in an unconventional way. She married Gideon in 1838, the book said.

Catherine Holden Riggs. It came to me with a crash. Annie'd said in her letters that she looked like Catherine Holden Riggs. Her friends all said so. Catherine who bore children when Annie never would. Was Catherine *Holden* Riggs related to David Holden? Maybe, maybe not, since we knew David had come from somewhere else.

"Look at this!" I called to Ted. "This is the woman that Annie said she looked like!"

I felt closer to Annie. I knew she had spunk. Like the spunk in Catherine Riggs's eyes. Whatever Annie had had to do all those years ago, she'd done it with pride and determination.

She'd come home from a joyous wedding party to find what? A bullet hole in the wall. Anything else? Blood on the floor? Or just a bullet hole and thundering silence. She and her father and the servants—yes, in those days a house that large would have had servants, maybe slaves. They would have searched every inch of the house, every bit of the yard. I saw them in my mind. Perhaps they sent someone on horseback back to the house where the party was, to find out if David or Buddy had showed up there. Perhaps her father went. Her father the lawyer, with his Irish temper, or so Annie said.

No. With the bullet hole in the wall, they'd have been afraid to ask until they knew more. That pride in family would have closed their mouths. All the time Annie must have known that whatever they discovered was bound to break her heart. Known it and prayed it wasn't true. But they did discover something. Her letters made that much clear. Although the family story, handed down through generations, said only that the two men vanished. She knew how to keep her silence, our Annie. Yes, she was brave. And why hadn't she married? She grieved for David, I was sure. But why would she grieve forever? A beautiful girl with spunk?

Could that mean she knew that David was the killer who ran away? That she knew he was alive somewhere? And so she hoped—no, that made no sense. Besides, I certainly didn't want to believe it. I'd stick to looking for the facts.

"I haven't found the Thomasons," I said.

"Well, now that you've looked at the book backward, you're ready," Ted said. He turned to the right page. Yes, I was dissappointed. No pictures. Never mind. I knew what Annie must have looked like.

The Thomasons, the book said, were living in Mecklenburg County, North Carolina, in 1760. They had one son and eleven daughters; the father and son fought in the American Revolution.

Now I was into bare facts. Wilbur Thomason came to Williamson County, Tennessee, in the mid-1790s. His daughters all married into local families, but the genealogy wasn't complete. The book did say that Wilbur Thomason, Jr., (that would be Annie's father) practiced law, farmed, and was known as a man who would always buy land.

"Anyone hitting upon hard times had only to ask him for cash on the spot. It was said, however, that he did know how to cut a sharp deal."

Here came the part I wanted to know more about: Wilbur Thomason, Jr.'s, son and Thomason's law partner both vanished together in 1849, the book said. While there were rumors that foul play had been involved, no solution to the mystery was ever found. A year later a minister coming back from California told the family he had met one of the young men out there who had been mortally wounded in a barroom brawl. The young man was using an assumed name, and the minister never learned his true identity. But this man sent Annie Thomason two gold nuggets, which the preacher went all the way to Tennessee to deliver.

That was all. Nothing I hadn't heard. I sighed.

"This time, your backward way of casing books did pay off," Ted said. "Because now you know what Annie looked like. And maybe we know what Wilbur Thomason, Jr., kept in his hiding place under the hearth—gold to make those sharp land deals whenever he got the chance. He didn't keep his cash in a bank but hidden nearby to make a fast deal."

Money. Of course. A whole new factor. Back in 1849, was a man killed for gold?

CHAPTER
21

THE SPIDER

By the time I finished looking at the local history, it was still only twenty of nine. We ate a quick breakfast at the kitchen table and finished just as Azalea and Pop came in to join us.

"Welcome back," Azalea said as she wheeled Pop up to the table. "Ted told me yesterday afternoon that you've discovered some wonderful old letters." She began to sing "Zippity doo-dah" as she went back in to the electric coffeepot on the counter and poured them both cups of coffee. Everything else was on the table. She sat down next to Pop.

"But you let that Anthony guy steal those letters right from under your nose!" Pop complained. "Honestly, Peaches, you need to pull yourself together. You came all the way back from the mountains without my extra shirts. Now we have practically no time to figure who killed who, and you lose those letters. Those letters that you say Annie What's-Her-Name wrote could be full of clues, and isn't tomorrow the deadline for you to prove that Anthony is wrong?''

Azalea gave him a playful tap and said, ''Grouch,'' and laughed. ''We'll solve this. Just have faith.'' With a flourish she poured cornflakes and milk into her bowl.

''We *have* figured out what it was that Wilbur Thomason, Jr., kept hidden under the hearth,'' Ted said quickly. ''He kept gold for quick land buys. So gold may have been the motive for the murder of our body under the floor.''

''Of course,'' Pop said. ''Anyone could see that. But you need to know who took the gold. You and Peaches need solid proof.''

''I think you two are just wonderful,'' Azalea said, turning first to me and then to Ted, and she began to sing ''Oh, What a Beautiful Morning'' while she reached out and hugged Pop. Then she said, ''Thank you for bringing these two marvelous young people into my family.''

Young people! What a thought.

The phone on the kitchen counter rang. Ted got up and answered. He frowned. ''Yes,'' he said, ''tomorrow. We have some new evidence that I think will interest you, but no final proof yet.''

He sat back down heavily and explained that Adam Marlowe wanted to meet with us tomorrow at one o'clock to settle the fate of the house. My stomach constricted. We weren't prepared.

''We need all the evidence we can find to persuade him to give us a little longer.'' Ted said that cheerfully, but I know Ted. He thought the old man was going to be difficult, if not impossible.

Azalea said, ''We'll be ready. We have to be.'' She sipped her coffee. ''I've put up a new slogan in your honor, dear,'' she told Pop. There hardly seemed to be room on the wall, but she pointed it out, a small quilted hanging: IT TAKES A LONG TIME TO GROW YOUNG—PICASSO. Pop beamed.

So. Think positive. I'd try.

But Azalea could not divert Pop from an inquisition. He turned to me. "How will you get those letters back from Anthony?" he demanded.

"I'll get them," Ted said. "I'll go by to see Anthony on my way to the archives. If there was nothing in those letters to prove his case and nothing to prove ours, he may just give them back, to save himself the trouble of the lawsuit I'll promise him if he doesn't. Judging by the way those letters started out, they may not answer any of our questions about who died."

"Is there much to do at the archives?" I asked.

"I need to go back, although I spent some time there after I looked through the records at the courthouse," Ted said. "Those old papers are unindexed and pretty well mixed up. There's a volunteer who's a member of the Historical Society presorting them, but I need to go through them all to find out if there's anything I've missed related to the mid-1800s. It's a long shot, but I have a feeling it may pay off."

Good! If he could do that, I had a project of my own in mind. "I want to look over the shed that used to be on Azalea's property before the boundary changed," I said. "If it was part of the Thomason property in 1849, something could have been hidden there that's related to how our skeleton got to be dead. First I'll just look, and if anything turns up, maybe we can get Frank to do a dig there."

"Oh, that's a marvelous idea!" Azalea cried. "That young man never comes up empty-handed, does he?"

I restrained myself from saying that I wished he had.

"Then," I said, "if Azalea will lend me her car, I'll join you at the archives, Ted. An extra hand never hurts." Azalea nodded yes.

Meanwhile Alice came in yawning, still in her bathrobe. She'd slept late, dreaming of Ed perhaps. "I'll be ready to take you to the doctor at ten, Azalea," she promised. She'd have to hurry to eat and dress. Lucky she had a car of her own, so I could use Azalea's. The clock over the stove said nine o'clock already.

Ted drove off to the archives, and I made sure I had my notepad and pencil and my camera in case I found something worth recording. One picture is worth a thousand words. I think Confucius said that. One photograph has certainly got a memory a thousand times as good as mine.

I drove down to the old house. Yellow crime-scene tape was still up, but nobody appeared to be at the site. I walked around behind the house over to the rusty barbed wire that separated Azalea's property from the place next door. I hoped the creatures in the field were cows, not bulls. Hard to tell about the one that was lying down. I pulled the strands of barbed wire apart and managed to get through without entanglement. The animals merely watched me without much interest. I walked over to the small gray board building. If there had ever been a door, it had fallen from its hinges and moldered away. A modern-looking shovel leaned agaist the building by the door. How odd.

It was dark inside since there were no windows. But I saw a flash of movement. Someone was there. My heart beat harder. "Who's that?" I called. Maybe it was just the farmer who owned the building.

But the face that appeared in the doorway was Anthony's. "Hello," he said, almost friendly. I must have looked shocked, because how did he know about the changed property line? Why else would he be here?

"Never let anyone in the archives hear you say what you've found," he said, "or someone is sure to hear it and repeat it. This is a small town, and we like history." So Ted must have mentioned the property-line change, perhaps to the archivist.

Anthony came outside. He was carrying a long metal rod with a crosspiece handle on one end and what looked like a pointed bullet on the other. "Archaeologist's probe," he said when he saw me staring. "To see if there's anything worth digging for."

He had such strange hands holding that probe, thin and long, an introvert's hands, but with huge stiff thumbs, the thumbs of stubbornness. "I'm a better detective than you are,'' he said cheerfully. ''I know you searched my house last night. And I know you didn't find anything.'' He sounded so sure of himself I could have kicked him. ''I know there was nothing in my house for you to find. And I know you broke in because you dropped your flashlight with the name tape glued to it. Breaking and entering is illegal. You know that.''

Oh, damn! I hadn't dropped my flashlight in Anthony's house—I'd put it down on his desk and forgot to pick it up. Marking things is great just in case you forget them, but not if you forget them where you're not supposed to be. I am not designed to be sneaky.

''We did not break in,'' I said hotly. ''We were passing your house, and we hoped we'd find you,'' I said. ''You did steal the old letters that I'd found.''

He continued to smile, as if congratulating himself, and said nothing.

''Someone had already broken into your house and left the door wide open,'' I said.

He laughed. ''You expect I won't believe that, don't you? You expect me to say you're lying.''

Of course I did.

''But I do believe you. You see what a nice guy I am? That would be the Kid who broke into my house,'' he said. ''He was due there about then. He's a damn fool to think I leave valuable things out to be found. So how did you like my place?'' he asked wryly.

He stood there under the small sapling that bent over the shed. The leaves cast a moving shadow on his face. For just a moment his eyes looked eager. He wanted me to like his stuff. He was human.

''I think you take remarkable pictures,'' I said. That was something I could mean.

He smiled broadly. He was pleased. Then the smile faltered. ''So you wonder,'' he said, ''how a bastard like me can take great pictures.''

I thought maybe it would actually help to tell him how I felt.

"I wondered why anyone as talented as you are goes around deliberately making enemies. How you can be sensitive enough to take those pictures and yet have contempt for yourself and for everyone else you meet."

He grimaced in rage. I'd gone too far.

"If I have talent, who do you think gives a damn?" he yelled. "They want cute babies. They want sugarcoated virgin brides. And they want them all to look alike." He was shaking. I could have imagined him hitting me over the head with the probe. Except he would have preferred an ax.

"Maybe," I said, "if you weren't so angry, you could keep friends who would help you sell your talent. Your father-in-law still thinks you're great."

He shrugged. "He's a gullible old man." He made a face exactly like Adam *Figleaf* Marlowe's. In Adam's voice, Anthony said, "It's important to obey the word of the Lord." Only, somehow, Anthony made the words sound ridiculous.

"If you ridicule your friends," I said, "how can you keep them?" Why was I wasting my time telling him that? But I thought of Alice. She had cared about him. I suspected that mixed in with her anger at him now, there was still some caring. He'd wanted to hold on to Alice. But he knew only how to threaten her. I found that unbearable— that he was systematically destroying his life and pulling down the people around him. If he could just see . . . But he couldn't see. Except perhaps through a camera lens. How could that be? Well, Van Gogh could paint, but he also cut off his own ear. Anthony was merely cutting off his nose to spite his face, as my mother used to say.

"You don't have your camera," I blurted. It had seemed so much a part of him, hanging around his neck, that he looked naked without it.

"The shutter sticks," he said. "It's being fixed." He pulled a small camera out of his pocket. "I have this if I need it." He stuck it back in his pocket and stood there awkwardly holding the probe.

"Don't let me stop you from probing," I said. "We both wonder what's here." He hesitated, then shrugged. I followed him into the shed.

"Why inside?" I asked.

"Because I've already done the outside. And besides, it seems that whoever buried things in 1849 did it in buildings, didn't they?"

The bullet-shaped end of the probe went into the ground as he put weight on the crossbar. He pierced the dirt floor again and again in a straight line along one wall of the shack, then back down a line next to that. Methodically he covered the floor. "Nothing of any size under here so far," he said. "Are you disappointed?"

Of any size? What was he expecting to find? Suddenly it came to me. He expected to find a spider. What did Annie Thomason's letter say? Something about a spider protecting a secret. A black iron pot with spider legs and a close-fitting lid was called a spider. Like the one on the hearth at the Vance birthplace. Whatever was buried in a spider would be preserved, wouldn't it? I began to quiver with excitement. But suppose Anthony destroyed the secret, whatever it was? I needed some other witness besides just me. I looked out the door—nobody working today. The old house was deserted. Across the gravel road I could see the glimmer of Goat's house through the trees. But no person in sight. In desperation I looked up the road, and here came Alice and Azalea in Alice's car, like the answer to a prayer. On the way to the doctor. I waved my arms madly, hoping they'd turn our way and see me. Luckily Alice did. She stopped, and I beckoned her to come over.

When I turned back, Anthony was probing the last of the floor. "Nothing under here," he said.

I didn't believe him. He was just a whisker too smug. "Let me show Alice how this works," I said, taking the probe from his hands.

Alice arrived, and that distracted him. He seemed uncertain what to do next. I took the probe and began to push it down just beyond the last place where I'd watched him do it. If he'd struck anything after that, my back would have been turned. The rod pushed down easily, and I felt small things, pebbles, perhaps, bits of broken pottery or glass, but, as he said, nothing large. I handed the probe to Alice. "Push it down here," I said, pointing to a place just beyond but still in a straight line. The probe went down about two feet, and we heard a sound between a click and a thud. Alice turned to me, amazed. "This thing won't go any further." I was excited.

"I'll dig," Anthony said gruffly, and went outside to get the shovel. Of course. He'd brought it just in case. "We need to see what you've hit," he said. He'd evidently decided he couldn't get rid of us. Or maybe he wanted to impress Alice. I took off an overshirt that I'd put over my tank top in the cool of the early morning. "Put the dirt on this," I said. "We can sift it for small stuff later."

I watched him to be sure he wasn't up to any tricks. My eyes had grown used to the dim light. He dug straight down, and after about two feet I heard his shovel strike metal.

Alice caught her breath, then asked "What is it?" She leaned forward.

I kept my eye on Anthony in case of tricks. He reached to pull whatever it was up, but it stuck. He tried to shake it loose, but couldn't. Did I hear something rattle inside? He dug around the back of the thing and then around the front. Delaying? But he could be sure we wouldn't go away. In fact, I heard a car door shut in the distance. Azalea was coming to join us whether her ribs hurt or not.

Anthony pulled a black pot on legs up out of the hole and said, "We can see better outdoors." The pot was in fine shape, only a little rusty. So that *was* what the letters meant! A spider pot. Anthony carried it outdoors. I was ready to trip him if he tried to run off with it.

I stuck right next to him, but he'd evidently given up on flight.

He set the spider down on the scraggly grass in front of the building. I got down on my knees to see better. Azalea stood close by, and Alice stood protectively beside her.

Anthony tried to lift the top, but it stuck. He struck the pot lightly with his shovel, and it made a clear metal ping. He tried again. He lifted the top off, and there in the black interior lay a pistol—an elegant one, if you could call a gun elegant. It just fit in the spider.

The curved handle was a polished dark wood, with gold inlaid initials: *E. R.* E.R.? That didn't fit. The handle flowed into the metal part of the gun, which was silver etched with flowers and scrolls and a small inlaid gold rose. The trigger with its guard seemed large in proportion to the gun, and the barrel was as wide as the rest of the gun. I looked closer. The barrel was not just one barrel. There were five in a bunch. Five places for bullets to come from. We all stared.

"This must be some special gun," Alice said. "I never saw one like that, not even in a movie. And look at those initials. E.R."

This got more curious every minute. "Why would Annie bury this pistol?" I asked out loud. "Who on earth did it belong to?"

"Buddy was a carpenter," Anthony rejoiced. "He sure wouldn't have a gun like that!"

"David wasn't the type to own a gun like that, either," I said quickly. "Besides, if we're just talking about those two men in the family story, if the gun belonged to the one who survived, why didn't he take it with him when he ran away? If it belonged to the dead man, why didn't they bury it with him?"

Azalea said, "We don't know who it belonged to or when." Of course, she was right.

"Don't touch that," I said to Anthony, who was just reaching out. "We'll get Nick to tell us where to send it to learn about it. He's the one we need. He sent the skeleton. He can send the gun. They didn't have ballistics tests back then, did they? But maybe this kind of gun had a particular ball an expert will recognize. Maybe that kind of ball will turn out to be the kind that was with the body."

"It's a beautiful old antique gun, isn't it?" Azalea asked.

Yes, and the handle was so smooth, it asked to be held. What could that beautiful antique gun prove about who lived and who died?

We had just one day before Adam *Figleaf* Marlowe's time limit. Had we found enough to persuade him to give us more time? I couldn't tell what the old man might do. He was irrational. Worse than Pop.

Anthony was smiling at Alice. "Tomorrow," he said, "the house will belong to me. Even that charming little pistol, which once went with the house, will be mine."

"No," I said firmly. "The gun will belong to the man who owns the land we stand on. The property line was changed about the time of World War One. This bit of land will not be yours, no matter what."

It was a small victory, but it pleased me.

CHAPTER
22

THURSDAY

We stood near the weathered shed and actually made an agreement with Anthony. Alice would call Nick, the head archaeologist, on the nearest phone and explain how we'd found the gun and the spider on land that now belonged to Azalea's next-door neighbor. Alice said she knew the man, a farmer but also a history nut. She was sure he'd let Nick explore this site and take the gun and spider to be identified by date, and in any other way an expert knew.

We agreed that Nick should make the results available to Anthony and Azalea. Both at once.

In the meantime I took photographs of the spider and the pistol from every angle. So did Anthony, of course. We were a photographers' convention.

Then Alice took Azalea on to the doctor's office, promising to stop on the way to leave my film to be developed and call Nick. She didn't have a car phone, and I had Azalea's car, which didn't have one either.

Meanwhile, in order to protect Azalea's interests, I stayed with Anthony.

"You can have those stupid letters back," Anthony told me angrily as he squirmed with impatience, waiting for Nick. "They're in my car. They don't tell anything worth knowing." So he'd hoped they'd prove his point, and they hadn't.

I could only hope Anthony had missed something. I wanted to say, Can we get the letters now? But with Anthony, it was better to be cool. He might not want me to make him look unreasonable in front of Nick. Anthony the letter stealer. But if I pushed him, he could get contrary.

When Nick arrived at the outbuilding, of course he was excited at our spider find. He'd called the farmer and got permission to dig all around the area where we found the spider. The man himself was sick in bed. He was ninety-three years old, Nick explained, and needed to take care of himself.

"Boy, that's a beauty!" Nick said when he looked at the gun. "Perfectly preserved." But he said he'd rather confer with a gun expert before he gave us details. "I don't want to be wrong."

Nick found bits of glass around the the place where we'd dug, but nothing to suggest this had ever been a kitchen, where a spider would normally be found. He agreed that someone probably brought the spider to this out-of-the-way shed to bury it, perhaps because this was a place where no one was likely to look.

But why, if it was related to the murder, wasn't the gun buried under the floor with the body? Nick had no answer to that, except that maybe the murderer discovered the gun had been left after the floor was back down.

By about three o'clock, Nick was finished at the scene, and Anthony actually gave me the letters. I was jubilant. I drove straight to the archives, where I was due to meet Ted. This time I would copy the letters right away.

The archives were down a set of stairs in the basement of the courthouse, but nevertheless the place had a cheerful atmosphere. The folks who sat at long tables and studied old records seemed rapt, and one man even chuckled, perhaps at some historical oddity.

The nice archivist welcomed me and said Ted was off in another room where the old papers were being sorted. She let me use her copying machine. And, thank God, the letters really were in the folders. I let out a sigh of relief. I had half expected Anthony would give us back the letters I'd already seen and nothing more except a sheet of paper saying, *April fool.*

Ted appeared as the copying machine let out its last hum—before I'd had time to more than glance at the letters—and led me off between the file cabinets and shelves of records to the room where an older woman was sorting papers. A case of old leather-bound books covered one wall behind her, and a big window threw light on stacks of papers that covered the table she was working at. This part of the archives must be at ground level. Ted introduced me to her: Madeline Guthrie, the Historical Society member who'd volunteered to evaluate the papers. She was short and wide and cheerful and brisk, with vibrant blue eyes and hair that was obviously dyed red. She was well aged, with kindly wrinkles and an air of having grown wise as well as old. "We have an exciting find," she said. "You're here at the right minute. We just found this stuff three days ago in Mary Etta Morgan's attic, when they cleared out her house after she died. Some of these papers go back to 1830."

"I have letters from 1849!" I told Madeline. I turned to Ted. "I can hardly believe that Anthony gave them back. Can you? While you went to his house to talk him into it, he did it on his own. He says they don't say much, but we need to look close." I was hopeful in spite of myself.

"Ted told me," Madeline said. "The letters are exciting, too."

I opened the first folder, the one that held what I'd already read. Old letters on the bottom, copies on top. I gave Madeline the first letter to skim. She was more used to the old-fashioned writing than I was. Maybe she'd spot something I missed.

The second letter I'd originally read told about Catherine Holden Riggs and how our Annie believed she looked like her. Then: *I was so happy when David asked me to marry him, and I believed that my life was on a straight course forever. How little I knew,* the letter ended.

I thought of the bright-eyed hopeful picture of Catherine Riggs. Annie must have been like that. Then her hopes were crushed.

I opened the second folder: the unread letters. Just a few. I prayed again that Anthony had missed something. I read aloud:

> *Oh, Mother, I don't know what to do. I wish you were here to advise me. I have put the weapon in a safe place. It would be recognized. Now my dear brother and the man I meant to spend my life with are both gone forever.*

I stopped. "Could they both be dead?" I asked aloud. "But one evidently ended up in California."

"Where she was never likely to see him again," Ted said.

> *Father is broken* [the letter said]. *I never saw him worse. He tells me to remember that we are a proud family. We do not give up. He keeps up his life, finding someone to take the hogs to market in Alabama, and writing a will for Allen Durer.*

Yes, I thought, remembering the stories in the history book. They were proud people who came here. Proud and ingenious. Some bad ones mixed in, of course. I read further to try to find out who had killed whom in our old house.

*And I get strength from HIM. He came on the
fateful night. He knows all and forgives all. I must
do the same.*

A second person knew what happened! This mysterious
HIM.

*I must not show what I know. I must appear as
amazed as everyone else. I must say, "How could
two grown men disappear?"*
*I have to be brave for the children, David's son,
David, and Bud's little Bud. Bud's poor Agnes has
no means of support now. She can sew prettily, but
she needs help to raise her son. Father has invited
her to live with us. At least to visit for a while. Her
brother who lives in Carthage can look after her
house and cow. We must never let her know what
happened.*

I was provoked. Anthony was right. Annie was not going
to tell much.

Another letter talked about the children. David Jr. and
little Bud.

*I wish their names did not remind me of our
sorrow* [she wrote]. *Then I see David smile through
his son's eyes and I am happy. Yes, happy.*

The letters told more about the children, about how
Bud's wife finally took her child and returned to her own
family. That was all.

I was so annoyed I could have thrown those letters in
the trash. That must be how Anthony had felt. Totally frustrated. He threw them at me so I'd be frustrated, too. At
least I didn't have to wonder what they said.

"We do have one clue." I made myself think positive.
"The mysterious 'HIM' must have been a minister." I

looked back at the earlier letters. "Annie said her brother 'wrote to me through "HIM" such a good and helpful servant of God,' " I said. "Then, in the later letters, she says, 'He knows all and forgives all.' "

"He could well be a minister," Madeline agreed. "It's possible," she added, pointing at the boxes of yellowed papers and the stacks on the table, "that some of these papers here will tell."

She turned to Ted. "Thank goodness Mary Etta Morgan's heirs didn't burn the lot when they emptied her house." She shook her head sadly. "Mary Etta hadn't been able to get in that attic for thirty years. She was the worst pack rat you ever saw—speak no ill of the dead. I suppose years ago she offered to store these papers when the library moved, and then she went through them herself. Poor girl, she never had a sense of order. I went to see her one day and found her toothbrush on the coffee table in the living room. She thanked me. She'd been looking for it." She raised her eyes to the ceiling in comic horror. "She kept tissue paper from Christmas, and you never saw so many magazines. But if you're a pack rat long enough, you're a resource—isn't that right?" She turned to one of us, then the other. A woman with tennis-match eyes.

Also, she was a rambler. But sometimes ramblers ramble onto something useful.

"These are papers from several people, right?" I asked.

"As I understand it," Madeline said, "Annabel Story, the woman who gave these, was a pack rat herself about old papers. Also she moved around. When she gave away these papers, she lived in west Tennessee, which may be why these papers got lost between the cracks here in middle Tennessee. But she originally came from around here, and she'd kept records from both sides of her family. There is a letter from her that says that several of her ancestors were ministers."

She said that as if it wasn't important, as if she didn't want me to hope one was HIM and be disappointed. But, heck, sleuthing is trying one thing and being disappointed and trying something else. In fact, that's life!

"Perhaps Annie Thomason was brave enough never to tell a soul what she knew, not even on paper. But that's hard for any frail human being. We do like to tell, don't we?" she asked with a smile. "And we like to hear first-hand what happened. I was so pleased that Ted could tell me all the details of how they found the skeleton," she said. "And I'll look extra carefully for any possible clues in these papers." She pulled up another cardboard box marked *Story papers*.

"If you want to help sort, we're putting them in piles by who wrote them, as best we can, and then by date if there is a date. If there's no other clue, we sort them by hand-writing, to get each person's words in one pile."

I sat down and tried to help. I'm not good at sorting papers. I get interested in reading each piece, so it takes me forever. Like a whole account of the bloody Battle of Franklin. At least I'd figured one thing out. Madeline must be the one who lent Ted the local history book with Annie's look-alike in it. I was grateful.

At five-thirty we had to quit. Madeline could probably have gotten permission to stay, but she had to go to her daughter's birthday party. She was unwilling to leave us in the archives alone with her precious papers, still largely unsorted. But tomorrow was the day we had to have our proof. Ted stayed calm. I had stomach quavers.

Ted and I went back to Azalea's, and we all gathered around the kitchen table: Azalea, Pop, Alice, Eudora the sitter, Ted, and me. Eudora had on a shirt with scrolls of movie film and various couples in clinches all over it. Unusual. Alice had circles under her eyes. But she and Eudora had fixed a delicious supper: roast chicken, baked potatoes, and salad. As we ate, Ted and I told about the slim pickings at the archives, then we all talked about the modern murder.

"We don't know who the killer was this week or in 1849," I said. "We are unanimously ignorant."

I went to bed, annoyed, and lay awake. I did know something. I could feel it. About the past? About the present? I didn't know what.

So never mind. I'd try Sleepthink—a wonderful process if your brain doesn't always percolate the way you wish it would in the daytime. You frame a question as clearly as possible. I did that: *What do I know that's right at the edge of my mind that I need to be aware of and won't come clear?* I wished I could be more exact, but that would have to do. You frame the question just as you are slipping into sleep.

Sleepthink almost always works. I prayed that when I woke up I'd have an answer.

CHAPTER
23

Sometime in the night or toward dawn, I either heard a door slam or dreamed I did. I didn't entirely pull up from sleep.

I came wide-awake when the clock radio by the bed said seven o'clock. I knew what I had to do right away—go look at the newspaper clippings on the upstairs wall of the old house. But I'd already looked at those, I told myself. *Just go,* said Sleepthink. *Now.*

The crew usually came to work at the house at eight. Would they come today? Probably not.

I slipped on my skirt and the new red T-shirt that Ted kindly got me when he bought himself a shirt. He slept so peacefully, breathed so evenly, I wanted to lean over and give him a kiss. And wake him up? Let him sleep a little longer. I left him a note and said where I'd gone and that I'd be back shortly.

It was such a pretty morning, still cool, that I could not

bear to drive down to the house. I needed to walk and smell
the early-morning air and the grass wet with dew. I walked
uphill first, which was why we couldn't see the old house
from Azalea's windows, then down a long hill where the
old house appeared small and then larger and larger. Everything was bright electric green due to the recent rain. Too
much rain. Bright green but here and there wisps of early-
morning fog.

The yellow crime-scene tape was gone. Hoorah. Azalea
must have been breathing down the neck of everyone in
the county to have it removed and get the restoration work
back on track. I picked my way around standing puddles
to the board ramp, climbed up, and looked inside. The log
pen on the left seemed virtually undisturbed. The hole
where the skeleton had been found was covered again with
blue plastic, but in my mind I saw it glaring empty the way
it was when I fell into it. No doubt an expert could spot
the place where Walt-z had sat, and where he'd put his
guitar case while he composed his ballad about "All that's
left are the bones, oh." A memorable line. And was there
still a mark in the dirt outside where Hector had lain? Poor
Hector, who knew so much and died so young.

I walked over to the ladder. I tested each rung with my
hand before I stepped onto it. Solid. I climbed up to the
second floor, and since there was no railing to hang on to
at the top, I crawled out onto the floor. There was plywood
to walk on up here, just as below. I headed straight for
those clippings pasted over the walls of the house. Had I
seen something from the corner of my eye that pulled me
back?

I walked over to the wall on the left and found a headline
that said KLAN SUBMITS TO GOVERNOR. That was in
Oklahoma. Must be from the Nashville daily paper that
would have carried national as well as local news. Another
headline said COOLIDGE ACCEPTS. Not helpful. I was diverted by a picture of women in those down-over-your-ears
hats, which I think were from the 1920s. Nearby, an ad for
"The Woman's Tonic." For cramps, perhaps? Some tonic

that women needed and men didn't. This was not what I was looking for.

Ah, the word *Tennessee,* maybe something local. An ad for McCormack corn harvesters, mowers, and Tennessee wagons. What were Tennessee wagons?

How could this help me? I came across the story of the Civil War veterans, about how they swapped battle stories. I had an odd feeling that meant something, that it had to do with what I was looking for. That didn't make sense. Besides, most of the story was cut off by the corset ad. Quite a chesty corset. Almost good enough for Madonna. But empty.

HAPPY-GO-LUCKY CLUB, large letters proclaimed. A story about the Japanese navy was catercornered to a tale of "Nearsighted Christians." I skimmed most of the wall. What was I looking for? Rats! No luck.

I went back to the bit of wall where I'd begun. I noticed a small, unassuming headline that I'd missed: LIBRARY ACCEPTS PAPERS. I caught my breath. The story said, *Annabel Story, daughter of the late Reverend John Baird of Franklin, who served in the Civil War, has given all her father's papers and a number of others to the American Legion Library in the Masonic Temple building.*

Annabel Story! She gave the papers Ted was sorting! The Reverend John Baird. My heart began to hammer. Suppose that was HIM, the minister who was there the night when whatever happened happened. But he would have had to be very young when he helped Annie, and rather old to serve in the Civil War. That was his business! I prayed for him to be the one Annie confided in! He must be. And Ted would find his papers. Just a chance. But I hoped until I was hot all over.

I stared at the name and thought Baird begins with a *B*. I thought of the ring with the *B*. What an odd thought. How could the Reverend Baird's ring end up next to the skeleton under the floor? No, that wouldn't work.

All this was a long shot. Calm down.

I heard car wheels, which brought me back to here and

now. Workmen arriving? Someone driving past? Would they go right back to work as if nothing had happened? I thought I heard a noise at the back of the house. A small crash. I walked over to the door at the back of this upstairs room, the one that opened onto air because for some reason the next room had been removed down to the dirt subfloor. I looked into the distance, but I couldn't see anyone. I felt discombobulated. I must get word to Ted to look for the papers of the Reverend John Baird. I must do it right away, not be distracted. I started to raise my arm.

Unfortunately I also looked down into the small room that was almost like a corridor between the two parts of the house. Where the floor had once been was a huge puddle—really a small pool, reflecting blue sky and the walls of the house at crazy angles. And something else. No, that wasn't a reflection. A man was floating on his back in the water. Good Lord! His arms and legs were at odd angles, one arm close to the body, one flung out, as if he'd been flung down. Good God, as if he'd been thrown from right where I stood. But thrown backward. His face was up. Hair wet and wild, around blood at the top of his head. Blood in the water around his head like a halo. Trash floated around him, too. No, it wasn't all trash. Mixed with bits of wood scrap and a green plastic 7UP bottle, were yellow roses. I wondered if my eyes were working right. Yes. In that muddy water that reflected helter-skelter beams and blue sky, fresh yellow roses floated. Several were lying right on the body, the one on the face making identity unclear. I felt dizzy. I stepped back from the edge. If he was murdered, was someone crazy in the house? Maybe still here? I pulled my arm down. I *needed* to be distracted!

I scurried down the ladder. No matter what, I had to look more closely, see who was dead. I ran across the plywood path to the rear-door hole of the front log pen. I stood near the edge of the pond that had been a subfloor, close to the floating body. Good Lord, it was Anthony! I should have known him from above. That dark hair, that mustache. But it's hard to see what you don't expect. A yellow rose was over, or almost in, his slightly open mouth. His skin was gray white. Those long lashes looked artificial around his open eyes, already glassy. Plainly he was dead. What had killed him? Some blow to the head? How long had he been there? I tried to feel sorry. No luck.

Who had been here in the night or in the predawn hours? Or were they still here? I remembered about how Walt had come back to compose his ballad. But that was two nights ago. Who else might be drawn back to that house now that the tape was down? Why? I remembered a door banging in the night. Or had I dreamed it? Someone leaving Azalea's house?

Why had someone strewn Anthony with roses? Anthony who stank. The flowers weren't just flung in the water, or they would have splashed and become dirty and even sunk. Each floated cleanly, fresh roses next to a soiled man. Almost arranged. In addition to the one over his mouth, there were two on his chest.

I looked around for anything a killer might have dropped aside from roses. But among the floating bits of construction trash, nothing I spotted seemed remarkable. Of the many footprints on the plywood where I stood, I couldn't tell if any were fresh.

I heard footsteps on the planks up to the door and turned, startled. This could be the one who—I held my breath. There was Ross the Boss. I was so relieved I let my breath out in a sigh.

"Good morning," he said.

I was so startled by his normal manner at such an abnormal moment that I was speechless. He wore a white T-shirt, a pair of chino pants, and a red cap, which he took off, turned round in his hands, and put back on.

"Anthony," I said. I pointed toward the open doorway to the topless room.

He walked over, looking at the ground as I'd seen him do before. An odd habit. I heard a sharp intake of breath. "First a skeleton," he said, "then Hector. Now this." He shook himself. His voice vibrated with despair. "There's a curse on this house."

He looked at the square-cut logs around him in what I can only call an affectionate way. As if the house was his friend.

"No," he said, "I won't say that. The curse is on the damn fools who come here. Too many fools." He sounded angry.

I realized I was angry, too. Dammit. We had enough to figure out from the past. This could make things more difficult. We might prove that Anthony was wrong. It would be a lot harder to prove that none of us went berserk and killed the skunk.

Alice was right. Dead or alive, Anthony was going to make trouble. The fangs of a dead rattlesnake can still inject poison. I learned that from my mountain neighbors. Anthony was a dead snake.

CHAPTER
24

AZALEA AND ALICE

FRIDAY, JUNE 28, ABOUT 8:00 A.M.

Ross called the sheriff on his portable phone. Is everybody wired? As Ross hung up I saw Alice through the front doorway. Alice? She was the last person we needed with a dead man in the house. A man she wanted to see gone. She was walking slowly down the road toward us through the early-morning wisps of fog, a dark-haired ghost in white shorts and T-shirt. She seemed disoriented, picking a wildflower here and there, not as if she wanted the flower, but as if it was something to catch hold of. I went out to meet her. My skin prickled with foreboding. Why was she here? Why was she so plainly upset?

"It's a lovely day for a walk," she said with a forced smile. She was holding several daisies and a yellow rose. *A yellow rose?*

"You know about Anthony," I blurted. Or maybe Alice just happened to pick the rose. This was yellow-rose day. Didn't I wish!

She stopped in her tracks. "I couldn't sleep," she said, staring at the rose. "I went for a walk." She turned her eyes to me as if she was searching for some kind of help. What could I say? *What a dumb thing to do, to take a walk at dawn near the place where you know two people have been killed?* But I'd done the same dumb thing, as if something pulled me.

"I couldn't just lie there." She began to shiver. "I got up and went out in the yard, and Chubby came up to me, and I thought, 'Oh, good. I shouldn't be out here alone.' I felt so rotten, I just followed along the way Chubby led. At least I wasn't lying in bed, worrying and feeling sick about the dumb things I've done. I stopped and picked some wild roses because I felt so rotten, and they were so pretty and smelled so good. Most roses don't smell." A tear ran down one cheek.

"I wished for him to be dead," she continued, as if she hadn't changed the subject. And then in a stronger voice: "And I meant it. Or I thought I did." Yes. She must have seen Anthony lying there dead in the pool of water. I hoped to God she hadn't killed him. I wanted to put my arms around her. But I mustn't stop her story.

She raised the yellow rose to her nose and sniffed it, as if that might comfort her. Or bring back the memory of Anthony dead? His ugliness lingered. We were standing just down the plywood ramp that led to the front doorway. She turned toward the house. "Chubby brought me here."

It was the dog's fault! Now, who would believe that? "I understand," I said.

"When we got near, Chubby began to bark. He ran inside and then out again and then inside, like he wanted me to come. I was scared because I knew that meant something was wrong. After a while I figured that if anybody bad was there, they'd have run away, with Chubby barking like that. I was so curious and scared of what I'd find that I had to know. So I followed him inside."

I reached out and touched her arm. She started. She was dead cold and damp from the fog. I put my arm around her. She leaned against me as if it helped her to stand up. "Go on," I said.

"And I found him," she said. "Floating. Dead." Her voice was calm and amazed. "I couldn't believe it. I'd said I wanted him to be dead. I'd said that."

She began to tremble nonstop. She stuttered out words. "Anthony. I hated him and he's gone. Good." She stopped and shook her head. "No."

"You're not glad?"

"I looked up to Anthony!" she wailed. "I used to look up to him and I felt sorry for him. Both at once." The tears streamed down her face. "He was part of who I was as a kid. He took great pictures. He really did. That Anthony is dead, too."

I remembered his bitterness about his pictures. He'd never take another. Not a creative one, not a commercial one, not a cruel one.

"There he was with his eyes all open and glazed that ugly way. And blood. Dead. I guess it was a crazy thing to do but I put the roses that were in my hands on him and all around him as a kind of good-bye to that other Anthony. Then I panicked and ran."

"Why did you come back?" I asked.

"Where could I run to?" she demanded angrily. "He was with me. I couldn't get away. I had to talk to somebody who—and I heard you, and I came back."

"You kept one rose," I said. Why did that make me feel so sad?

She laughed. This was no time to get hysterical. She said, "One rose to remember the good part of Anthony by." She turned to me, alarmed. "But I didn't kill him. They'll think I killed him, won't they? They'll find my footprints! I didn't do it. You've got to believe me." Her eyes were huge with fear.

Ross came out the front doorway of the house. Where had he been? Standing out of sight listening? Checking out the rest of the house? He turned to Alice, face puckered with worry.

"I didn't do it." She broke away from me and hurried toward him. "Honest to God."

Ross stepped close and put his arm around her. "We know that," he said urgently. "We believe you." I'd seen how protective he was with his wife. He was that way with Alice. As concerned as if she was his child.

But the sheriff might not believe her. With a start I realized how time raced. Deputies might be here at any moment. "Before you talk to anyone else, you need a lawyer," I said firmly.

Ross handed Alice his portable phone. With a shaking hand she dialed Information, then someone named George Dean, who I assumed must be the family lawyer. She might be upset, but she was pulling herself together, at least enough to look after herself. Good.

Meanwhile two things happened—one comforting, one predictable. Ted came walking toward us down the hill. Boy, was I glad to see him. Also, I heard a siren in the distance, coming closer. Help or more trouble?

CHAPTER
25

FRIDAY, 11:00 A.M.

"Does the fact that the deputies won't tell us anything mean that we're suspects?" I asked Ted as soon as we had a chance to compare what we'd been asked and what we'd learned. Rhetorical question. Of course we were.

They'd questioned us separately, and all we'd found out was that Anthony had been hit over the head with a heavy object.

The deputies had found Ted giving me moral support as I waited near Anthony's body, but Ted could tell them he'd just arrived. I'd found the body.

Neither of us had a good alibi for the earlier hours when Anthony must have died. We'd both been asleep, not even able to say positively that the other was asleep in the same bed. Lord knows poor Alice was in the worst shape of all. She'd put roses on the body—that still rocked me!

Ted and I walked back toward Azalea's house, passing the guilty bush of wild yellow roses by the road. The sher-

iff's investigators hadn't released Alice, which worried me.
I huffed a little going up the hill. I must exercise more.

"Anthony's murder will shock the pants off Azalea.
More than Hector's did," I said. "Even if Anthony tried
to make trouble for her. And may yet succeed, though dead.
She's known him a long time."

We hurried in the house and found Azalea and Pop and
Eudora at the kitchen table, all drinking coffee. Azalea
seemed subdued, no makeup on yet, still in her white ter-
rycloth robe. Pop wore a red shirt and red plaid pants, as
if to thumb his nose at death. Eudora, who always acted
out her thoughts, wore black shorts and a black T-shirt, as
if in summer mourning.

"I heard," Azalea blurted. "On the morning news. But
only a flash. Now, sit down and tell us everything about
Anthony. You saw him dead?"

"This is amazing," Pop stuck in. "We would all have
wanted Anthony to be killed, if somebody had to be wasted,
wouldn't we?"

"Wasted?" Where did he get that word? I wondered as
we sat down with them at the table. I felt sick remembering
the floating body. Hit over the head. Hector's head had
been crushed with a rock. Was it the same killer?

"Murder doesn't usually work out that well, does it,
Peaches?" Pop said cheerfully.

"You'd better not talk like that," I said dryly, "unless
we all have good alibis. I don't think a single one of us
has a witness to confirm where we were before six this
morning. That's when Anthony must have been murdered."

"May he rest in peace," Azalea said. "He wasn't a
happy young man. Let me pour you two a cup of coffee."

We both said thanks. I definitely needed coffee.

I wished I hadn't remembered reading about a killer who
was so sweet and good that she suddenly went berserk and
murdered her father. Did Azalea kill Anthony to end his
misery? No, she never would. Azalea was not crazy. She
poured us both coffee from the coffeemaker on the counter
and passed us sugar and cream.

With the comfort of coffee in hand, we told Azalea and Pop and Eudora all we knew about Anthony's death. I told the first part. Then Ted chimed in.

"They still have Alice down there where Anthony . . . Don't they?" Azalea asked. For once, she wasn't cheerful. "Oh, this is terrible," she said.

I told her Alice had called her lawyer. Perhaps they were waiting for him. "So she'll be protected," I said hopefully.

"We're going over to Adam Marlowe's," Ted said. "Maybe, if we're very lucky, Anthony told Adam if he meant to meet someone at the house—and, if so, who it was."

"Maybe," Pop said hopefully, "someone working on that old house is the head of a drug ring, or killed his wife in a fit of rage, or has kidnapped his own child. That happens, you know. Maybe the person was broke and couldn't pay his blackmail bill, and the killer arranged to meet Anthony and killed him, quick, before Anthony exposed him."

"That would be appropriate," Eudora said. I noticed she had on black lipstick. Talk about appropriate! But a death sentence seemed a little much for blackmail. Had Eudora known and hated Anthony somewhere before?

"Adam may know about Anthony, and he may also be at the point of conjuring up some crazy scheme to sell the old house," Ted said. "We need to stop him."

Azalea flinched. "He wouldn't! Not with Anthony gone—"

"This is the day," Ted said, "our time was up to bring him positive proof of who killed who. Adam's being pushed to sell the land. You can be sure of that. That house is on lovely rolling land, prime for development."

"I can't believe," Azalea said, "that Adam would destroy history. But then, I can't believe that anyone would ever suspect Alice of murder! Oh, why do catastrophes all happen at once?"

Was Azalea really using the word *catastrophe*?

"Adam is a strange man," I said. "He has a strange

pride.'' In a way, a very Tennessee kind of pride in family,
I realized. ''If he's still convinced that your ancestor killed
his ancestor, he could go off the deep end. And suppose he
jumps to some wild conclusion about who killed Anthony?'' As soon as I said that, I wished I hadn't. Azalea
went dead white.

''He could cause all kinds of trouble!'' she moaned.
''I'm coming with you to talk to Adam,'' she said firmly.
''If anybody can handle him, I can. You stay here, dear,
and call us if anything happens on this front,'' she said to
Pop, who was just opening his mouth, no doubt to an-
nounce that he'd join us, too.

''We need you here,'' Azalea told Pop urgently. ''Let us
know the minute Alice gets back.'' She kissed him on the
forehead.

Eudora patted Pop's hand. ''We'll be the first to know
what the sheriff's folks told Alice,'' she said in a hushed
expectant voice, ''and the sheriff may want to interview
us.'' She said *us* as if she spoke of royalty. ''I bet he'll be
along soon.''

That cheered Pop up about staying put. Eudora might
like to play parts, but she wasn't dumb. She knew what
made Pop happy. Action, attention, and suspense. Of
course, I worried about what Pop might say if he was questioned, but there was no way I could bottle him up.

So Ted and Azalea and I headed on the double for Adam
Figleaf Marlowe's horse-and-Bible farm. I felt better doing
something. I hoped Adam hadn't already done anything
precipitous while we were preoccupied with murder.

Ted drove. I ruminated. Adam was the person Anthony
would have been most likely to tell his business to, I reminded myself. For a minute that cheered me. It was a lead
to follow. But would he confide in anyone at all? It wasn't
likely. I remembered the closed look on his face and how
he always held his hands closed tight. People who hold
their hands shut keep their mouths shut.

''We will hope,'' Azalea said.

''The Kid said Anthony blackmailed Goat.'' I saw the

Kid in my mind's eye, punk streak in hair, a guarded look in his eyes.

"Yes," Ted said, "and the Kid was willing to meet Anthony at his house at an odd time of night, so he said. Or if that was a lie, why was he searching the house unless Anthony was blackmailing him, too?"

"And Pop could be right! That would explain why Anthony was murdered. Because he had other people's secrets carefully hidden somewhere," Azalea cried. "There would be better suspects than my little Alice!"

I was for that. "But a blackmailer has to have proof," I said, out loud but really to myself. "There was nothing like that in Anthony's house! But wait a minute," I went on, "I have an idea. No, not exactly. I have a hole in my head in the shape of an idea." I reached up and touched the ceiling of the car to remind myself not to let that idea get away. "I've heard something somewhere," I said, "about where Anthony might hide the blackmail proof." I tried so hard to think, I got a headache. No luck. I made myself relax. Still no luck.

"If Adam had a safe, he'd have let Anthony store anything he liked there. He wouldn't even have looked at it," Azalea said bitterly. "He trusted that boy too much." Things were really bad when Azalea got bitter. "But we'll find what he hid," she added. "When things get tough, the tough get going!"

A safe? Maybe a safe place! The hole in my head began to take a shape. If you can just hold on to the edge of an idea, it grows. I kept my arm up in the air as Rose had instructed, to anchor the idea. "Adam may not have a safe, but he has an attic!" I said. "It's hard to find things in attics! Like that woman had all those historic papers in her attic, and no one knew. There has to be some photograph of Goat misbehaving. Something like that, if Anthony got money to be quiet, right?"

Ted grinned. "A good thought!"

I began to get excited. "How can we search Adam's attic?"

"Don't worry," said Azalea. "We'll find a way. I know how to handle Adam."

"You can pull your hand down," Ted told me. "You caught the idea."

I felt downright gleeful at the hope of finding a better suspect than Alice! But not for long. In my mind, I saw Goat holding his child on his shoulder. I saw her laugh and look at him with eyes full of love. Suppose he killed Anthony to protect that child? Please. No.

"I hope to God that Goat didn't do it," I said. "If that stinking Anthony blackmailed one person, he may have blackmailed lots." I comforted myself with that. There had to be an alternate murderer I didn't know.

I looked out the car window at Adam's white fences and horses. The three of us walked up onto his white-pillared front porch, full of hope and fear. Azalea knocked.

Adam opened the door and said, "He was a soul capable of redemption, and he was cut down before he could repent." He stared at each of us accusingly. He was still dressed in pajamas and an old seersucker bathrobe. He looked harmless. I knew better.

"Repent what?" Ted asked.

Instead of answering, Adam said, "I understand that Alice was by Anthony's side when they found him, but she had some means of disposing of the gun."

"Who on earth have you talked to?" I asked, aghast. Where did he get this gun idea?

He turned to me. "I understand that you were nearby, too. Did you dispose of the gun?"

"I never saw a gun," I sputtered. "The deputies never mentioned a gun. He was hit over the head. Anyone could have come and met Anthony there in the night or the early dawn." I heard myself say, "Even you."

Azalea nudged me. Was I going too far? Adam glared at me, but he said, "Come in and sit down."

We followed him into the living room.

"It always impresses me what a lovely room this is," Azalea said, glancing from a photograph of an old lady in a lace collar to a portrait of a glossy bay horse, head held high. "So filled with the pictures of those you have loved." She sat on the couch and made herself comfortable with a small pillow behind her back.

"Who have you talked to?" I asked Adam again.

"I want to know how *you* are involved in this," he growled, and this time his frown matched his voice. "I don't have to answer questions!" He looked around at each of us. We all waited for him to make the next move. He was not a man who was good at silence.

He turned to Azalea, formal as a diplomat. "I am sorry you have been unable to persuade me that your ancestor didn't kill my ancestor. In fact, the proof seems solid the other way," he said. He actually sounded regretful. "I have signed a contract with the Anderson Construction Company, promising that if you can't prove your ancestor's innocence, I will sell them the house and land right away."

"But you have no real proof of who killed who," Ted said quickly. "Only a signet ring that wasn't on the skeleton's finger, just near the body. And the *B* on the ring matched Buddy's first initial, but signet rings usually match last initials. And furthermore, we have found the gun that killed whoever died in 1849. And the initials on it are E.R., not Buddy's or David's."

This was true, but it wasn't getting us to the attic. Patience, I told myself. All in good time.

"You have proof that gun fired the fatal shots? You have proof that gun was not borrowed or even stolen?" Adam demanded.

"Not yet," Ted said.

"Certainly," Adam said, "the fact that Alice has killed Anthony—with a gun or any other way—I'm not nit-picky—means that she believed he had the solid proof to get the house." He smiled with pleasure at his own twisted logic.

"Alice had no reason to kill Anthony." I began to get mad. "And the way you're acting proves it. The fact that he's dead is no help to her or Azalea, not at all." Besides, if anyone had the motive to kill him for endangering the house, it was Azalea. But I didn't say that out loud.

"You had until today to bring me proof!" The old man began to sound petulant. "You failed."

"We haven't failed," I said. "We have been delayed because someone committed murder. We have discovered that there was enough gold in the house to tempt thieves. We have the name of a preacher whose diary is in a box of papers at the archives. A preacher who could even have been on the scene when the shooting happened in 1849." After all, why shouldn't the Reverend Baird in that newspaper clipping be HIM? "Ted is going to go through those papers. By the end of the day we may have the proof that your ancestor killed Azalea's ancestor." I wanted to say, What we need to know most is who killed Anthony. But if Adam had made up his mind it was Alice, what then?

Why wasn't Ted putting in his two bits' worth? Because he'd vanished. I hadn't seen him leave, but he was gone. The old man didn't seem to notice.

"I don't believe you," the old man said, turning pink, "and I'm going to sign the final contract shortly. If you don't get out of here and leave, I'm going to burn that house down. It would be good practice for the fire department, and it's still technically my house." Could he be serious? That fanatic light I didn't trust burned in his eyes.

"Why, Adam," Azalea said sweetly, "that's not like you. That's not reasonable." She got up, walked over to him, and took both his hands in hers. "Why, I remember when you were accused of having something to do with fixing a horse race—you kept your cool and waited, and the other people didn't have the proof they needed, and you prevailed, just by being cool."

By now Adam was bright red. He pulled back from her. "Those dirty, lying, low-down—" He sputtered and ran out of words. "You know I never did anything underhanded. You know that, Azalea." He quivered with anger. I had the feeling he might burst into tears.

Where was Ted? Gone off to the bathroom? Or gone to

search? He wouldn't even know how to get to the attic. But Ted was good at finding his way anywhere.

"Tell us exactly what you think happened to Anthony," I said. At least I could keep the old man distracted.

"If Alice asked Anthony to meet her anywhere, he would have gone. He was mad at Alice but he was sweet on Alice."

"He had a strange way of showing it," Azalea said.

Adam nodded. "Yes, he did."

"So what happened next?" I asked.

"Alice invited him to the house after work hours, when it's deserted, in order to kill him," Adam said. "She killed him and felt guilty, so she covered him with roses. Peaches helped her dispose of the gun. Now all of you get out of here."

"You have no right to order us out!" Azalea said. I never heard her sound so confrontational.

"Get out!" Adam shouted even louder. Then he looked around wildly. "Where is your damned husband?" he demanded, eagle eyes riveted on me. "If he's sneaking around my house, I'll kill him." The way his eyes blazed, I wasn't entirely sure that was an empty threat.

CHAPTER
26

NOON

"Here I am, Mr. Marlowe," Ted said. "Are you hiding something in your bathroom you don't want me to see?" He stood in the doorway at the end of the living room, which must lead to the bathroom—and, I hoped, to the stairs to the attic.

Adam was fortunately so upset he didn't ask questions—he just kept yelling, "Get out!" He opened the drawer to a pretty little table with a white leather Bible on it and pulled out a pistol. He waved it at us. "Get out! Get out!"

Never challenge a nut if you can help it. We hurried outside, jumped in the car, and took off. Ted and me in the front. Ted driving. Azalea in back.

We drove out past the white fences and the horses, all so deceptively peaceful.

"Did you get to the attic? Did you find anything?" I asked Ted. I wished for a trunk of pictures of people in compromising situations: picking pockets, in the arms of their best friends' husbands, bashing heads. You name it, and Anthony would have photographed it. None of them would be Alice, and all would be likely suspects. But no. I'd better rethink that. Suppose those pictures made trouble for some of my favorite people? If they were evidence, we'd still have to give them to the sheriff.

"There are dozens of boxes in the attic," Ted said. "There's a dressmaker's dummy, stacks of magazines, and a few old rolled-up rugs. I didn't have time to go through the boxes, but they didn't seem to hold papers as much as old clothes and bric-a-brac and books and magazines. But papers could have been under those."

I was disappointed. The attic had begun to seem like a sure bet. But maybe somehow we could find out what was in the boxes.

The car phone rang. That would be Pop, curious about what we found. I picked it up.

Not Pop. It was Alice. "They are through with me for now," she said, sounding discouraged. "I don't know what they think. They just made me tell my story over and over, and all about how I knew Anthony." Small silence. I wondered if she'd held the hurtful details back.

"I asked the photo shop to rush those pictures," she said. "They must be ready by now. Be sure to pick them up on the way home." Oh, yes, the gun pictures. She'd dropped those off on the way to take Azalea to the hospital. That seemed so long ago, I'd almost forgotten the pictures. How on earth could she remember those now, in the midst of our troubles?

"Come as quick as you can," she said, sounding more upbeat. "Eudora's boyfriend is here. And tell Azalea I'm all right, so far."

If there was one thing I was not ready to do, it was to entertain Eudora's boyfriend. That's what I thought first. Then it came to me: Eudora's boyfriend is the antique-gun expert! That's why the pictures could be important. Might even help us understand Anthony's death in a roundabout way. If the past and present were connected, Eudora's boy-friend might have the key. Hallelujah!

We stopped at Capital Photo, and I ran in and picked up the pictures, blessing them for the rush job.

I opened the envelope and was delighted. The prints were clear, showing the elegant little pistol with its silver etching and gold inlay, the pistol that put four bullets in the man who died. What kind of anger did that show? Nick's expert might eventually learn a lot from the gun itself, but we could have instant gratification and learn something about it now.

Ted slowed as we passed the old house. No human being in sight. The house sat solid, in contrast to the electric-yellow crime tape, all around it once again. I hoped that Adam Marlowe was too moralistic, too set on the rules, to cross the crime-scene tape with kerosene and matches in hand. At least not until the deputy or whoever had talked to him. By then, Incendiary Adam might have cooled off. I hoped.

Or maybe we would somehow have learned from the gun that Azalea's ancestor definitely did not kill Adam's.

The gun had looked solid, well made. Expensive, I imagined. Buddy didn't have much money, and he drank.

David did not sound like a man who would lose his head. But I had his description from the girl who loved him. She would be prejudiced. I'd noticed in newspaper descriptions of crimes how often the neighbors of the killer said they were surprised, that the killer had seemed like a quiet young man—or a quiet young woman.

So, which man lost his head and killed another back in 1849—evidently in a fit of rage? I couldn't imagine how the gun could tell us that. And yet I had illogically high hopes.

CHAPTER
27

12:45 P.M.

I knew what Eudora's boyfriend the gun expert would look like. He'd be heavyset. He'd be somewhat somber, with jowls. He'd have gimlet eyes. After all, his business was to know about killing, about how to do it in the historically correct way.

Of course he didn't look the way I'd imagined at all. He was one of those slender young men who seem to be in love with facts. He had curly brown hair and eager blue eyes. Even his hands were not those of a heavy. His fingers tapered slightly, though the tips were squarish, and the flesh was high and rounded under his thumb. My cousin Fern the hand reader would have said he was emotional with that high padding, versatile with those tapered fingers, and that a small hand like his meant he liked to think big. In other words, enthusiastic! I supposed advising movie people was *big*. Fern would have said his long little finger meant he'd be good at telling stories and, if necessary, lies. Interesting to look at hands and watch to see if what they "said" came true. He certainly had no reason to tell me lies. Not that I knew of.

We'd come in the front door and found him in Azalea's living room. Azalea was showing him the scrapbook of the old house, with Pop and Eudora in eager attendance, all sunk in the depths of Azalea's overstuffed chairs and couch, except for Pop, who was in his wheelchair. Well, I thought, good for Eudora! She'd outdone herself in the boyfriend department.

"We sure need to save an interesting house like this," Boyfriend was telling Azalea and flashing a pleased grin. "I hope I can help."

Eudora stood up and introduced us: "This is Harvey August. These are Mr. and Mrs. Ted Holleran."

"Peaches and Ted," Pop said. "And Peaches writes under the name Peaches Dann. Dann is the name of her husband who died. You should buy her book!"

A literary plug is nice, but this wasn't the time.

I said Harvey sure had come at the right moment, and looked in my pocketbook for the photos of the gun. Good grief, I'd left them somewhere. By the grace of God, they were still in the car. I guess I should use Travelcount even when I'm not traveling. I brought the pictures in and laid them out on the coffee table. He sat on the couch in front of them. I pulled up a chair to the side of the table.

"Oh," he said, "this is a wonderful pistol. A rich man's gun. Look at the gold inlay."

"Tell us about it," I said.

He picked up a picture where I'd managed to show the business end of the pistol. "This is an Allen and Thurber pepperbox," he said without hesitation. "What year was it buried?"

"We think in 1849," I said.

"It was a state-of-the-art pocket pistol that year," he said. "Point thirty-four-inch caliber, patented in 1845, and capable of shooting a bullet from each barrel before reloading.

You know those long coats men wore? This would slip right in the pocket.''

Boy, what a memory he had! I was impressed and jealous.

"Was that a usual gun to have here in Tennessee?'' Ted asked.

"Very *un*-usual,'' he said. "It would stick out like a sore thumb anywhere, especially on the frontier.''

And perhaps identify the killer, I figured.

"Would it have unique bullets you could match with it?'' I asked.

"No, not at all. Just ordinary round bullets. You see, a pepperbox was like a revolver. You loaded all the chambers, and they all turned. So you could fire five shots without reloading. Some pepperboxes fired six.''

He studied the other pictures. "Not a military weapon,'' he said. "Not powerful enough to shoot a horseman at a hundred yards. This was a close-contact gun. This gave a gambler a chance to back out of a saloon, shooting.'' He smiled broadly, and I was sure he'd created scenes like that. Gambler backs out, shooting, while hero rescues bar girl, who turns out to be a faithful virgin at heart. Or maybe she's a diamond in the rough who dies later to save his life so he can marry the surprisingly sexy schoolteacher. In real life, we'd need more than a gun to protect Alice if she was accused of murder!

"So if a man had been seen with this gun, people would be likely to remember it,'' I said. "If they found it at the scene of the murder, they'd know who the killer was likely to be.''

"He'd be hanged in short order,'' said Harvey enthusiastically. "But there'd be no question who he was with his initials on the gun.''

But the small gold initials, E.R., inlaid on the gun handle, weren't Buddy's or David's. Would someone lend an elegant expensive gun like that? Neither Buddy nor David sounded like the type to steal. So who owned that gun?

"We figure on a vicious crime,'' I said. "There was one

shot in the wall and four in the skeleton. Whoever shot, he fired again and again.'' Why had he been so angry?

"Not necessarily vicious," said Harvey. He pointed to the five barrels, which made the barrel end of the gun as thick as the handle.

"You'd load 'em all, and if there was not enough grease in each chamber, a spark would go into the other ones, and the pistol would chain-fire. It would discharge all the bullets at once."

"Chain-fire?" Ted asked.

Harvey explained. "The chambers were designed to fire one bullet at a time, first one and then the next, set off by a spark when the trigger was pulled. But when sparks leaked to all the chambers at once, they all fired.

"Revolvers also chain-fired sometimes," he said, smiling at the picture as if he was defending the pepperbox. "Revolvers were even worse for that. The revolver had a frame, and the bullets would sometimes hit that and blow up the gun and destroy it. Not good for the man who held the gun. At least these pepperbox bullets all went flying into the victim. So your killer fires once and misses. That bullet goes in the wall. Then he fires again, and all the rest of the bullets discharge at once. Were there broken ribs?" he asked hopefully.

I described them.

"This gun would do it," he said, blue eyes shining with pride. He obviously loved the old gun, even in a picture.

"So a rich man would have owned this gun," I said. That didn't fit.

"You're looking for a man who always wanted the most up-to-date gun and could pay for it. Or he could be a successful gambler," he said. "There was lots of gambling on the frontier. A man who lost a gun like this had probably lost his most valued possession." He said that wistfully, sorry for that man long ago.

"He may have lost it to a man who ruined his life with it," I said. "What's the old expression? You win some, you lose some. Sometimes you win and lose at the same time."

CHAPTER
28

1:30 P.M. That Day

Ted, who sometimes skips lunch, went straight to the archives, where Azalea had urged him to search hard for proof from the past.

The rest of us grabbed a sandwich, then Pop took a nap, exhausted from the excitement. Eudora went off with What's His Name, the antique-gun expert, in great excitement to meet the casting director of his movie.

Which left Alice, Azalea, and me sitting in Azalea's living room, wondering what to do next. Alice was jumpy, as if she expected the sheriff to arrive at the door with handcuffs at any moment.

At least we were comfortable. Azalea's chairs were so soft that mine sighed when I sank into it. Her couch was deep, with big pillows to lean against. Alice chose the couch, took off her shoes, and tucked her feet up. She looked very young and vulnerable, still in her white shirt and shorts. Alice, who'd strewn yellow roses on the man who meant to do her wrong. Because she'd known him when he was first hurt. Before he hardened. Her first thought when she saw him dead had been sorrow, not self-exoneration. Or so she said. I hoped she wouldn't have to pay the price for being sentimental.

Azalea, who never worried, was worried about Alice. She sighed and clutched the smooth arms of the big rocker where she sat straight and did not lean on the cushion.

"Azalea," I said, "Adam Marlowe feels a debt to you because you stuck by his son. He may hurt you because he's so darn rigid, but he likes you." I noticed a picture of Azalea's husband—Adam's son, Hunt—on the table near her chair. "He's grateful to you," I emphasized, "while Ted and I make him mad. Could you go to see him alone? Could you tell him right up front that Anthony may have been involved in blackmail? He might believe you. Ask him if he knows of a place where Anthony could have hidden the proofs that a blackmailer needs. Then maybe you can get around to asking if you can look in the attic. Could you do that?"

Azalea thought about this for a long time. She stared into space as if she was seeing that scene in the air. Then she said, "No. That won't work." Hey, where was her faith and determination?

"Azalea," Alice said, "they think I killed Anthony. Me!" She hugged one of the big sofa cushions to her like a shield. "I just know it. They're looking for proof I did it. But I didn't." Amazing how Alice had shrunk. She appeared so much smaller on Azalea's couch than she had in the mountains with Ed. As if she was wool and we'd put her through the dryer on *hot*.

"We need to help Alice," I said, "and we need to keep Adam from doing something crazy. He believes Anthony was killed because he was proving the house should belong to him. Adam threatened to burn down the old house. You saw that gleam in his eye."

"Only a fool would believe that Anthony was killed for a dumb reason like that," Azalea said, rocking her chair forward like she might take off. "So how can he believe it?" she asked angrily. "How?"

"But he does believe it," I said. "He said so."

"I know how," Alice said. "Adam can't admit he's been wrong. He never has. Even the time he hired that crooked trainer. He said the man was framed. Adam is a pill. He let Anthony fool him. And if Anthony was such a fine person, like Adam thinks, who'd kill him but me?"

"We have to find out," I said.

"The past is mixed up in this," Azalea said again. She began to rock as if the chair could soothe her. "Ted will find something in those papers at the library. He'll prove that what happened back in 1849 is the clue to what's happening now. And it has nothing to do with Alice. Nothing!" I half expected her to sing "Tomorrow Is a Better Day," but she only said, "I know he'll do it."

"He could find some clue," I said doubtfully. "But we can't count on it." Who knew whether the Reverend Baird, if he was HIM, ever wrote down anything about the men who vanished, even if he was there to lend moral support to Annie Thomason the whole time. "That still leaves Alice as the A-number-one suspect for Anthony's murder."

Azalea took a deep breath. She took a long look at Alice clutching her pillow and a long look at me sitting forward on the couch, wanting to take action. She straightened her shoulders. I expected her to say something like, We have to believe that the sheriff's folks will do a good job and find the right answer. I thought I'd scream if she did.

"Adam always leaves his back door unlocked," she said. "Like we all used to do out here in the country. If I lure Adam out of the house, will you and Alice search the attic?"

I guess the good thing about being a super-optimist like Azalea is that you don't mind risks. I mind, but when I get curious enough, and sure enough that someone is going to be hurt in a way that's not fair, I get a little reckless.

"Don't worry," Azalea said, serene again. "If Adam finds out you two are searching his house, I'll say I told you I was sure he would say yes. And you're lucky because this is the housekeeper's day off. That woman would defend Adam to the death from any intrusion. She was his horse trainer's wife. The trainer left, but she and her daughter stayed. They live in that little cottage out back." She stood up, and the rocking chair rocked behind her. "I'll tell Adam that I knew he wouldn't want his own great-granddaughter to be accused of murder, so I told you to search. Then he can't say you snuck in his house without permission."

Yeah, and I'm the Easter bunny.

"If I'm caught, you just tell him I offered to search instead of Alice because Alice is in enough trouble," I said. "Also, tell him I talked to someone who suspected Anthony of blackmail, so I knew what to look for." That was an exaggeration. Never mind.

"I'll call Adam right now," Azalea said. When she took to being devious, she dived right in. "I'll tell him he needs to come and look at something at the old house which will prove one way or the other whether Alice killed Anthony."

Alice and I both sat up and said, "What?" in chorus.

"Oh, I'll think of something when we get there," she said with a shrug. "When he gets curious I can handle him." She smiled to herself. "When I was a little girl, I knew Adam's mother. She was old as the hills but nice to all the kids. We lived on the same street in Franklin. You know what she told me? Adam was so curious that when she did that old trick about 'I bet you I can make you say *who*, and if I can't, I know who can!' he fell for it every time. Can you imagine that?"

She marched right to the telephone. She picked it up and dialed with her index finger. She said, "Hello, Adam, this is Azalea. You and I have been friends too long to quarrel. I have something to tell you that I think you'll want to know. I'll be right over." She hung up fast and then winced. "Dern ribs," she said. "Won't let me forget them.

"Never give a stubborn man a chance to reply," she

added as the phone began to ring. "Answer on the sixth ring and tell him I'm gone," she said to Alice. "Start for Adam's house in fifteen minutes," she told me. "I'll keep him occupied for an hour if I have to sit on him." That must be a figure of speech, since her cracked rib was better but still strapped and still made her wince with every sudden motion. She paused at the door. "You, Alice, stay right here. Don't leave Harwood alone." She marched out, and the door slammed.

On the sixth ring, Alice picked up the phone and did what Azalea had said. "You can tell my grandmother that when she gets there, Grampy," she said, and hung up.

Alice grinned. "And some people think Azalea is wishy-washy!"

I remembered how Azalea'd zeroed in on Pop. "She knows what she wants," I said dryly. And what I wanted was for this not to end up as a disaster for Pop or Azalea or Alice. Or me.

I went to Pop's room and peeked at him. He was still asleep, quite peacefully, sheet drawn up to his chin. No sign of nightmares. Pop is an optimist, too, in his way. He never expects the worst. He leaves that up to me. Particularly when he's in the middle of an adventure. Leaves me to wonder what would happen if Alice was convicted of murder and the old house was destroyed because Adam *Figleaf* was just plain pigheaded and self-righteous and too handy with matches.

I was damn well going to do everything in my power to see that those things didn't happen.

I went in the kitchen and got a pair of rubber gloves. If I was going to take up a life of crime, I should be circumspect. I put them in my pocket, ready when needed. I timed my departure just like Azalea said by the clock over the mantel, the one held up by two cherubs. I drove along our road quite cheerfully until I realized I'd lost the sheet of paper that said where to turn and what to do next. I called Alice on the car phone. Busy. Oh, boy. I picked a road that looked friendly and turned in by a huge dead tree that looked like a modern sculpture. I wrote a big *R* on my notepad to show I'd turned right. Not a bad road. I was hopeful. After about five minutes I worried. I should have come to some landmark I recognized. I called Alice again. Line still busy. The trouble was this rolling country all looked a lot alike. After about eight or so minutes I came to a huge green barn right by the road that I knew had not been on the road to Adam's. Time was passing. Now I had to go back to the place where I turned off. So I reversed myself, grateful that the dead tree would tell me when I got back to my original turn. Then I had my right-right rule. Retracing is simple to folks with a good sense of direction. But I need a rule to help. If you turn off a road to the right, when you come back turn right again. Then you'll be going the same way you were before you turned off. Always works. I tried Alice once more. Still busy. Now, where was the next turn? A crossroads loomed. I tried Alice one last time. At last she answered. "Ed called. I'm sorry." I was sure she tried to be sorry. She sounded euphoric. Oh, well. I asked her the time. I'd left my watch by the bathtub. I had wasted twenty minutes. I wrote down her directions and drove as fast as I dared.

Of course, I recognized Adam's house with the horses leaning over the fence. I debated whether to park in front of the house. If I hid my car, Azalea would have trouble saying I knew I had permission to search. On the other hand, I could hardly believe that Adam would accept her explanation that she told me it was okay to look through his house without his say-so. I parked on the road down from his driveway among the cedars and ledgy rocks, and trotted across a meadow full of horses to the house. The horses all ran off to the other end of the field, but they had left horse droppings I had to avoid. An obstacle course. Perspiration dripped in my eyes, and I wiped my forehead. This was a scorcher. I couldn't stop to cool off. I'd already wasted twenty minutes. I could count on three quarters of an hour max to search.

I rang the front doorbell in case the housekeeper was

there. The housekeeper who moved as silently as a cat. No answer. I went around and sneaked in through the big old-fashioned kitchen with the white enamel table in the middle. Fortunately, the driveway was long enough so no one was likely to have seen me arrive except the horses. I called out, "Yoo-hoo," just to be sure the house was empty. No answer. I looked for the living room and the door Ted had disappeared through in the morning. That seemed days ago. I felt as if the eyes of all Adam's nicely framed family and horses were following me.

I found the hallway where he'd been, then a staircase, and hurried up to the second floor. I stopped and put on the rubber gloves, pink, ugly, and hot. Oh well. Several rooms surrounded the stairwell, but I couldn't see a stair to the attic. I opened each door. The first was a simply furnished bedroom, the second was completely empty, and the white walls needed paint. The third door led to a narrow staircase with boxes, mostly of magazines, but one with empty glass jars along the side of the stairs. There was just room for me to pick my way past. At the top of the stairs was a steamy hot room with a slanted ceiling, and boxes on every inch of the floor except a thin path through. It smelled of age and neglect. The boxes went right over to the eaves, and were stacked two boxes high in some places. They teetered at odd angles because some of the bottom boxes were not carefully packed and sealed, but were full of odd-shaped junk like an electric fan. I could have used it, but I didn't see an outlet. Rolled rugs were in a stack on the right. Oriental rugs. I shuddered to think of the moths. The dressmaker's dummy stood at the end of the room farthest from me in the highest part.

There were too many boxes to search in forty-five minutes—not without leaving the place a telltale mess. I should pick the ones where the dust was disturbed, of course. But up here in the attic where there were no open windows, and where I guessed even the door rarely opened, there was almost no dust. Where would Anthony hide whatever? Somewhere not too hard to reach but where the old man wouldn't be likely to happen on it. Under magazines? I began to look in the boxes of *National Geographic, People,* etc. I got hotter and sweatier. I started to look at my watch to see how fast time was passing. Oh yes! I'd left it on the bathtub again. I must get a waterproof watch. This was ridiculous. I didn't want to stop looking in order to go see the time on the clocks below. The best thing was to hurry.

I finished the boxes of magazines, surviving the temptation to stop and look at Reagan's inauguration, for example, as reported by *People,* and went through several boxes of books. Nothing out of the ordinary. I felt let down. Suppose there were no papers of Anthony's in this attic? All this for nothing. My hands were sweating like they were in dishwater. I moved down to boxes with clothing in them. Stuff that must have belonged to family members, now long gone. Yellowed shirts, a velvet dress, even an old black lace shawl.

I began to listen with all my strength. At least a half hour had passed. I had to leave soon, but not empty-handed. I got more careless. The boxes looked a little tossed, but not too bad. A movement caught my eye. The door to the attic opened. Mary the housekeeper stood in the door. In her right hand was the pistol that Adam had waved at us. Black and ugly, more businesslike than the pepperbox.

"Why are you here?" she asked evenly. "Mr. Adam never lets anybody in this house when he's not here." She stared at the pink rubber gloves.

"He let his daughter's husband, Anthony, come in, didn't he?" I asked.

"That gives you no right," she said, standing perfectly self-assured in the sea of boxes. "Walk in front of me." She waved me toward the stairs.

I did not want to confront crazy Adam. And even without the gun, Mary was built like a champion wrestler.

I also did not want to get shot. Mary leveled the gun at me. "Walk."

"Anthony was a blackmailer," I said. I watched for her

reaction. "I want to find the papers he used to get money from people." No reaction. "Listen, Adam's great-granddaughter may be accused of murder if I can't prove that lots of people had a reason to kill Anthony."

"Alice?" she asked, still weighing me with her eyes. "Alice is a good girl. She wouldn't kill. Now, *I* could have killed that man. But I was with my sister last night. The paper said he was killed last night. It was my night off."

Her eyes swept the attic. "Why are you looking here?" Her eyes demanded an answer quick.

"I knew Adam Marlowe had an attic," I said, "because he said he kept his daughter's things in the attic and I thought—" And then it came to me. "The blackmail stuff must be hidden in the things that belonged to Anthony's wife. Mr. Marlowe would certainly have let Anthony look through those. Please let me look," I begged.

"Anthony was a bad man," she said. "He gave my daughter a baby. He said it wasn't his." Was she softening? But the gun still pointed.

She reached in her pocket and took out a small stainless-steel turnip-shaped object, hanging from a chain. She held the end of the chain between her thumb and index finger, stared me in the eye, and waited. What on earth? Time was passing. Slowly, slowly, the steel turnip began to move, began to circumscribe a circle. She smiled. "Clockwise. You tell the truth."

I thanked God the turnip, whatever it was, liked me. I said, "Please let me look." But I knew it might already be too late.

"Mr. Adam is good to me," she said, "but that Anthony was evil. And Alice is a good girl."

She waved the gun at the dressmaker dummy. "Under there."

I was weak-kneed with relief, but spurred on by hope. Yes. That was a box the dummy stood on, a closed box. I picked up the dummy.

I heard a car drive in. I caught my breath.

"Go out the back door," she said. "I'll keep him in the

front.'' And quickly but silently she ran downstairs. I moved the dummy aside, brushed the sweat off my forehead, and opened the box. Books. Oversized ones. *The Historical Atlas of the United States, Birds in Our Lives.* Oh, great! I sagged with disappointment. But I looked deeper. What appeared at first glance to be a large flat book was not a book at all. It was a box. My heart beat faster. A box about the size and shape of the one that had held Annie's letters. But this was cardboard, not wood. I opened it as quickly as I could in the clumsy rubber gloves. There inside I found a newspaper clipping that told about ancient Indian artifacts found when Hector did a dig on the property where a famous country musician was restoring an old house. But what was wrong with that? Perhaps this stuff was all innocent. Under the clipping were picture folders. The kind that brides' portraits come in.

I opened a folder. There was a photograph of the same automobile accident I had seen hanging framed above Anthony's desk. But this picture was from farther back, so the license-plate number on the car that seemed to have hit the other car could be seen. License-plate number. That would give power to blackmail. Good. But now I had to get out of here quick with the box. Downstairs I could hear the rumble of Adam's voice. I prayed Mary really would keep him in the front of the house while I sneaked out the back.

I took the small box out, closed the bigger box of books, and set the dummy back on it. And then nearby on the floor I saw a two-handled shopping bag, the kind that stands up by itself. On the top was crammed a smooshed-up newspaper. Odd. I leaned over and pulled the paper out with my free hand. In the bottom of the bag was broken wood. Two sharp pieces. The ladder rungs! And down in the very bottom of the bag was a tube of glue. ROGERS ALL-PURPOSE GLUE, it said. Not Super Glue, which might have mended a rung safely, but all-purpose which would leave it almost sure to break with weight. Why on earth were they here? Oh, Anthony had left them, I could see that. And if he had the glue as well as the rung, he must have set the trap. But why not burn these things or throw them off in the woods? Why have them here to be found?

Did he half want to be caught? Or did he save that broken ladder rung and glue to plant them and throw suspicion on somebody else. Immediately I knew that was it. That was true to character. He had simply been killed before he had the chance to frame some innocent person for his own meanness.

All that flashed through my mind in nothing flat. I left the two-handled bag to whoever found it. I ran across the attic and hurried down the stairs. I almost knocked over the bottom box of magazines on the steps and said a prayer of thanks when I managed to catch it. My heart was thumping. I heard footsteps. My heart stopped. Maybe I could convince Adam that what I'd found was worth trespassing. But he was too unpredictable to take a chance. The footsteps went back toward the front of the house. I ran down to the first floor. I found my way through the other end of the hall from the stairway into the kitchen.

I ran out and dashed for the patch of woods across the horse pasture where my car was hidden. Several horses whinnied as they ran away before my flight. Don't let Adam come to see why, I prayed. I jumped over horse droppings left and right. If I stepped in one, I could slide and fall. I almost tripped on a low rocky ledge. But I caught myself before I fell, and before I dropped the box. I reached the woods panting, and was so glad to see my car I almost cried. I put the box in the trunk and threw an old shirt of Ted's that was in there on top of it. I shut and locked the trunk and got in the car.

I started the car up and drove out into the road as quietly as possible. I turned and hadn't gone far away from the Marlowe house when a sheriff's department car came toward the house and passed by me.

Was what I'd done stealing? Removing evidence? Would the turnip stay my friend, and Mary keep her mouth shut? I couldn't take the box back now. Besides, I had to read the contents.

CHAPTER
29

As I passed the old house I noticed the crime-scene tape was down again. A man was standing in front of the house with his head bowed as if he was praying. When he heard my car, he quickly turned and looked at me, erasing a look of anguish. Could I be wrong about that? It was Ross the Boss.

I sure wanted to get back to Azalea's and look at those papers. But something was very wrong here. I pulled into the driveway near him, got out of the car, and said, "Are you all right?"

If I'd been correct about the anguish, he'd largely recovered, though he still seemed sad. "I was thinking about all the tragedy in this house," he said. He sighed. "This morning's paper had a story about a woman of seventy who was mugged and a twelve year old who shot his brother. There's a hell of a lot of evil in human beings. I guess there always has been."

Good grief. Philosophy. He needed to be talked out of his gloom. "And also there's good in us," I said, working to believe it. "Most of us try." He seemed so solid, so feet-on-the-ground, and yet so sensitive. I'd seen that in the way he protected his wife.

He shrugged. He crossed his arms as if he was cold. "When I was a child I believed that most people were good and kind and I had to work to be that way, too. I wish I believed that now." Yes, there was anguish. He couldn't keep it out of his voice.

"You do a job that's good for the world," I said. "You try to save history." I waved at the house. "Some people make bombs."

He put his shoulders back in a determined way and changed the subject. "I'm here," he said, "because there's something I wanted to show you and Azalea. But before I got up to her house to tell you both, she showed up and now here you are!" He shook his head in amazement.

"She showed up with Adam Marlowe?" I asked.

"Yes," he said, frowning. "Adam said he'd be glad when this house of death was gone!"

"He's a little nutty," I said. I was glad he hadn't brought his matches. "But what have you found?"

Ross pointed at a window to the left of the front entrance, an old one with wavy panes of glass. "I found *this* last thing yesterday," he said, "but I had to pick up Rose. She hates to drive after dark. I figured if this had been there a hundred and fifty years, it could wait for us to look one day longer. I stopped to look at it once more on the way up to Azalea's house, and then you both showed up right here."

What was new about the window? Except that neither that nor anything else in the house would be there one more day if Adam had his way. "Azalea thinks that somebody killed Anthony because of what happened in 1849," I said. "Are you going to show me something related to those days?" So get on with it, I thought.

"If history causes murder, this could be important," Ross said.

"So?" I waited.

"I don't know how we missed this for so long, but look." He pointed to one of the small square panes. I looked closely. There did seem to be some scratches on it. He reached in his pocket and pulled out a magnifying glass. "Maybe this will help."

I held the glass out from the window, and I realized the scratches were writing. Faint, but definitely words. Two above two. "The top two words," I said, "are *Annie Thomason.* On a window? How odd. The bottom two words are *David Holden.* But this is glass. How did someone write their names on glass? And when?"

"It was a custom here in Tennessee in the mid-nineteenth century," he said, "for the bride and groom, at the time of their wedding, to do that—to write their names on a window in their new home, using the bride's diamond ring."

"And David and Annie did it when they were engaged," I said, suddenly enthralled.

He shook his head. "That was never the custom. Perhaps they were secretly married."

"Perhaps he came back," I said. "In secret. Perhaps they were married in secret. I want that to be true! But it doesn't make any sense."

"You have another mystery," he said. "I wish all mysteries were as pleasant as that."

His words jarred me. Why? Because they seemed phony. I still had the feeling he was here for some other reason I needed to know. Some unhappy reason. But he'd brought a magnifying glass to show us the writing. So, what was true?

"But why did you come here now?" I asked.

"I was passing by on my way home," he said. "I felt drawn here. I felt that if I came, maybe I'd have some inspiration about what happened here. I know that's foolish. But that's how I felt."

"And did you?" I asked.

"No," he said. "All I felt was terribly sad. This is a house of sadness. I was thinking about Hector and what a waste it was for him to be killed."

"Nobody seems to grieve for Anthony," I said. "I believe Anthony was actually blackmailing several people. Have you seen anything that might make you think that?"

He sighed deeply. "I believe Anthony would have enjoyed harassing any poor soul that he could scare," he said. "But God knows how you'd prove that."

"How about Hector?" I asked, remembering the clipping about Hector in Anthony's blackmail file. The clipping had seemed perfectly innocent, just about a dig for a famous man. But why was it in that file? "What was there Hector could have wanted to hide? That Anthony could have blackmailed him for?" I asked.

"I didn't know him well," Ross said. He fidgeted as if he didn't want to talk about that. "His father was a well-known archaeologist, but not active in anything I know much about. Something about the Mayas in Mexico. But Hector was very touchy about whether he was good enough to live up to that. If you could prove he cheated or fell short in any way, you'd have him by the short hairs. If someone tried to blackmail Hector, I'd half suspect Hector of killing *them*."

Yes, I remembered how Hector needed to feel important, to be admired, even for the arrowheads he found. I suspected that if you humiliated Hector, he would be wild with rage. But Hector was dead before Anthony. So what did that prove?

"How did Azalea act when she came here with Adam Marlowe?" I asked.

Ross liked that subject better. He relaxed. "Strangely," he said. "I told her I had something I wanted to show her that might be important, and she shot me one of those please-go-along-with-what-I-say looks and said, 'Yes, that's what we came to see!' So I showed them the writing, and Azalea told Adam, 'See, the handwriting is the same, on the top name and the bottom name. She wrote both names to prove she married him in her heart. Because she knew somehow that her David was dead.'''

"And Adam?"

"Said she'd wasted his time with a lot of hogwash."

I could imagine.

I borrowed the magnifying glass and looked at the words again. Yes, the handwriting was the same for both names.

But, boy, I must not forget that Azalea could think fast. I must not forget that when she felt it was necessary she could lie like a trouper. If she could persuade Adam Marlowe she had brought him to see something that, in fact, she hadn't even known existed, what else could she have lied about?

CHAPTER
30

I didn't stop to look at the papers in the car. Suppose a deputy came along. I'd be a sitting duck. I took the box into Azalea's house, through the back door into the kitchen.

Alice was sitting at the kitchen table—everybody's favorite spot. She said, "Pop's asleep, taking a nap." I swear he sleeps twice as much in Tennessee, probably because when he's awake, he's in a constant state of excitement.

Just for a second I stood there, looking beyond Alice out the window at the sassy zinnias in Azalea's garden, feeling anything but sassy, and not sure what to do next. I had the blackmail box under my arm. I felt furtive. "I may have been a fool," I said to Alice. "I stole some papers and pictures from Adam's attic. I think they prove blackmail." I heard myself and was half-surprised. "I guess I'd better be sure the deputies don't know I have that box! Not until I look at it."

I didn't explain that by the time I found the stuff, I had

to leave quickly, because I got lost on the way to Adam's house and that took twenty minutes. I wanted to kick myself in the butt. Actually, that's not easy.

"Where's the proof?" Alice cried. "Let me see!"

But I knew I'd made a mistake to bring that box—that hot box—inside the house. I wasn't thinking clearly.

"The sheriff might show up at any moment and decide to search—I can't look at blackmail papers here. And you just forget I mentioned them." My eye hit a handmade sampler on the wall. It said VIRTUE IS ITS OWN REWARD. I read it out loud. "How about taking risks?" I asked myself out loud. "Is that its own reward?"

"Listen, I'd have done the same thing. Grabbed those papers. I think you're wonderful! And you did it to help me." That's why Alice was in trouble, following her heart, not her head. She rushed over and hugged me and almost knocked the box on the floor.

She pulled back to look me in the eye and burst into a big smile. "We'll find out what happened! Maybe we'll even know who killed Anthony and Hector!

"Take it off into the woods," she said, lowering her voice.

Then in a stage whisper: "A wood road goes up in back of the house, up out of sight. Drive up there and look through the stuff. And come back quickly and tell me!"

I was compounding my crime, but I was red-hot curious. I stopped near a bank of cedars and opened the trunk. For once I was glad there was no breeze, even though I was sweating. Nothing to blow stray papers away.

Fortunately, I'd cleaned out the trunk of my car a few weeks ago. Virtue *is* its own reward. I had a fair amount of space to lay out papers in piles. I opened a folder and pulled out the picture of the strange wreck, with one car totaled against a tree and another car hitting the rear end of it, with what appeared to be a glancing blow. The light was getting dim. Good thing I hadn't waited any later. Beneath that picture was a page of sheet music. What could that mean? Then, a copy of a letter from a parole officer concerning Goat. So the Kid had probably been right that Anthony was extorting money from Goat. There were two newspaper clippings. One I'd already seen, about ancient Indian artifacts and Hector. Another told about a fatal accident on Giles Hill Road, where a car went out of control around a curve and hit a tree. Skid marks and dents showed that a second car came around the curve, hit the rear of the wrecked car, then sped away. That's how the sheriff reconstructed the scene. If the second car had stopped and called for help, the story quoted the sheriff, the man in the first car might have been saved. He appeared to have slowly bled to death. I shuddered. Someone had panicked, perhaps thinking they'd done more of the damage than they had. Perhaps thinking they'd killed the driver. They'd fled the scene. Probably not knowing they could have saved the driver's life. And then to read this story in the paper. What a sickening shock.

And how did Anthony get pictures like that? Partly by luck, of course. Partly, no doubt, by having a telephoto lens. Binoculars, too? His camera was always with him, and he'd watched for every possible chance.

The driver of the hit-and-run car was a girl. Melody the poet carpenter? I'd hardly seen her after the first day in the house. Hard to tell from the back of a head. She looked to be too young. The clipping was dated ten years back. But there are girls who look half their age. I knew that.

The clipping about Hector must be related to blackmail somehow, though I couldn't be sure how. I'd heard of archaeologists seeding digs. Putting in artifacts that didn't belong there. Had he done that to please a famous client? When he was young and foolish? He'd be too proud to let that come out now.

There were other papers and pictures that made no sense to me at all. Oh, I could imagine what some of them meant. There was a photo of a beautiful horse. There was one of those white cardboard folders that bride and baby pictures come in. I opened it and found a man and women in bed together, both half sitting up stark naked and looking startled and terrified. Obviously, not a properly matched pair. But I'd never seen either one before. I closed the folder.

Anthony collected other people's guilt and despair for fun and profit. What an ugly life. Even for him.

I thought about what Ross the Boss said about all the evil in the world. I felt like that evil was pressing down in a black cloud.

I heard a car in the distance. It seemed to stop at Azalea's. It could be a deputy. I stuck the box back in the trunk. But if anyone searched my car, they'd sure search the trunk. I remembered the hiding place on the hearth where Annie's letters had been. I could put the blackmail box in that hiding place until I figured how to get it back to Adam's attic and how to get the deputies to find it there. Or perhaps I wouldn't help them find it unless Alice was arrested. What good would it do anyone to know about the human despair in that box? I parked near Azalea's house. No deputy in sight. Even Ted was not home yet. The archives must be open late tonight. I took a flashlight out of the glove compartment. Twilight was reaching the postviolet stage. I took a trowel out of the garage. That would do to prise up the slab on top of the hiding place on the hearth. I walked down the hill to the old house with the box of papers still under my arm. I could slip into the bushes if I heard anyone coming. Something moved in the bushes near me. I stood perfectly still and held my breath. Chubby came out wagging his tail and licked my hand. Good. I could use a protector. He walked halfway down the hill with me, past the troublesome yellow roses, and then veered off, chasing some small animal across a field.

The old house was dark and quiet. Still, I felt my way rather than turning the flashlight on. You never knew when someone might be watching, even in a deserted-looking place. The victims of Anthony's camera must have thought they were alone. I felt my way up the plywood ramp into the first pen. I turned on my flashlight, pointing it straight down toward the floor so it shouldn't be visible from outside and went over to the hearth. I began to prise up the stone with the box of papers still under my arm. Very awkward. I was still nervous about being spotted.

A flashlight clicked on and shone in my face. I let out a small scream as a voice said, "Quiet." I could see the business end of a gun and the glare of light. I couldn't see who held the gun and the flashlight. I was so startled I lost my grip on the blackmail box. It fell to the ground, popped open, and spilled papers all over: the mismatched lovers, the automobile wreck, all the ugliness. The flashlight pointed downward and I could see the face of Ross the Boss. "The first thing you're going to do is burn these," he said in a cold voice I didn't recognize.

"But Alice . . ." I said.

"We'll take care of Alice," he said. "This is the end of the line for blackmail."

I'd seen nothing in that box that implicated Ross. Unless—suppose that hit-and-run driver was Rose? Rose was afraid to drive after dark. Because she'd panicked and fled after she hit a car on a curve in the purple dusk? I blurted, "Anthony was blackmailing Rose!"

"I wouldn't lose my head and kill for anybody else," Ross said bitterly. "Now, hurry up."

Kill! Ross?

I turned my flashlight on him. His face was hard and bitter, as if killing made him into a new man. A ruthless man. I was afraid of him. "Come on," he said. "Pick those up. We're going to the back fireplace." I picked up the papers awkwardly, still holding the flashlight in one hand, and shoved them back in the box. It hardly mattered if I wrinkled them now, did it? He waved me in front of him and we made our way through the dark house, flashlights still pointing down at the plywood walks across the dirt subfloor. I was afraid I might trip. I was afraid that in his dark mood he might shoot me even before I burned the papers. His slight limp somehow made him more sinister.

He paused in front of the fireplace in the back room. "She was very young," he said. For a minute I saw the old, kind Ross in his eyes. "She spent her whole life helping other people, to help make up for one stupid night. And you see, I have to take care of her.'' He said that last as if he wanted me to understand why he had to get rid of all the evidence. For a moment his eyes were pleading. Then he was robot killer again. Stiff and angry. And I was part of the evidence, wasn't I?

"He was ruthless," Ross said. "Anthony killed Hector."

I had thought so, too. "How can you be sure?" I asked.

"I accused him of it, and he said, 'You could never prove that, Ross,' and then he said, 'Hector thought he was smarter and faster than I was, but he was a fool. Only a fool would agree to meet under a scaffolding full of stones.'"

"So you assumed that he meant to kill you," I said. "Or he would have protested more than that."

"No," he said sadly. "I would never have exposed Rose by telling on Anthony. He knew that. I simply lost my temper." Tears came to his eyes.

"You hit him over the head?"

"With a hammer some fool left here," he said. "I was so angry I lost my head. I have Lou Gehrig's disease," he said. "Nobody knows yet. Because I can work now. But when I can't anymore, what would he do to Rose then? And I lost my head and grabbed the hammer and I killed him." He said that with such regret and despair in his voice that I almost expected him to say he was sorry. All he said was, "Poor Rose."

Except for that limp, Ross looked healthy, but I knew some diseases didn't show at first. And, yes, he still held his hands closed. Why hadn't I tried to find out why? Fool that I was.

"There's a pile of old newspapers," he said, hardening again. "Crumple them up and put these damn blackmail papers on top. I have matches. Don't miss a single one. I want all that viper's poison to be gone."

I put my flashlight down on the hearth and began to do what he said, as slowly as I could get away with. If he destroyed these papers and killed me, there'd be no suspicion except against Alice. And besides, I'd be dead. I meant to live. I prayed that someone would pass the old house. Could you see smoke from a chimney in the dark? Yes, if it was white smoke. I prayed those blackmail papers would make white smoke.

The newspaper caught with a rustly crackle and orange flame leaped up. The papers on top soared up in flame. The accident picture caught at one end and the flame raced across. A black folder writhed in the flame: must be the cardboard picture folder with the man and woman in bed. A hot romance. One newspaper clipping took fiery wings and disappeared up the chimney. I was both glad and sorry to see those instruments of torture burn. I was also scared to see the flames end. Ross was staring into the fire. He seemed hypnotized. As the flames subsided his face filled with fatal resolution. He waved me toward some loose wires sticking out of the wall. Certainly, those had been protected in some way. I couldn't remember how. We both stood and looked at the wires. "These will do the work," he said. "Electrocution is fast. It doesn't have time to hurt much. Remember that."

It didn't seem like I'd have very long to remember. Short-term memory would do me fine. Shocking things are easiest to remember. Why does my crazy mind make jokes when I'm in mortal danger?

"If Rose finds out you killed Anthony, she'll forgive you," I said. "If she finds out you killed me in order to protect her, she'll be destroyed."

He stared at me as if he'd reached the stage where he was so set on his purpose that he couldn't hear. "And besides," I said, "I don't intend to tell about the blackmail unless I need to, to save Alice from being charged with murder. Let it die with Anthony." I hoped he might trust me if I said that. No reaction.

I walked closer to him. "You'll be sorry," I said. That sounded trite, but my purpose was to get close enough to kick him and grab for the gun.

As if he was psychic, he grabbed me with his free hand

and pulled back the gun in the other. He was strong as iron. He pushed me around and held the gun against my back. With one of his hands free again, I heard him rummaging for something. "Turn around," he said, still keeping the gun close to me. He handed me a pen and a bill for lumber. "Sit down on the hearth and write on the back of that," he said.

I sat. I held my flashlight on the paper with one hand, ready to write with the other. He began to dictate. " 'I killed Anthony because he was cruel and destructive. I killed him in a rage. No one but me should suffer.'

"Give it to me!" he said roughly. "Now turn your back again."

My eyes searched for an object to use as a weapon, something to distract him. Anything. My flashlight picked up only dirt floor.

And then I heard a strange noise in back of me. A kind of half scream and a crackle. An ugly acrid smell shocked my nose.

I whirled and the light fell on Ross holding the loose wires, or maybe they were holding him. His body vibrated with the current. I screamed in horror and relief. I was alive. But Ross must be dead.

I didn't dare try to pull him loose from the wires. I knew that if I tried to do that without a rubber mat or something to break the current, I'd electrocute myself.

In the edge of the light I noticed the lumber bill on the ground. I picked it up and reread the note I wrote. Ross had signed it.

I remembered what Rose had said about this house. That she believed this was a house that made heroes. I looked around at the solid log walls. This was a house that endured. I ran toward Azalea's house. Up the dark road with the wildflowers along the side, glimmering faintly in the dark. The scent of roses and ferns intensified in the cool of evening. I don't cry often. But as I ran I realized I was crying.

CHAPTER
31

THREE MONTHS LATER

Perhaps the old house should have been draped in black. But the garlands of flowers and leaves that Alice had draped through the banister of the new wide upstairs porch seemed just right. Pots of chrysanthemums made the front of the house seem almost landscaped. The house was finished. It stood squared and clean, the logs chinked, chimneys pointed up, new steps leading to the mellowed poplar front door with a small brass knob. The original door had turned up in the rafters of the old shed where the gun had been buried.

I arrived early, entered the new-old front door, walked across the beautiful new-old ash floors, and admired the table of exhibits in the front left room. At least Azalea hadn't put up any super-cheerful quotations yet. I was tired of slogans and quotations. There wasn't much furniture yet, either, but a long table with a white tablecloth held all the artifacts found in and around the house, including twelve-thousand-year-old arrowheads and the elegant pepperbox pistol and several small round bullets, turned milky white with age, like boiled fish eyes.

Pop had arrived early, too, and he called me over to his wheelchair near the hearth. He was dressed to the nines in a dark suit and a tie with some kind of coat of arms on it. Could it be we had a family coat of arms? I didn't believe it. We are named Smith.

"I am new in this community, Peaches," he said grandly, "and it befits my position as Azalea Marlowe's husband to have a certain dignity. Azalea, as you know, is descended from one of the founders of this community. Today, you and I will meet some of today's leaders and see others that we know already."

I refrained from saying, Get off it, Pop. He might as well enjoy being grandfather of the bride.

"Therefore," he said, "I must ask you to try not to make a fool of yourself, not to use any of your more outrageous memory tricks like going around with a string on your finger. The best people in Tennessee do not wear strings on their fingers to socially important weddings. People will get the impression that we are not well connected."

Thank God, Azalea wasn't stuffy, or I could see that Pop would become impossible. But I wanted him to be happy, so I didn't bring up his cousin Zeke who was in Craggy Prison, outside of Asheville, for stealing whiskey.

"I promise I will behave," I said. "But folks will have so much to see here they'll hardly notice me."

I waved at the artifact table with the box of Annie Thomason's letters on one end, and next to it some papers written in a round flowing handwriting in faded brown ink. Also the magnifying glass so folks could look at the signatures of Annie Thomason and David Holden scratched with Annie's engagement diamond on the windowpane.

I kissed Pop on the forehead and walked over to the other front room to check another long table being laid out with small sandwiches, little cakes, and other goodies. At one end, champagne glasses were set out.

Alice was admiring the spread. She wore a white dress with lace trim and looked as lovely and as happy as I'd ever seen her. "Adam outdid himself," she said. Ed stood glowing by her side, solid as ever. The man to count on, and now resplendent in a navy silk jacket.

"This is a jewel of a house," he said.

The guests began to arrive. Neighbors, pleased to satisfy their curiosity about the old house, even patted the new plaster walls. The crew that made it happen filtered in. Walt with his guitar, dressed like a country singer in fringes and a high-crowned hat. Goat with his drums. Melody with bass, and the Kid with a harmonica. They had volunteered to make music. I wondered if they would play "All That's Left Are the Bones, Oh" and if we would like that or be horrified. Ted was going to tell about the history of what had happened in this house and read us what the Reverend Baird and Annie herself had written about it.

That might seem a strange way to embellish the celebration of a wedding, but Ed was a curator himself, and Alice was descended from the players in the drama here. I noticed a small antique table stood right above the spot where we'd unearthed the skeleton of a bridegroom shot dead before he had the chance to tie the knot. On the table stood a beautiful bouquet of mixed chrysanthemums and daisies.

Azalea touched my arm, and I turned to be introduced to the head of the Williamson County Historical Society, a man with a wonderful shock of white hair and long slender bony hands. I remembered to look dignified.

"We owe such a debt to you folks and to Azalea and to Adam Marlowe for preserving this house," he said. Adam? Ha! If Mr. Historical only knew. But perhaps he did, and was being tactful.

Yes, my family could take credit. I noticed Pop was busy doing just that, enthroned in his wheelchair next to the table with the flowers. Three admiring older women hung on his every word as if he had restored the house with his own hands. Adam Marlowe was encircled by even more admirers. We'd shown him the proof he wanted, and he'd been so completely converted that he'd insisted on hosting this reception for the bride and groom. Alice had wanted a celebration of her wedding and a celebration of what happened in this house one hundred and fifty years ago, both together.

Even Rose was there. "You don't have to come," I'd told her. She had called, and I'd answered the phone.

"I want to come," she'd said. "I know—and I think you know—that Ross died because he was protecting me. I don't know the details. But I know in my bones that's how it was."

I had kept the details to myself. Anthony was unpopular enough that Ross had lots of sympathy. "I could have wrung that Anthony's neck myself," I heard a county commissioner say. "He took a picture of my wife kissing her brother from New Mexico. I think he thought she was kissing a boyfriend and he could embarrass me."

And nobody needed to know any of the ugly blackmail that Ross had died to keep secret.

"That is a terrible house in a way," Rose said, "but I'll be near Ross in that house." So she came, and we all hugged her. And it seemed all right.

Eudora was on hand, done up like a nineteenth-century barmaid and telling anyone who would listen about her part in the movie about Davy Crockett. Her boyfriend was there, too. Oh, dear, I forgot to memorize his name. Harry October? "No," he said, "Harvey August." Well, I was only two months off.

Adam announced that Ted had done a great deal of research in some newly discovered papers and that he would read us selections that would dramatize for us all the sad events that happened here. "And highlight the evil of drink." Adam liked getting in that commercial for virtue. He smiled smugly.

Azalea, God bless her, had been smart enough to emphasize that angle to Adam and encourage him to dwell on how drunkenness destroys lives. She'd asked Ted to explain what we'd found.

Ted looked distinguished in his blue blazer as he talked

about the past. He held up a picture of the skeleton, half-unearthed and with broken ribs and the usual skeleton grimace. "This is the gentleman found buried under this floor," he pointed down. "Frank Morton is the archaeologist who dug him out." He indicated Frank, who stood nearby sipping a glass of champagne. "Nick Fielder, our state archaeologist"—he nodded at Nick—"sent our skeleton off to the forensic folks at the University of Tennessee." Ted kept introducing all the people who helped.

He even mentioned Hector the Collector who had helped to date the house at around 1795. Hector's murder had not been officially solved, but I was sure that the clipping about him among the blackmail papers was the key. Anthony had all but told Ross he killed Hector. I could picture proud Hector threatening to kill Anthony if he spread the word that Hector had done something unprofessional like seeding a dig. And what would Anthony do to protect himself? He could hardly call the sheriff. Hector must have asked Anthony to meet him at the house, maybe even specifying the spot near the chimney. Hector must have had the knife with him to kill Anthony, or at least to threaten him. That's why the knife was in his hand.

I looked at the artifact table. We should have Hector's knife among the objects that told the story of this house. That part of the story would be lost, like so much of the past is.

Anthony must have suspected Hector would threaten him, and had slipped up to the platform at the top of the chimney, quietly edged a rock to the edge of the platform, and dropped the rock on Hector's head. He had good aim, I'll say that for him. All accomplished before first Walt and then Ted and I arrived. I didn't tell anyone my thoughts but Ted. The blackmail evidence was gone. And Hector and Anthony were both dead. Let them rest in peace.

I was alerted by Ted saying my name. "Let's begin by hearing the letters that mention all the folks that took part in this tragedy," he said, and he introduced me as the one who found the letters.

I read about Annie's love for David Holden, who "was like my right arm" and "like fair weather." I noticed Rose had tears running down her face, but I couldn't stop. I read about Annie's brother, Buddy, whom she helped to raise after her mother died, and about how both Buddy and their father had "that Irish temper, as Father's father had before him," and how they both were prone to hold a grudge. And how Buddy took to drink.

I could see by frowns that my listeners were as frustrated as I had been that Annie would not say who actually killed who on that fatal night in 1849, or give the name of the man of God who helped her through that dreadful time. Oh, people knew those things. The story had been in the newspaper and on TV. And some of it had even been explained when Walt's song was played on the radio. But our guests hadn't heard Annie's own words about the man she mentioned only as HIM.

"This house held the clue to the man called HIM." Ted pointed to a copy of the newspaper clipping from the upstairs wall that told about how the Reverend Baird's papers ended up in the library. From there, of course, they landed in the archives. Ted explained how the land records showed that the Reverend Baird lived quite close to the Thomasons.

"I want to thank the archives and the Historical Society for letting me be in on the original sorting of those papers, which had somehow found their way to an attic and were recently rediscovered." Ted walked to the end of the table, where the gun shone darkly against the white tablecloth.

"The reverend wrote these words," he said, "which I believe must be about this gun."

It breaks my heart to see a young man feel his whole self-worth is in his gun. Alas, his father has contempt for him. He had one good friend who went off to the Mexican War and came back with that pistol—won at the gaming table, no doubt. He also came back with injuries to his stomach that killed him in a short time, and he left this beautiful inlaid pistol to my young friend. Even for drink he will not sell it. It is always near to his hand, constantly flourished, especially when he is angry and in his cups. I pray to God no mischief comes of this.

Quivering silence as we waited for the next quote from the reverend. Obviously mischief had come.

My poor young neighbor came to get me in the night. Praise God I am not far. She begged me to come and read a Service for the Dead, and to help absolve the living.

Ted found another section.

My young friend is distraught. And yet we did the best that we knew how. I thank our good Lord I learned something of carpentry as a boy. We laid out that poor boy, shot down by the power of drink in a fit of anger. (His killer was repentant, I praise God for that. I prayed with him.) She took the locket from around her neck, put a lock of her hair in it, and laid it on his chest. I said the Service for the Dead. We buried him. All of us worked together to put the house back to rights before dawn. Even my young friend, God give her strength. A strange job for a woman. A strange job for a preacher of God's word to take part in.

Ted sorted through and found another paper.

We found his gun lying on the table after he was gone. Why? He would need it in the West. I like to think he left it to throw away the violent and proud part of himself. But perhaps in his devastation at what he had done, he merely forgot to take it. He had to leave quickly, to be far gone before daylight. He would not dare return for any reason.

"You will notice," Ted said, "that like Annie, Reverend Baird did not use names. So is there any chance that this skeleton"—he held up the picture again—"belonged to Buddy Marlowe? Not according to the experts at the forensic anthropology department at the University of Tennessee, where Nick sent the skeleton to be studied. By matching stress lines on the teeth with known years when David Holden was ill, they have confirmed this is David Holden's skeleton." He turned to me. "We were lucky that Annie mentioned his illnesses in her letters."

Yes, we were. That's what convinced Adam. I went and got myself a glass of champagne. The guests were busy crowding around looking at the old letters and the other artifacts.

Rose came over to me. "Could I talk to you alone?" she asked. She darted her eyes around as if she was afraid of being overheard. I nodded toward the stairs and we went up the narrow staircase. Much better than the ladder, but still narrow because that's how most staircases were built in 1795. I led her into the back bedroom over the kitchen and shut the door, and because she was actually trembling with nerves, I latched it.

"I wanted to share this with you," she said, "because you were with Ross when . . ." Tears came to her eyes, but she choked them back. "I found this note in the book I was reading just before Ross died. He knew I'd find it there after . . . I've been shy about showing you this," she said, pulling a piece of paper out of her pocket, "because it's personal. But I think you know what a fine man he was and I want you to share this. In fact, I think eventually, when the impact of all this is past, this note should be among the papers that show the history of the house. You're going to have a little museum in an outbuilding, is that right?"

I said yes, and we'd be proud to have something by Ross in it.

"These are the last written words of the man who killed himself in this house." She took in a deep breath and paused until she could go on. "And if no one knows the details, except that he admitted he had killed a man, perhaps with good reason, at least this shows what kind of man Ross was."

She finally handed me the note, gingerly, as if it might explode.

It was written in black ink on a piece of plain typewriter paper in bold clear handwriting.

Whatever happens, Rose, believe that I love you more than anything else in the world. Please never let the past be quicksand to get stuck in—make it a lesson, no matter how hard, to help improve the future. That's what I want for you.

All my love,
Ross

I hugged her hard.

"Take it and make a good copy," she said. "I want it to be part of the history of this house. I want it to be preserved now, and maybe in a year or two, you can put it in the little museum."

There was a knock at the door. "Peaches, are you in there?" Ted's voice. "People are wondering where you are."

"Can I show Ted now?" I asked Rose.

"Yes," she said. "Ted will understand."

So I opened the door, and we showed Ted the note. He handed it back to me and gave Rose an even bigger hug than I had.

Right at that moment we heard shouting downstairs. We ran down and found that Chubby had stolen a piece of wedding cake. Not a big deal but it seemed to cause pandemonium. Pop in his wheelchair yelling, "Stop!" Azalea trying to catch the dog, knocking over a chair, almost falling flat. At the same time three people were asking me questions. I mustn't lose Rose's note. I stood perfectly still. I put my hand up in the air. Sudden silence. All eyes on me. The head historical honcho and the county commissioner looked amazed. I felt like a fool. My eyes fell on Pop. He had turned beet red.

I stood stock-still. If you just don't panic, there's likely to be a graceful way out of almost anything. That's what it says in my book. I took another deep breath and acted like there was a perfectly sensible reason to have my hand straight up in the air in the middle of a wedding reception.

"I want to make an announcement," I said.

An announcement? I looked around praying for inspiration. "I'd like to say something about the connection between the murder, in 1849, and the murders this year," I said. Someone had asked me the connection. Maybe I could answer that. What was the connection? The early murder was used to manipulate Adam Marlowe and almost destroy this house. My eye fell on Adam, mouth half smiling, eyes smug. It would not be tactful to talk about manipulation. Then my eye fell on Ed and Alice holding hands. "The connection has to do with love," I said. Now what?

"The killers," I said, "were both deprived of love. Anthony and Buddy had fathers who believed that they were no good. Then Anthony lost Dolores, the wife who loved him. And Anthony and Buddy were both so jealous and angry that they became killers." I saw skepticism in some eyes. "I see Ross as having been infuriated by Anthony because Ross was loving and Anthony was cruel."

That was certainly a gross oversimplification, though Anthony had probably mimicked and humiliated lots of the people here.

"And why didn't Annie ever marry?" Azalea asked. Hey, wait a minute. This was Azalea's ancestor. Why did she ask me? But I'd thought a lot about Annie. About how it was to know her lover lay there just beneath her floor for all those years.

"I believe Annie was a strong woman," I said. "She knew her brother killed her lover. But she protected her brother. She even buried his prized gun where it would be safe. The gun that ruined his life. Then she raised her lover's little son, right in this house with the body under the floor.

"I think she was married to her terrible secret," I said. "How could she marry another man with David there, under her floor?" I pointed to the vase of flowers just over the spot.

Azalea of the smiling face let out a long sigh. Not like her at all. "She must have been a very lonely woman." Azalea reached out and took Pop's hand.

"She was a strong woman," I repeated. Then, I was the optimist. "Perhaps, it wasn't a horror for her to have the man she loved right there, under her feet. Perhaps it was a comfort. If he had to be dead, at least he was close by." I wanted to believe that. "Perhaps Annie put flowers on a table over his burial place, just as we've put them over the place where he once was. I hope so."

The President of the Historical Society nodded. Several people glanced at Alice, encircled by Ed's arm. We all wanted to think that love can comfort even in a tragedy. We wanted to believe that, especially at a wedding.

"Perhaps," said Mr. Historical Society, "her spirit is glad that they are now buried side by side in the Riggs Cemetery."

Azalea asked him to tell a little about the belated funeral in the old cemetery, and then we all drank champagne to the bride and the groom.

And we weren't gloomy about the past. We were glad for the future. Ed was looking for a job in Tennessee, and if he found one, he and Alice would live in the house. It would be open to the public on Thursdays.

After the bride and groom took off and the guests departed, I turned to Ted. He laughed. "Quick recovery from the hand-up maneuver," he said.

"You knew what I was up to all along," I said dryly. "Just trying not to seem old and stupid, and embarrass Pop."

"You are never dull," he said, and then he began to spout what sounded almost like a recitation: " 'Age cannot wither her nor custom stale her infinite variety.' ''

I must have looked startled.

"Shakespeare," he said, "describing Cleopatra. Weddings make me feel poetic."

Then he winked at me. "Try Marlowe—Christopher, not Azalea: 'Come live with me and be my love, and we will all the pleasures prove—' I don't know the rest, but that's enough. Let's get home quick before somebody finds another body."

Perhaps quotations are not so bad, after all.